April '15

TIGGER

Memoirs of a Cosmopolitan Cat

To Jill,

a fellow cat lover.
I hope you enjoy our story!
   Susanne, Tigger + Bilbo
      ♡

SUSANNE HAYWOOD

Matador
9 Priory Business Park
Kibworth Beauchamp
Leicestershire LE8 0RX, UK
Tel: (+44) 116 279 2299
Fax: (+44) 116 279 2277
Email: books@troubador.co.uk
Web: www.troubador.co.uk/matador

ISBN 978-1784621-216

British Library Cataloguing in Publication Data.
A catalogue record for this book is available from the British Library.

Printed and bound by CPI Group (UK) Ltd, Croydon, CR0 4YY
Typeset in 11.5pt Bembo by Troubador Publishing Ltd, Leicester, UK

Matador is an imprint of Troubador Publishing Ltd

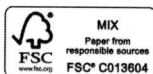

MIX
Paper from
responsible sources
FSC
www.fsc.org   FSC® C013604

To my family

TABLE OF CONTENTS

"For he will do
As he do do
And there's no doing anything about it!"

T.S. Eliot, *Old Possum's Book of Practical Cats*

PART 1

From Perth to Maryland

1

I HAVE A REALLY BAD START,
BUT EVENTUALLY FIND MY FAMILY

Have you ever felt the pleasure of gliding silently through a green tunnel of long, soft, swishing grass? Or of feeling the radiant warmth of hot summer earth on your belly as you lie stretched out in your favourite hiding place while the breeze gently strokes your ears? Or of pouncing on long-awaited prey and the satisfying crunch as your teeth sink into a warm, trembling neck? No? Then you're probably not a cat. Never mind.

I am. You can call me Tigger, and this is the story of my turbulent life, which is all my family's fault of course. They are a restless lot, off at the drop of a hat from one continent to the next with me in my travel box. They're not *bad* as humans go, mind you, just really hard work. And let's face it: they need me. Left to their own devices, they would be hopelessly lost.

My story starts in Perth, in Western Australia, where my brother and I were born and lived at first with two humans in a small house in the suburbs. My brother, I am sorry to say, wasn't careful enough − trust me, you can never be careful enough. He was friendly with anyone who came along, which is what killed him that fateful day, when strangers came into our yard while our humans were out. We were only tiny kittens, but I knew to disappear as soon as they opened the gate. I've asked myself a thousand times why he didn't follow me instead of trotting off to meet them, tail held high. What a stupid thing to do!

That was the last time I saw him alive. By the time darkness fell and our people came home, he was lying limply on the paving stones at an awkward angle, and blood was trickling from his mouth. There were stones and beer cans lying all around the yard and a scent of violence was in the air. He looked peaceful, stretched out on the ground, but he felt cold and smelt different. I knew he had gone. So I wandered off on my own and felt very strange. We had always done everything together – played, eaten, and slept together. Now a part of me was missing – the trusting part. I knew I would never trust anyone again, ever, and decided to rely on myself for all things. I've never regretted that decision.

The very next day, I came to live with my family. It was considered safer for me to move to a different neighbourhood, in case the people who had killed my brother came back for me.

That made sense to me, but still I wasn't looking forward to moving. Taking on a new set of humans is always risky. I knew that even as a kitten. Think about it: humans are so poorly equipped. They have no tails and no fur, so you have to take a guess at their moods. They can't move their ears at all, which restricts their hearing, and I don't think their eyes are much use either. They definitely can't see a thing in the dark. So all they have left to express themselves with are their paws and their mouths. The paws are good. They may not get much use from their claws, but they can grip and handle delicate things with their long, thin fingers. They use their mouths to make lots of different sounds, quiet ones and loud ones, high ones and low ones. You can tell they're all supposed to mean something, but it's very difficult to be sure what. After a while you get the general idea, but for a kitten it's a challenge. As for understanding *us* – well, some of them are quite slow, and it may take years of patience and persistence to teach them our language.

I didn't know all this at the time, but I suspected much of it and therefore reckoned it would be safest for me to spend my first day with the new family under a shoe rack in the corner of a small, dark room. The smell of the shoes was unpleasant, but the humans left me alone there, and that was a good sign. I would have hated living with a family who didn't respect my private space.

Eventually hunger, curiosity and the need for a pee made me leave my hiding place and meet them. There were three young ones sitting on the floor, listening to a grown-up, who was sitting in a very comfortable-looking armchair and holding what I later came to know as a Story Book. It was a peaceful scene, no scent of danger, and I was ready for company. So I strolled up to the chair and sat down at a safe distance from the children. A familiar smell drifted over to me from a pair of feet; I recognised the owner of the smelly shoes on the shoe rack. We would have to see about cleaning habits in this house.

If the humans were pleased to see me, they didn't show it. They just said hello, and one of the children leaned across and stroked me lightly. I moved away an inch or two; she took the hint and left me alone. So we all sat there quietly, listening to the strange sounds that the person on the chair was making. It was comfortable on the soft carpet; the regular sing-song of the human voice almost lulled me to sleep after a while. But then the voice stopped, the book closed with a snap and everyone got up. They showed me where my food and drink bowls and a litter tray had been prepared for me. I made use of them all.

That done, I followed the young ones to their rooms, where we attached a piece of string to a ball. I showed them how to pull it around the room while I gave chase. They loved it when I pounced on the ball and held it tight; we had several repeats. It was clear they had never played a cat game before and needed help. When they had picked up the basics of a couple of the simpler games, I encouraged them to run along and let me have a rest.

It was time to look for a suitable place to take a nap. My corner under the shoe rack had served its purpose. From now on I would rest in comfort. There were a couple of beds in the room. I tried each one in turn until I found a convenient corner spot on one of them that gave me cover from behind and a good view of my surroundings. It was an excellent choice; I was asleep in minutes.

2

I ANSWER A CALL OF NATURE AND THE SERVICE IS BRILLIANT

I woke up because I needed a pee. I was still very sleepy. As I wandered around the house, it seemed quite different from last time. The room with the litter tray had disappeared. Back in the room where we had listened to the story, I found a pile of papers. It brought back memories of when I was a very small kitten in a box with my Mummy and all my brothers and sisters. She had taught us how to use the paper to go to the toilet – what a stroke of luck! I ran over to the pile of paper, scratched it into shape, squatted down and did my business.

I had to hand it to those humans – their service was first class: no sooner had I finished than they came running from all directions to remove the wet paper. They even seemed quite worried about not being quick enough. I tried to tell them they were doing just fine, but they had already disappeared, taking the paper away with them. Oh well, I reckoned they would relax once they realised I was fairly easy-going about these things.

There was a nice patch of sunshine on the carpet next to the armchair, just the place for a thorough clean-up. I was doing the inside of my left hind leg when they came back, carrying my litter tray. They looked pleased about having found it again, scratched about in it and made cooing noises. I gestured 'well done' with my free foreleg, but, finding myself in a very difficult position, lost my balance and fell over backwards. How embarrassing! Sure enough, I heard a giggle. I collected myself, sat up, and gave them one of my sternest looks. I think they got the message, because the giggling stopped and they all looked sorry. They went off with the litter tray, and I must say to their credit that they never lost it again after that.

Life with my new family settled down nicely; I had made a good choice. Mealtimes were regular, the beds very comfortable, there was a garden with several good climbing trees and a swimming pool that had fresh, blue water in it for me to drink. Next door had a garden shed with a tin roof leaning against a brick wall. It was warm and sheltered, the best place for a nap in sunny weather; no smell of dogs for miles around. My family consisted of two grown-up humans and three young ones. The bigger one of the grown-ups had been away when I first arrived. He came back one evening in a shower of rain with lots of bags and seemed surprised to see me, but was very polite when he was introduced to me and asked me what my name was. I couldn't tell him of course, as cats' names are a secret and must not be given to any human, however friendly. Luckily, my family had already chosen my every-day name, because of my ginger stripes and some tiger in the Story Book. I didn't mind it too much; actually, I've come to think it even has a certain ring to it, and I am of course a tiger in many ways.

I approved of the bigger grown-up – even though he wasn't often around – his name was Dad, and of the smaller grown-up, who saw to my food, drink and the litter tray and generally seemed to be in charge around the place. Her name was Mum. The young ones were Caroline, the eldest and clearly the most sensible of the three. When she sat down to read a book or watch TV, you could settle down next to her knowing she would stay there for a while, without fidgeting. She was friendly without fussing, and occasionally we would have a game of drafts or chess together. Robin, the youngest, was a different matter: never in the same place for more than one second, very unpredictable. The times that child has accidentally landed on me over the years! I'm not saying he's not kind and loving, but you do have to be careful around him and his toys. The one in the middle, called Emily, was my favourite straight away: her bed was the most comfortable, her voice the softest, and she seemed to guess my every wish. In return, I occasionally made an exception to my number one rule (no cuddling!) with her and her alone.

3

I SETTLE DOWN AND EXPLORE

In their different ways, each member of my family helped me settle down in my new home. The bad memories of my earlier life began to fade in their company, as gradually they filled the void my brother had left.

During the day, the children and I played chasing games in the garden. In the evenings I would lie on one of their beds during Story Time and afterwards let Mum or Dad share my armchair while we watched TV. When the children were at school, I went off exploring on my own. I always found something interesting: furry caterpillars crawling on the warm paving stones were grateful for a helping paw to speed them along; blossoms gave off rich, fruity scents on hot summer days; and up on the back garden wall, I was able to watch events unfold in four separate gardens. In our front garden I built myself a hiding place under some bushes from where I watched cars pass on the road and people walk by, without being seen myself. Whenever my family went out, I waited there for them. This enabled me to mysteriously appear at the front door to greet them when they returned home. It clearly puzzled them how I managed to do that – it took them months to find my hiding place and work it out.

I also began to do some hunting for my family to reward them for their faithful service. I usually managed to find something – a lizard from the patio, a bird from a nest or a rat from under the roof. The frogs were a real challenge because of their shrill squeaking when cornered; I always had to let them go because the noise hurt my ears. The craftier ones jumped in the pool to save themselves, and I certainly wasn't about to follow them in there! I had my own door at the back of the house and so was able to take my gifts inside to deliver them personally. Without fail, my family were excited by my presents and rushed off with them immediately – presumably to eat them while they were fresh. They never left me any, but I didn't mind. Sometimes there is enough pleasure in giving.

One particularly exciting day, I caught a bird and brought it into the house. Nobody was home, so I thought I might as well have a game with it while we were waiting for Mum's return from the shops. It was so much fun – the bird fluttered all over the place. I managed to chase it through the passageways right to the back of the house and into Mum and Dad's wardrobe. There, it disappeared between the clothes and I lost it. When Mum came home with the shopping, she was immediately impressed by the scene I had prepared. She put the shopping bags down to follow the trail of feathers through the house, muttering to herself as she discovered specks of blood on the walls. Finally, she found the bird in one of her dresses. It was dead, but still quite fresh; I thought she might have it for lunch. I was quite tired after my morning's excitement, so I went off to sleep on Emily's bed. I heard the vacuum cleaner going for quite some time, but fortunately Mum had shut the door to my room. She knows I hate that machine.

At night, much to my annoyance, my family locked my door, and try as I might I could not get out. That was frustrating, because everyone knows that the best time for hunting is in the dark. Sometimes humans can be extremely annoying. There was nothing for it but to curl up next to Emily and go to sleep.

Life took on a nice, regular pattern over the following months. I was happy with my family. Very rarely was I on my own, as Mum worked from her study in the house. I advised her on her writing from my favourite spot on the sofa beside her desk. When the children came home from school, the house became livelier, especially when they brought their friends back to play. I usually retired to the tin roof then, where they never found me. On rainy days, my hidey-hole was under Mum and Dad's bed, where they also never thought to check. This was without doubt the safest place in the house and still is my haven when times get a little rough.

Sometimes I came along in the car with Mum when she went to collect the children from school. I loved going in the car, because I was able to stand up with my front paws on the window and pull faces at the dogs that walked past. I could hiss at them and bare my teeth, safe behind the thick glass. It was great fun watching them get really annoyed. Once we had two or three dogs running after our car, and their owners running after *them*, but our car was faster.

When my family went on holiday, I stayed at the local cat hotel, where plenty of staff were available to entertain me and the other guests. I was able to unwind there without having to worry about my humans. It had nice, big apartments containing indoor and outdoor areas. The indoor area was cosy and dark, with a raised bed covered by my favourite soft blanket from home. Each outdoor area had its own climbing tree for a daily workout and views of a fish pond, where juicy goldfish darted about under the water lilies. They were a real treat to watch, though I would have preferred to get closer to the pond for a bit of fishing. Nevertheless, I always returned home refreshed and ready to face the demands of my family. Those were calm and pleasant times, but they were not to last.

4

WE LEAVE OUR OLD HOME TO FIND A NEW WORLD, AND I LEARN TO FLY

Something strange was afoot by autumn. There was a sense of excitement in the house. My family talked a lot in the evenings and looked at pictures in brochures. Strangers came wandering through the house at weekends. Nowadays, I would recognize these signs immediately, but I was still a young and inexperienced cat then, so it took me ages to work out what was happening. In fact, it wasn't until the day when three big men came into the house and started carrying the furniture away that the awful truth dawned on me: we were *moving*! I hate moving. I am a creature of habit, and as far as I'm concerned, things should stay the same, always. It takes a long time to find sunny patches on the carpet for each particular time of day or year; to assess draught-free spots for naps; to locate food and drink bowls with ease when half asleep; to feel safe and comfortable with the sounds and smells of a house and garden; and to know where bolt-holes are in case of danger. So naturally I was alarmed. I made straight for the big double bed and stayed under there for the rest of the day, sulking. Unfortunately, nobody seemed to notice; they were far too busy rushing about.

The next morning, they started packing up the big double bed! I was just going to scratch the muscular forearm of one of the men as it reached under the bed when Mum and the children came in, picked me up and carried me out into the car. I was relieved to find that our car, at least, was still there just as before. I imagined we were going to the cat hotel, which was probably the best place for me to be until they had sorted themselves out. But no, this time we went to a different place. A *kind* of cat hotel, but much bigger than my usual one, and definitely not as good: I could hear dogs whining! I refused to leave the car and dug my claws into the seat cushion, but they prised me off and in we went, like it or not.

I stayed in that place for about the usual length of time and made the acquaintance of several other guests. Some of them had strange accents and talked of having lived in far-away places and of having flown to Australia just recently. I thought they must be soft in the head, because they clearly did not have wings, but decided not to argue with them. The dogs were kept away from us, thank goodness, though we could hear them yapping and whining in the distance, stupid creatures. Everyone in the cat wing agreed they would never stay in a mixed-species hotel again.

Then one morning one of our care takers came along, carrying a container with lots of holes in it. I had watched other cats arrive and leave in one of them, but this time they stopped in front of my compartment. I didn't like the look of the container, but went in without making a scene — it would never do to make a spectacle of myself in front of the other cats. They carried me to a van, which drove me to a very noisy place that smelled like our car service station, where I had spent many happy times annoying dogs in nearby cars as we waited for our humans to buy fuel. But this time I was driven across a big open space to a huge, roaring machine and lifted inside. Many other boxes were piled around my container, and I was sure I saw a dog in one of them before they moved it further down the narrow corridor. It was all very disturbing. I stood in a corner of my container with my hair on end, hoping that someone would soon get me out of there. But nobody did.

Instead, the men closed the big doors to the outside world, the noise level increased to a terrible pitch and I was being jolted about in my container while the machine bounced about and screeched until I felt quite light-headed and nauseous. It was a good job I had no food in my container, because I could not have eaten one bite. There was some water, but I didn't even want to touch that. I felt miserable! At long last, the noise settled down to a continuous hum and the screeching stopped. We were still moving though, I could feel little bumps every now and then, and it finally occurred to me that I must be flying! This was obviously what those other cats had been talking about. Did this mean that I was going to a far-away country where cats had funny accents? I curled up on my soft blanket and fell asleep wondering, and the journey continued for a very long time.

At one point, we landed with more bumping, screeching and noise, and my container was unloaded. I was taken to another cat hotel (cats only this time, I was glad to see) and a man in a white coat came to check me over. I told him I had a migraine and was off my food, but he just patted me on the head and said everything would be fine, not to worry. He didn't sound Australian at all. I had a few hours of rest in the hotel before it was time to get back in the container and off again. This time I knew what to expect, so the flight was slightly less frightening, but almost as long as before. Flying was definitely not something anyone would do for fun. I had hated the airport food, the cabin was cramped, and this time I was next door to a really fat cat who kept burping into my ear. If my family ever wanted me to fly again, it would have to be in greater comfort.

Finally, we landed again with an extra big burp from the cat next door. I was exhausted. The fat cat and I were loaded on to a trailer and taken into a building, and there, just the other side of a swinging door, was – Dad! I had never been so pleased to see him, and he seemed just as pleased to see *me*, so I completely forgot to be cross with him for bringing me to this strange place. Instead, we said fond hellos before he carried me out of that noisy, smelly place into a car – a different car from our usual one – and drove me home. Oh, how glad I was to be going home at last!

We arrived very late at night. Mum was still up, but the children were asleep. It wasn't our house and garden at all, but some new place with different smells and weird noises. Still, I was just glad to come out of my container, stretch my legs again (I felt quite wobbly and the ground swayed under my feet), and to have a snack and a drink from the bowls that had been prepared for me in the new kitchen. I was so tired! I collapsed on Mum and Dad's soft, warm, quiet bed, where Mum stroked me until the room stopped swaying around us and we all went to sleep together.

5

I DISCOVER A NEW HOUSE AND SOME VERY ANNOYING CREATURES

The next morning, the children gave me a boisterous welcome that left me quite exhausted. It was great to see them, but I was still very tired. It was a relief to find that there was a safe hiding place under Mum and Dad's bed in that house, too. I spent the rest of the day asleep there.

By the evening I felt better, but it was getting dark and they would not let me go outside to explore. I had no choice but to check out the inside of the new house instead. It was much smaller than our old one and smelt musty. The furniture was strange as well. Emily and Robin shared one room, and Caroline had a room with a big bed all to herself. I reckoned there would be space on there for me. There were a couple of armchairs and sofas in the lounge, but not nearly as comfortable as my old armchair. I wondered what had happened to it. The food was different and not very nice actually, but I didn't want to offend my family and ate it anyway. The water was really dreadful, though. It had an evil taste and left ugly brown stains in my bowl. I simply refused to drink it. They gave in pretty soon and served me milk instead – my favourite, so I was glad I had remained firm.

After a couple of days in the house, I was ready to investigate the great outdoors of this new mystery place. Mum wasn't keen to let me, but I slipped outside one day when someone opened the door. It was terribly hot and stuffy outside – in Australia it had been winter when we left and quite cool, but this place seemed to have its seasons quite mixed up. It was definitely summer here – I would have to moult all over again immediately, which was a nuisance. There was a small back garden with a shed containing old garden furniture and some tools. The door didn't shut properly, so that was soon explored. No pool unfortunately, but given the taste of the water in my bowl, that was probably no loss. There was a deck out the back with a reasonable view, and very high trees all around the garden. Some creatures in those trees gave off the strangest noises: a solitary rattling sound first, then others chimed in, until the whole garden seemed to vibrate with a sound that made my ears throb. Probably not a good place for outside naps; it sounded a bit spooky, too. It might be wise to stay away from those trees for a while.

From the deck, I could see several other houses quite close by. There were no fences anywhere, which was a worry in case of dogs. There was one now, ambling down the small brown dirt road as though it owned the place. Where had I ended up? There was a cat, too, a black one, sitting on the neighbouring deck. We eyed each other for a bit. It looked alright, but I was not really in the mood for socialising. I could also hear children's voices everywhere. They seemed to be as unrestrained as the dogs, and I didn't care for either. I decided this would do for my first outing and went back inside – Mum had thoughtfully left the door half-open for me.

Over the days that followed, I had several more outings and ventured a little further each time. It was an interesting place, if you took care to avoid the straying dogs and children. At twilight, little sparks of light went flying through the air, turning themselves on and off at will. They were impossible to catch, but I had some success with the rattling creatures in the trees — they turned out to be big crickets, quite harmless, and it was fun pouncing on them while they were rehearsing: silencing one caused all the others to lose their beat. We had a lot of stop-start concerts after I discovered that. The trees were very high indeed, of a kind I had never seen before, and difficult to climb as the lower branches were way up. I tried a couple, but couldn't make it.

As I was resting in the shade one day, recovering from my latest climb, the most peculiar creature ran across the grass right in front of me. It was about the size of a rat, but grey in colour with a very big, bushy tail. Strangest of all, it seemed not a bit scared of me, but set about collecting seeds from under a tree as though I didn't exist. For quite a while I was too stunned to move. Back home, I had developed a certain reputation among the creatures of our neighbourhood: they all knew better than to mess with me. There, bird guards had sounded the alarm as soon as I stepped outside for my morning walk. I had single-pawedly chased a whole colony of rats from their nests under our roof in a matter of days. Frogs had thought twice before leaping into our garden. And here was that bushy-tailed creature, ignoring me!

I collected my hind legs under me and shot forward to grab the intruder by the neck, but it sensed my approach and scampered up a tree unhurriedly and effortlessly, as though it was flat ground. Up I went in hot pursuit, really mad by now at the creature's cheek. I positively raced up the trunk in the same way as the creature had done and managed to climb up quite a bit further than on previous attempts, but still I was out of reach of the lowest branch. I had to stop for breath, which took away my momentum, and found myself stuck to the tree in mid-climb. I held on for as long as I could, but the bark was smooth, my claws gave way, and to my dismay I felt myself slithering back down the way I had come, landing on the ground with a thump. I was badly shaken. Bits of tree bark were wedged in between my claws so I could hardly retract them. I felt dizzy from my sudden descent and shook my head to clear it. When I looked up, there was the tree running creature sitting high up on a branch, laughing its head off and showering me with seed husks. Alerted by his hysterical giggles, other tree runners appeared from all directions, dancing deftly along branches and joining in the fun – at my expense. It was unbearable! Never in all my life – not even on my flight in the container – had I been so humiliated, and all by some scrawny rodent whose head I could have taken off with one bite, had I just been able to catch it. I held my tail high as I retreated towards the half-open back door of my house. As I slipped back inside the cool, dark interior I made the second big decision of my life: I would catch one of those creatures one day and get my own back, if it took me the rest of my life.

Mum must have been watching from the kitchen window, because she met me at the door and tried to comfort me with soft cooing noises, stroking my tail in the way I like. I rubbed myself against her legs and told her I was glad to be back. We went to sit on the sofa, where I cleaned my poor claws and licked the seed husks off my fur. Then I curled up next to her and we watched TV together. Just before I dozed off to sleep, I felt the sofa shake a little, and watching her through half-closed eyes, I saw her quietly laugh to herself. There must have been something funny on TV.

6

I HAVE A VERY NARROW ESCAPE

After the incident with the tree running creature, I went out every day to look for possible ways of catching one, but it proved more difficult than I had imagined. They were incredibly nimble and fast, and soon I knew that only trickery could succeed here. Meanwhile, they missed no opportunity of mocking me as they scampered through the trees and chased each other up and down the long trunks, giggling and jeering all the way. It was quite intolerable, but I put a brave face to it and made a point of sauntering along carelessly, pretending not to notice them at all. I could tell they were annoyed when I did that. Occasionally I stopped to sharpen my claws at the base of a trunk, just to let them see how long they were.

I ventured out a little further each day. Once I followed an interesting creaking noise into someone's garden. The noise turned out to be a swing, creaking on the rings that attached it to a tree branch. A small child was swinging to and fro. I don't care for small children, so I took a detour and found myself at the back of a garden shed. Wondering what lay beyond, I rounded its corner – and stared straight into the face of a large dog. One look at his sharp teeth and at his ears, which were pointed sharply forward in anticipation of a good chase, convinced me I had no option but to bolt. And here's the thing about bolting: you don't get long to decide on your direction. You have to make up your mind on the spot, then trust your instincts and take off like there's no tomorrow, or else there'll *be* no tomorrow.

In this case, the dog's athletic build and long legs made me decide against the wide expanse of the lawn in favour of the garden shed. The door was very slightly ajar; I squeezed through and darted up onto a tottering pile of crates that started wobbling even as I landed. Fortunately, they were stacked against an old wardrobe that looked much sturdier, so up I leapt and crouched down low.

The dog, meanwhile, was frantically working on the door to prise it open further. The shed shook from his efforts – or perhaps it was my heart hammering in my chest, I'm not sure. His mission accomplished, he stormed in, upsetting the crates and crashing into tools that fell over each other with a clatter. The handle of a heavy shovel hit him hard on the head, and for a moment I hoped he might have been knocked out, because he staggered a little. Alas, not for long. Either the blow had affected his judgment, or he wasn't very bright in the first place, even for a dog, because he made no effort to locate me rationally; he just wrecked the whole place. The noise was deafening; my hair stood on end as I watched tools flying and workbenches toppling. Of course the silly creature never found me. But the owner of the shed must have heard the commotion. He came storming across the garden, shouting abuse at the dog and chasing him from the shed, adding a couple of smarting blows to his other injuries. Then he came back and locked the door.

Peace returned to the shed and a warm wave of relief flooded over me. My ears gradually recovered from the noise, my hair settled down, and my tail deflated. I was safe! Even so, I had learnt from experience to stay put for a while after a crisis, just to be on the safe side. Through a crack in the wood of the shed wall, I watched the sun go down behind the trees, and by and by I realized it was dinner-time — time to go home. That was when I discovered that I was locked in just as much as the dog was locked out. There was no other escape route. A fine mess!

In my mind, I pictured Mum getting a tin of fish out of the

cupboard for me, opening it and spooning it into my dish, then filling up my other dish of dry food and my milk bowl. I could almost smell it all, it seemed so real! Sure enough, a little later I could hear her calling, "Tigger! Fish!" from very far away. Normally, I'd be hiding somewhere nearby (I could go in and wait for my dinner in the kitchen, but I prefer to be called). On this occasion, however, just when I really wished I could be right next to her, I was far away and frustratingly unable to answer her call.

Goodness knows for how long I sat in that dark, messy garden shed and waited. It seemed like years. Night-time came and still I was a prisoner. Once or twice I heard my family calling for me; it sounded as though they were out looking for me. I tried to answer, but my voice wasn't loud enough and they walked past the garden. How could they ever find me in here?

Finally, it was quite dark and everyone had gone inside. I prepared myself for a long, lonely night of hunger and discomfort and had just closed my eyes when I heard a sound from the house. There were footsteps, and they were coming closer! A torch was shining towards the shed, and the man's voice called something to the people back at the house. Then – I could hardly believe my luck – he opened the shed door! I was ready for him: as soon as the door opened, I shot out between his legs. The man jumped and used some very bad language. I couldn't blame him; it must have been a shock to find me fly at him like that. I reckoned he would be even more upset once he saw the state of his shed, but I didn't wait to find out. I ran all the way home as fast as I could. They had left the back door open for me. I walked in and announced my arrival, and when my family came running to meet me, I rubbed everyone's legs in turn and told my story. They wanted to know every detail and were clearly impressed with my adventure. Outside, I could still hear the neighbour yelling. It was time to have my dinner and relax.

7

MUM AND I SOLVE AN EMBARRASSING PROBLEM

I was quite back to normal the next morning, but my experience in the garden shed had shaken me a little, so I chose not to go outside for a few days. I watched TV for a while after the children had gone to school, strolled around the house, helped Mum with the cleaning by chasing the mop around the kitchen floor, looked out of the window and generally kept myself busy.

I woke up from a long sleep around lunchtime with an annoying itch on my neck. Scratching did not help much; the itch just moved further along. Then another one started on my leg, then one on my back, and soon I was jumping all over the room, trying to make it stop. I realized with a shock that I had picked up fleas! It must have happened in that shed, of course. I went to tell Mum. She knew as soon as she saw me and reached for the spray. I hate flea spray! We did our little chasing game around the room, as we usually do, but it wasn't much fun because the fleas itched so much, so eventually I let her spray me. It was no use; there were too many fleas. Before long I was beside myself with itches and could not sit still even for a minute.

Mum was worried about me. She got into the car and left for the shops. When she came back, she carried a collection of plastic bottles and made for the bathroom to run a bath. I thought it was strange that she should want to have a bath in the middle of the day, but I love watching the bath fill up, so I came to stand beside her with my front paws on the side of the bath, and together we watched the water rise.

When it was full, I was surprised to see her put on rubber gloves, but not for long: before I knew it, she had picked me up and sat me in the water. Yuck!! I was so stunned, it took me a while before I could even move, by which time she had already soaked me to the skin and covered me in some very smelly shampoo. I tried a tentative struggle, but she had a tight grip on me and I was going nowhere. I simply could not believe she was doing this to me, so I pretended it was not happening and closed my eyes. She continued to rub shampoo into my hair and all over my head until I could hardly breathe. When I opened my eyes again and saw my reflection in the mirror, I nearly screamed — there was a white froth cap on my head, my body looked thin and scrawny and my tail stuck out at an angle, dripping slowly. That could not be me, surely? Mum noticed my stricken face and made soothing noises. I wished she would stop. Anyway, the shampoo was blocking my ears. Eventually she took pity on me and hosed me down under the shower. I never thought I would actually welcome a shower, but it was a relief to get the shampoo off me.

Finally, Mum lifted me out of the bath and wrapped me in a large, soft towel. I saw my chance for escape and struggled hard, but once again she would not let go. She rubbed me dry until I started to feel like myself again. Only then did she let me go. I had a good long shake to get the rest of the water out of my hair, and guess what? The itches had stopped! Mum and I bent over the bath and looked at the dirty water. I still could not believe I had actually been *in* there. There were dozens and dozens of dead fleas floating about. Mum gave me a lecture on how silly cats caught fleas and smart ones didn't, but I wasn't listening. I was beginning to feel deliciously warm and almost dry again, and very sleepy after my ordeal. I trailed off to the lounge and curled up in a sunny patch, where I dozed off immediately.

Later Mum put me in the car while she sprayed the whole house to get rid of the fleas in the carpet and on the furniture. Phew!

8

WE MOVE AGAIN AND I AM REUNITED WITH MY ARMCHAIR

After several days spent cooped up inside, I became seriously bored with my life. I still did not fancy going out because of the children, dogs, tree running creatures, the general noise and fleas. This was no fun at all. I missed my quiet garden in Australia. I spent hours by the window, watching people out on the road and dreaming of my tin roof back home. When I heard water running, I thought of the crystal-blue pool back home, now very possibly taken over by freely marauding frogs no longer kept in check. When other children came to play with ours, I hid away morosely.

However, I need not have worried: my travel-happy family helped me out almost immediately. The packing started again, and this time I was excited to think that this boring place was not to be our home for good. We packed our luggage into the car (there wasn't much this time, since our furniture had not reappeared) and drove off. It was quite a long way, but I sat on Emily's lap and looked out of the window. By and by, the tall trees gave way to open fields with big, dangerous-looking creatures in them. I was glad to be safely behind glass.

After a while, we turned into a lane between high trees, then off that into a long driveway that led uphill to a big house with a veranda and bright, white steps leading invitingly up to the front door. This was it? We jumped out of the car to investigate. I led the way and the children followed. We went all the way around the house, across the lawn that surrounded it to the trees that surrounded the lawn, and back again to the car, now parked by the garage. At the end of our tour I could not believe our luck! This was *the* best place! No sign of dogs or children, no sign of any neighbourhood at all. Just us and lots and lots of space. I loved it and launched into a loud purr to tell everyone. They were pleased that I approved.

Then we went into the house, and there – wonder of wonders! – were all our things! It was still a bit messy, boxes everywhere, but I could see my armchair in one corner of the sitting room. Caroline's piano stood in a large room in the basement alongside Robin's toys. Upstairs, Emily's bed had arrived, and Mum and Dad's big bed… It didn't matter at all that this house was different from our old one back in Australia – we were home anyway! I spent the rest of the day saying noisy hellos to all the furniture, while the others unpacked the boxes, made the beds, put things away and generally sorted the house out. I discovered my bowls in a corner of the kitchen and checked they were all full. I strolled through the house, explored everyone's bedrooms and nearly all the cupboards. It was a big and interesting house. I had a feeling we would be happy there.

When evening fell, we were exhausted from our hard day's work and had an early night. I chose Emily's bedroom, because my coat looked particularly stunning against the dark turquoise of her carpet, but of course I didn't sleep there. I lay on the bed by Emily's feet and purred her to sleep.

9

WE SETTLE DOWN IN PARADISE, I MEET MORE STRANGE CREATURES AND A LARGE YELLOW MONSTER, AND I MAKE A NEW FRIEND

There was much to be done over the next few days and weeks: our new home had to be explored thoroughly. I had to check out favourite places for naps, hidey-holes and lookout spots, noises and smells and, of course – hunting opportunities! As it turned out, this place had everything. I even found a spot high up on a deck at the back of the house that was ideal for secretly observing everything that moved below! It faced the morning sun, so I took to going there at the end of my early walk. I spent a couple of hours napping and watching in complete safety as all kinds of creatures went about their business on the lawn.

As for the hunting – it was very close to paradise! There were all kinds of creatures I had never seen before, and so many of them! Mice, of course, nice fat ones, and they were easily caught. I arranged them by the kitchen door for Mum. Literally hundreds of tree runners everywhere you looked. As we sat on the front veranda in the evenings, we could watch them chase each other all over the place. I was careful not to chase them, as I did not care for a repeat of the embarrassing incident in the other garden, but I watched their behaviour and favourite places and studied their strengths and weaknesses. Patience was the name of the game, and I intended to play it better next time.

There were other strange creatures that tunnelled under the lawn. If I sat still on the grass, I could watch as the turf lifted up in criss-cross patterns all around me. I could hear them as well as they moved the earth underneath me with what sounded like strong claws. Sometimes they came up to the surface, and you could always tell when that would happen, because a little mound of earth came up first. It was great fun pouncing on them when their heads popped out. Occasionally I managed to pull one out. They were a bit like mice, but bigger, and frankly, not much fun to play with; very sluggish. Once I brought one inside and set it down under Mum's desk, where it just lay still with its feet in the air. When Mum came in and sat down at the desk, she put her bare feet right on it and gave a little yell of surprise. I was proud of how well I had placed the creature. She picked it up, brought it over to me and told me it was beautiful. I was glad she liked it so much. She also said it was called 'mole' and that we should put it back outside where it belonged. I didn't think so, but you can't argue with Mum, so we took it outside and put it back on the grass. Then Mum picked me up, carried me inside and locked my door. I didn't think that was very nice, after all I'd done for her, but that's humans for you!

The days passed and my new life settled into a pleasant pattern. In the mornings, Dad and Caroline left quite early to go to work and school. They went in Dad's car, and I watched them leave from my observation spot on the back deck. A while later, Emily and Robin walked down the drive and to the end of our lane. Mum said they were old enough to go on their own, but I didn't think so, so I went with them to make sure they were safe. When we got to the end of our lane, I hid behind a bush, because I didn't much care for the big, yellow monster that arrived shortly afterwards and stopped in front of them with much rattling and flashing of lights. I could never understand why they got in there; you couldn't have dragged me anywhere near it. Emily told me it was called 'school bus' and that it was all right – well, rather her than me. I waited until it had roared off down the road, then went back home to report to Mum that all was well.

After that, it was time to explore! There was so much to see and do, and I found new delights almost every day. Some old tree trunks had toppled over each other in one corner of the garden, creating a wonderful hiding place and climbing stack. It was overgrown with moss, and there were often insects underneath and inside the wood that were fun to watch. They were so busy and nearly always hard at work. I helped them along a bit with my paw. From the top of the mossy wood pile I had a good view of the field next door, where the grass grew high and the green blades were like a jungle all around me as I walked along. Big, brightly-coloured insects with huge wings fluttered about. It was quite wonderful there, but you had to be careful, too. A big, black snake lived nearby and occasionally slithered along in the sandy soil. I didn't like the look of it and receded onto my high mossy wood pile when it was around.

One morning, as I returned from my walk and was about to climb the steps to the back deck for my nap, a small grey cat came sauntering across the lawn. He seemed quite at home and pleased to see me. I hadn't seen another cat in ages – not since my flight – and had not played with one since I lost my brother. I invited him to come up on the deck with me, and we had a nice time getting to know each other. He lived in a house not far away, but his owners expected him to live outside all year round – cruel people, evidently. So he used to come over to our house before we moved in and made the previous owners believe he was really *their* cat. They let him come into the house and fed him, but on balance he liked the food better in the other house, so he went back there occasionally just to keep his other family happy, too. Then the people in our house got a *dog*, and that, of course, was it as far as he was concerned. He left and never came back. Now he was pleased to see the dog had moved out and we had moved in. He asked whether I thought my family might want another cat, but I told him I was sure they didn't, because they already had me. He just shrugged and said he had to go now and would see me later. I had enjoyed our chat and told him to come by any time; then I dozed off in a lovely patch of sun.

At lunchtime I joined Mum in the kitchen for a bowl of food. Unfortunately, the cat food had not improved since our arrival. Mum knew that but said there was nothing to be done about it, as Australia was too far away to go back for cat food each week. But she made up for it by giving me little bits of cheese when she made her sandwich, and sometimes a slice of ham. I wouldn't have minded just eating her food, but she said that wasn't good for me. Typical.

After lunch and another walk around the garden, it was time to start looking out for Emily and Robin, who came back in the big, yellow monster mid-afternoon. It spat them out in the same place where it had swallowed them up in the morning. I was always glad to see them safely back and led them up the lane towards our house. We usually had a snack together in the kitchen before they went off to do their homework and watch TV. Sometimes I watched with them, but if it was a nice day, I liked to go with Mum in the car to pick up Caroline from her school. We went down a long, busy road where we passed big trucks and all kinds of scary things, but nothing could harm us, because the windows were shut tight. One day it started raining hard while we drove along and big puddles appeared on the road. A huge truck that passed us sprayed our windscreen with a great big splash of muddy water. I panicked and ducked under the dashboard. Mum thought that was very funny. She couldn't stop laughing all the way to school. I didn't think it was *that* hilarious. How was I to know we had a waterproof car?

Our evenings were usually spent getting dinner ready and watching TV. I always helped Mum in the kitchen when she cooked chicken; she needed me to check that it was all right before she cooked it for everyone else. That was always my job and still is. Caroline and Emily practised their music after dinner – piano and flute. That was a very good time to go outside for my last walk of the day, because the flute in particular was quite shrill. On warm summer evenings Mum and Dad sat out on the front veranda with their drinks, so I joined them when I returned, and we mused about the events of the day while the sun went down behind the trees.

I DISCOVER THE BENEFITS OF A BLACK BOX AND SOME WHITE STUFF AND REALIZE THAT MY FAMILY IS SOMETIMES RIGHT

As the weeks passed, it grew cooler, the crickets suspended their concerts, and in the early mornings dew covered the grass and the large spider webs that hung in the trees. They sparkled like silver in the morning sun.

Later still, the ground became very cold, hard and frosty-white. The trees changed colour from green to various shades of yellow, red and brown. As I sat still on my mossy wood pile, I could hear them slowly floating down all around me; they made a soft rustling noise. They were exactly my colour, so I became invisible amongst them, even to my family. When the children went off for a walk down the lane, I was able to stalk them through the undergrowth for ages without being noticed. Sometimes we explored the countryside together. A narrow path led off the lane deep into the forest. We liked going there, because the forest floor was covered thickly in pine needles, which muffled our footsteps and turned our walk into a silent and mysterious adventure. The lane led to a lookout platform high up in a tree. At dawn and dusk, big animals with branches on their heads walked through the forest. If we kept very still, they didn't see us.

As it grew colder, Dad collected wood from a large pile by the back door and used it to make a fire in a big, black box that stood in a corner of the large basement room. The fire hissed and roared, but Dad shut the glass door of the black box and locked the fire inside. After a while, I could feel heat radiating from it, and the whole room became lovely and warm. Through the glass door, you could see the flames licking the wood, which started glowing yellow, orange and red. Dad kept the fire going day and night while it stayed cold. The sofa by the black box became my favourite spot, where most of the family joined me in the evenings. Sometimes it got so hot the humans couldn't stand it any longer and went upstairs, where it was cooler, but to me it felt just right. When they left, I stretched out on the sofa until I was as long as I could be, and slept and slept and slept…

One morning I woke up on the sofa and everything felt different. Even the light in the room was different. It was a soft, creamy light, and everywhere was very still. I was on my guard straight away. I walked over to the cat flap my family had installed for me in the basement door. When I carefully lifted the flap, icy air stung my nose. Then I saw the whiteness everywhere; an ice cold, sparkly white substance that covered our entire garden, even the branches of the trees and every bush. The grass had disappeared under it, and with it the mole heaps and the russet leaves. No more hiding out there for me! My fur would stick out brightly for everyone to see! This was bad news, and I wondered who was behind it? I strongly suspected my family, who were always up to strange new tricks. I resolved to have stern words with them when they got up.

But for now there was really nothing for it but to go out there, because I needed a pee. I crept carefully outside — front paws first, then one back paw, then the other, then my tail, very gently, so no loud click of my cat door closing would give my position away to the enemy. Nothing unusual so far. All was eerily quiet, and although the white substance smelled cold, it looked very clean and soft. I gingerly placed one front paw on it. Freezing! I pulled back immediately and had to shake my paw hard to get the stuff off. I tried again with the other paw, but same thing. What was I to do? The cold made me even more desperate for my pee.

I could see a small bare patch under a big tree some distance from the house. The white stuff must have come from above, because the tree branches had obviously prevented it from landing under the tree. First mystery solved. I decided to make a run for that bare patch. If I ran fast I wouldn't feel the cold so much; so I set forth. The white was deeper and colder than I had thought. I had to take big leaps to stop it touching my tummy. Soon it clung between my toes, gluing them together. I tried to shake my paws while running, which proved almost impossible. Eventually I made it to the tree and did my business in the comfort of the bare patch there. Impossible to dig a hole though, as the ground was completely frozen. Too bad, it would have to do. No enemy in their right mind would come looking for me today, and if they did, I wished them luck.

Looking around, I could now see that the whiteness was not confined to our garden. The lane was white, and the two neighbouring houses that could just be seen through the bare trees also had it on their roofs, just like ours. Either my family had ordered too much of it, or they were in fact innocent after all. Unlikely, but I decided not to pass judgment until I was certain.

My business done, I had no choice but to leap back to the house, trying to keep to the paw prints I had made on my way out. I dashed in through the cat door and straight upstairs to announce the disaster to my family, but too late! They were already up, and the children were leaping about by the windows, screeching and laughing and clapping their hands. They had clearly gone mad overnight. I called them to order, but as soon as they noticed me, they scooped me up and dragged me to the window. They pointed to the whiteness out there as though it was the best thing in the world and were obviously very pleased with it. They must have ordered it after all. What would the neighbours say when they found out? And my new grey friend? How was I ever going to explain to him what my family had done? It was too embarrassing for words!

I was speechless all through breakfast, staring numbly through the kitchen window at the white hell outside. No sooner had the children finished breakfast than they threw on some clothes and ran outside, where they jumped about in the white fluff, threw themselves onto their backs into it, yelled and laughed. Mum and Dad joined them after a while, and all were clearly happy with what they had done. I sneaked out behind them and climbed up to my morning deck, which had a roof and was therefore dry. From up there, I watched them for some time, wondering what strange turn my life had taken yet again, when all of a sudden the sun rose from behind the trees and the white substance sparkled silver, pink and light blue. I had to close my eyes for a moment because it was so bright, but my goodness, was it beautiful! As far as I could see from my lookout place, the whole world was wearing a glittering coat of brightness, and above it the sky was a deep blue. I don't think my family had time to notice all this. They were too busy throwing themselves about below me, leaving imprints of their bodies with their arms spread out. Humans are very odd creatures.... But I lay very still on my deck and looked all around and was beginning to understand why my family had made everything white. It was actually quite nice for a change.

By the next day, it was much easier to walk on our white lawn because of the holes my family had made everywhere. I even went for a walk into the forest with the children, where we saw footprints made by rabbits and by the big animals with branches on their heads. We sat on the platform in the big tree, eating biscuits we had brought from home, and admired the stillness and the white all around us. After a while, more of it started coming down! I was a bit alarmed at first, but it didn't hurt. It fell slowly from the sky in small crystals that landed gently on the tree branches, on our heads and on the ground. When we kept very still — which was hard for Robin – we could actually hear it land with a very soft hissing sound, much softer than the rustle of the autumn leaves. The children told me the white substance was called 'snow', and I made a mental note to remember that word, because it was clearly of some importance in this place.

The snow didn't stay very long. Three days later, the weather changed and it started melting. As I lay on the deck in the late morning sunshine, I could hear it trickling away down the gutters and dripping off the tree branches. The children had made a little man out of snow with Robin's woolly hat on. I watched it getting smaller and smaller until eventually it collapsed and the woolly hat fell off. I was as sad as the children to see it go. The grass underneath looked brown and squashed when it emerged, and so wet that it squelched under my paws.

My family seemed to forget to order more snow for quite a while after that, which was surprising considering how much they had liked it the first time. The hunting was definitely better without it, but I still wished they would get more one day.

11

I DEFEND OUR HOUSE

The cat door my family had installed for me was too tricky for my liking. Similar to my Australian door, it only opened during the day and locked for the night after I came in from my last walk. In the morning, Mum or Dad came downstairs and opened it somehow. I watched them closely and tried to do the same thing with my paws when I was alone, but it never worked. I even tried to dismantle the whole door using my teeth and claws, but no luck. So I had to stay in all night, which was boring in summer. In winter, when it was warm and cosy by the fire and bitterly cold outside, I didn't mind so much. However, it has to be said in fairness to the door that it had its good point as well: it knew that it was my door alone and never, ever let any other animals in, which was pretty cool. A big, fat toad once spent hours glued to the glass panel, desperate to join us inside, but the door stayed shut.

While it was cold and snowy, I did not see my new friend the grey cat again. This may have been because his grey/white colouring made him invisible in the snow, just like I blended in with the autumn leaves. But as soon as the ground dried up a little, he was back. We sat on the deck together, and Mum came out to join us for a while. She was very friendly to him – almost a touch too friendly, perhaps – and he certainly did his best to endear himself to her, rubbing his head against her as she stroked him and purring into her face, the two oldest and cheapest tricks in the book.

38

When it was time for me to go inside for my lunch, he made to follow me. I stopped, glared hard at him and told him he could not come inside. He just sniffed at a flower, looked innocent and scratched himself behind the ear. I think he had fleas. When he was in mid-scratch and looked the other way, I ran towards my cat door as fast as I could and slipped inside. Halfway up the stairs, I heard a loud bang, and turning around I saw my new friend standing just outside the closed cat door, looking stunned. He must have banged his head really hard on the door, because he shook it a few times before trotting off.

I was grateful to the door and went upstairs to tell Mum all about it. She listened carefully and looked pleased. Then she gave me a piece of salami to eat, which was nice of her because, really, it was the cat door that deserved a reward.

My friend never tried to come into our house again. He returned a few days after the incident and bore me no grudge, so it was just as well I had made it clear whose territory this was. We were happily strolling through the garden together, when suddenly a large, fierce-looking dog came trotting up the driveway towards us. Escape clearly being the only option, I bolted, but in my haste I ran away from the house instead of towards it! There was nowhere to take cover except for a large tree. I raced up its trunk like one of those tree runners and amazed myself by making it to the lowest branch, which was almost as high up as the roof of our house. I clambered up onto the branch and turned to call to my friend to join me. To my amazement, he was still standing in the same spot, facing the huge dog — back arched, hair spiked up and teeth bared. He gave one vicious hiss and struck the dog on the nose with his right front paw. It happened so fast, the dog never had the chance to step back. It yelped, turned tail and fled! I called a loud meow of victory for my friend, who looked up at me blankly and asked what I was doing up the tree.

I indicated I was just coming down again, but when I tried to climb down, I found I was too high up and couldn't. Luckily Dad was home and had watched the whole episode. He got the long ladder from the shed and helped me down. My friend sat and watched us, and this time *he* looked impressed. I don't think his humans would have helped him like my family helped me. He would probably have been stuck up that tree forever. I was glad we were here now to look after him, should he ever get in trouble again.

12

WE CELEBRATE CHRISTMAS AND I NEARLY GET LOST

Christmas was coming. I knew because every day tantalising smells wafted down the stairs into the basement room from the kitchen, where Mum and the children baked cookies. They also made a gingerbread house decorated with colourful sweets. Some of them could be rolled along the table top with a front paw until they plopped on the floor to disappear under the fridge. The roof of the little house was covered in something white that looked exactly like snow, but wasn't cold and tasted sweet when I licked it. It was a very pretty little house; I had my picture taken next to it.

We also decorated the outside of our real house with green garlands and red bows that looked lovely against the white paintwork. Through the bare trees, we could see the neighbours' houses all decorated with coloured lights, some of them flashing. They were a bit alarming at first. I went to check them out, but after keeping watch from behind a tree for some time, I was able to pronounce them perfectly harmless. For some reason, the humans enjoyed these lights a lot. Soon there were houses and front gardens flashing everywhere.

Mum put some food out for the birds on the garden table, which stood on the veranda by the living room window. Whenever I got bored, I sat by the window and watched the birds peck at the seeds. They were so tempting, but unfortunately the window was shut tight – I checked. Sometimes tree runners would also come up and eat the seeds. That was really exciting, as it gave me an opportunity to study their strengths and weaknesses at very close range. The only weakness I could spot was greed! I didn't realize at that point just how useful that knowledge was going to be for me one day...

Mum and the children came back from school with a large tree tied to the car roof. It seemed a silly idea to bring a tree home on the car roof when we had so many growing all around the house. It took them ages to untie the ropes that were holding it in place. Then they carried it through the back door into the kitchen and on into the living room. I kept out of the way, because the tree was so big it filled the doorway completely and nobody seemed to be able to see where they were going. Robin stepped right into my water bowl. Finally the tree was put up in a corner of the living room. We all stood around and admired it. For all that it was strange to have it there right in the room, it did look magnificent – a bright splash of green that filled the entire corner. It smelt wonderful too, of leaves, pine cones and secret, dark pathways through the undergrowth. Just like having the forest in our house. I would have been perfectly happy to leave it there as it was, but my family had other ideas: they brought in boxes full of glittering ornaments and spent the rest of the afternoon hanging them on the tree's branches until it sparkled like the snow on a sunny day. Then they added little lights and switched them on just as it grew dark outside. It looked quite magical.

The tree was an excellent hiding place. Screened by green branches and dangling ornaments, I watched unnoticed as visitors' feet walked past. We had lots of visitors, and there were children everywhere who wanted to make a fuss of me. They tried to put a tinsel bow around my neck, but I soon got rid of that. There were often yummy leftovers in my bowl at night, and we lit candles as soon as it grew dark in the evenings. I loved watching them flicker.

One day, I was woken up at dawn by yells and laughter to find the children ripping colourful paper off parcels that had somehow appeared under the Christmas tree overnight, while Mum and Dad sat on the sofa, looking sleepy. Toys, clothes, story books and many other interesting things emerged from the parcels, leaving large swathes of wrapping paper scattered all over the living room floor. I played hide-and-seek in the paper with the children all morning. I would hide in one of the multi-coloured tunnels until they had forgotten about me, then pounce on their bare feet when they weren't looking. Poor Robin lost his balance at one point and fell on his new Lego castle. I helped him build it again later.

The children stayed home from school over the Christmas holidays, and there was more snow. It was very cold outside. The black box in the basement room was hissing away and puffing out heat to keep us warm. We had games in the snow together. I was quite used to the snow by then and didn't mind getting a little wet. We played hide-and-seek in the garden. It was not easy for me to hide in the snow; they spotted me every time. So I looked for a darker hiding place. There was a door under the steps leading up to the front veranda. Normally it was closed, but on that day, the wind was blowing. As I passed the door, it creaked open a bit. What a stroke of luck! I ran inside, and as my eyes adjusted to the dark I could see that I was in an open space underneath the house, with tiny windows all around. The ground was rough earth; it smelled musty. I heard the children running around outside looking for me and felt very smug in my hiding place. They would never find me here! After a while, they gave up and called me. I was just about to make a brilliant entrance through the little door, tail held high, when another blast of wind knocked it shut in my face. I tried to push it open again, but it was shut tight and I could not move it.

There I was, caught yet again. I was furious with the door, with the wind, and even a little bit with myself. I checked all the windows, but they were barred and I could only just squeeze my paw through in between the bars. I would have no choice but to call the children and ask them to let me out. So I called them. They called me, too. I heard them, but they obviously could not hear me, because they walked off after a while and left me to my dark hiding place. Soon it was evening and even darker. Dinnertime came and went. I heard them chatting and eating above me in the kitchen. The clunk of their cutlery on the plates made me quite hungry. I called again many times, but they made too much noise for my little voice to be heard.

When dinner was over and cleared away, Mum and Dad came outside with torches to look for me. They walked all over the garden, calling my name, but never near enough to catch my frantic calls. Oh how I wanted to get out of this stuffy place and sleep under their bed! But it was no use. They gave up after a while and went back into the house. I had been right: they would never find me here!

Soon everything went quiet above – they had gone to sleep. I dug myself a small hollow in the earth to get some rest. It was not easy to relax – the musty smell was awful and caught in my throat. But I must have dozed off in the end, because all of a sudden I woke up from a strange dream in which three tree runners were dancing up and down in front of me, giggling and carrying bowls of delicious food. It was the middle of the night and very still, but the click of the back door had woken me. I heard Mum's voice calling for me very softly into the stillness, then she stood quietly, listening.

My chance had come! I ran over to the window nearest to her and called her as loudly as I could. She *must* have heard me! I could see her slippered feet coming down the steps into the garden. It took her a while to work out where I was, and in the end I had to stick my paw through the bars of the little window and wave it up and down a bit. Thank goodness there was a bright moon – my white paw was clearly visible against the dark window. Mum saw me and gave a small gasp of surprise. I knew she was wondering how on earth I had got myself trapped in there, so I started explaining straight away. She had to walk all the way around the house to get to the little door. I ran alongside her on the inside, past all the tiny windows, telling her my tale, until she finally got to the door, opened it and let me out. I jumped up into her arms, so glad to swap the hard, smelly earthen floor of my prison for the soft material of her dressing gown and her night-time scent of soap and lotions. She held me tight and told me I was a silly cat. Maybe I was, but I didn't really care, because I was safe once again.

Mum carried me back into the house, and we were finally able to sleep in peace. The next day, Dad hammered some nails into the little door under the house, so it wouldn't open again. I sat next to him while he worked and made sure it was quite secure.

13

MY FAMILY ABANDONS ME IN A TERRIBLE PLACE

Dad got the travel bags out of the wardrobe – always a bad sign. With a sinking feeling I watched Mum pack for a 'long weekend' away. Where would I go and would I have to fly again? I prepared myself for the worst.

The very next day, Mum took me to the local vet clinic, where a mean-looking woman who smelt of smoke carried me into a room full of cages. There were bigger ones at the bottom and smaller ones stacked on top, all along the walls, with just one small window at the end. The window was shut tight, and the air was rank with the smell of unhappy animals. There were cats in all the smaller cages, but in the big ones underneath, there were dogs! They howled and yapped and jumped about as the woman shoved me roughly into a cage. I yelled, hissed and scratched, but too late – she had already locked the door. I was given some food, water and a litter tray; that was it. No warm blanket, no space out the back to stretch my legs and play, no goldfish pond. Was this going to be my home for a whole long weekend? How could I survive here, without fresh air, without a run or a climb – without my family? And how long was a long weekend, anyway?

I spent the rest of the first day trying to get out of my cage and run back home, but it was no use. The door was firmly locked, and there was no other exit. I tried to bend the bars, but my paws and teeth weren't strong enough, and eventually my paws were so sore that I had to give up.

All day and most of the night the dogs continued their racket. When they jumped about, they rocked their cages, which made a loud rattling noise, so sleep or relaxation of any kind were out of the question. I could not eat a single bite and just drank a little now and then. The rest of the time I rolled myself up into a tight ball, suffered quietly somewhere deep inside and vowed never, ever to let my family leave me here again. I have never forgotten the unhappiness I felt during those long days. Even now I can recall that smell, that noise and the discomfort of that horrible room as though it happened yesterday. My biggest disappointment was that my family left me there. They had never done anything to hurt me, and I loved them for it. Why did they do this to me now?

By and by, I started looking around at the cats in nearby cages. There was a straggly tortoiseshell, who looked as though she hadn't had a brush in years, a very fat old cat who seemed not to notice what went on around him as long as his bowl was full, and a scrawny kitten that shared a crate with his haggard-looking mother. They were a pretty rough lot; as far as they knew, pets everywhere stayed in hovels such as this one. I felt sorry for them.

One night, when there was a semblance of peace from down below, I told them about the nice cat hotel where I had spent my holidays in Australia – the personal attention, the peace and quiet, the excellent food, the climbing tree out the back with a view of the fishpond. What a difference! The cats looked at me with concern and clearly thought I was having hallucinations. I assured them I wasn't mad, but it was obvious they didn't believe a word I was saying and started whispering among themselves, darting furtive glances at me from time to time. I gave up trying to talk to them after that. What good would it do, anyway? It occurred to me that if I stayed in that place long enough, I might start to look, talk and think just like them. I curled my long, silky tail tightly

47

around myself to stop it straying into another cage, shut my eyes tight and kept as close to the centre of my cage as I could.

At one point, the mean-looking woman dragged in a particularly ferocious dog. It was straining on the lead she was holding, slobbering all over the floor and sniffing at our cages as it panted past. It must suddenly have realized what the smaller cages contained – us! – because all at once the room erupted into bedlam: the ferocious dog jumped up at our cages to get a closer look and in doing so, managed to dislodge the tortoiseshell's cage, which came crashing down to the floor, its occupant tossed about like a fur ball inside. It was awful to watch! The dog hurled itself onto the cage with a throaty growl, while the poor cat tried to squeeze herself into the far corner and screeched. All the other dogs in their cages, sensing battle, started to bark, howl and rattle their cages. This alerted the vet and several other staff members, and soon the room was a jumble of arms and legs, some belonging to humans, some to animals. Everyone shouted and shrieked in their own language.

It took them a while to bring the dog under control. Once they had caught it they had to put a muzzle on its nose to stop it snapping at everything and everyone. The poor tortoiseshell was hoisted back up to her old place. She looked terrible, her eyes huge, her fur even wilder than before, and continued shaking for the rest of the day. The dog was finally wrestled into a cage, where it continued to crash about and snarl viciously. It caused such a disturbance that all the other dogs remained restless and the cages below us kept shaking alarmingly. Eventually, after what seemed like forever, the humans came in again and took the dog away. None of us cared where they took it or what they did with it, just as long as it never came back.

More days and nights passed; they seemed like years. I was exhausted by the time the woman finally opened my door again, pulled me out and carried me to where Mum was waiting for me. The welcome smile died on her face when she saw me. I must have looked quite a sight after my ordeal, because she took me into her arms straight away and asked to see where I had been kept. They showed her; reluctantly, I thought. When she saw the conditions in which I had lived, she grew really angry: she yelled at the mean-looking woman, and when the vet came in she yelled at him as well. She even stamped her foot, and I would have stamped mine as well had I been able to. But I had to cling to Mum to make sure she took me with her. When she finally stomped out to the car with me, I dug my claws so deeply into her jumper that it probably hurt her quite a lot, but she never said a word. The whole way home I could not settle in the car and jumped around until there was hair all over the car and all over Mum. Mum said she was really, really sorry and that I would never have to go back to that awful place. She blamed herself for not having checked the room before she booked me in there and said that apparently, vets in this country could not be trusted.

When we got home, I ran straight away under Mum and Dad's bed, where I sat and listened to my heart pounding. Mum came to find me and sat down next to the bed. She talked to me soothingly until I felt myself relaxing, and then I was very, very tired. I crawled out from under the bed onto Mum's lap, and she laid me down in the middle of her soft bed, covered me with a warm blanket and stroked my head until I fell asleep. I slept and slept for ages; it stayed very quiet in the house the whole time. At one point I thought I heard the children come back from school, but I also heard an angry hiss from Mum, and they left me alone.

I felt much better when I eventually woke up, and when I came into the kitchen everyone was sitting around the big table waiting for me. I was so happy to see them again! I jumped up on the table and rubbed heads with everyone in turn. Then I had a big, delicious dinner and a whole bowlful of fresh milk as a special treat. Everyone was cross with the vet and promised I could stay home the next time they went away. I thought it had better be a long time before they left me again.

14

MY NEW FRIEND IS INJURED AND WE HELP HIM

In late winter, my new friend the grey cat needed our help. I was just hanging the washing out with Mum when he came limping slowly and painfully across the lawn towards us. When Mum picked him up, we saw that he was bleeding from one of his front paws. It looked pretty bad to me. Mum carried him into the kitchen, where she sat him down on the table and went to make some camomile tea. He looked surprised, but pleased to be inside our house and sat patiently on the table, holding his injured paw up. I sat down next to him. When the tea was ready, Mum put it in a bowl and cooled it down. Then she told Emily, who wants to be a vet and always looks after me when I'm unwell, to dip the grey cat's paw into the tea and wash it carefully. Emily was very gentle and my friend didn't flinch; he just sat there with his paw in the tea and looked mournful. As Emily washed him, she discovered a thorny twig that had lodged itself between his toes. She pulled it out and we all had a good look at it. It was very sharp. I was glad it wasn't in *my* paw. Emily finished cleaning the wound, then put a bandage around it and told my friend he would be fine now.

I was pleased that we had been able to help him and expected him to leave now, but he had other ideas: he wanted to be shown around our house. I didn't like that much, but Mum and Emily told me to be nice to him since he was wounded, so off we went.

I noticed his limp was already improving. He admired everything and said our furniture was much nicer than his family's. He sat in my armchair for a while and pronounced it very comfortable. He sniffed at my food and looked under the big bed. When I suggested he might like to go now, he looked mournful again and gave a sad little meow that had Emily come and check on him. She shot me a sharp look, then she asked my friend to rest for a while, until he felt better.

I squeezed onto the armchair next to him and we rested together. Emily also stayed with us; she named my friend 'Piglet'. I think he liked his new name. He certainly purred loudly enough, rubbed his nose against her hands and stayed until Dad came home from work. As soon as Dad walked in, my friend decided to leave. He told me he didn't like men. I thought that was strange, but also quite convenient. It was good to see him run off with hardly a limp, and even better to have my house and family to myself again.

15

I DISCOVER THE JOYS OF SPRING AND PROTECT MY FAMILY FROM A DANGEROUS BEAST

Spring arrived in a flurry of apple blossom and sweet, sweet scents. Previously dead trees pushed out tiny leaves practically overnight, and in no time at all the russet forest had turned bright green again. My camouflage was gone.

Birds twittered everywhere, busily building nests. I watched them lazily as I lay on my deck in the morning sun, soaking in the pleasant warmth, wondering whether one or two of the birds might build their nests in accessible places. In fact, a pair of finches had the cheek to build theirs in one of Mum's hanging baskets, right on the deck! I knew, of course, long before Mum discovered the little eggs while watering the flowers. From then on, both Mum and I watched the nest very carefully. We both knew I could easily jump up to the nest from the deck rail, and there seemed no way she could stop me. Or so I thought. But when the first egg cracked and I was just sharpening my claws in delicious anticipation, Mum and Dad appeared on the deck with a wooden board brimming with sharp, shiny nails and fastened it on to the deck rail just underneath the nest. It looked lethal and ran nearly all the length of the rail. No way was I going to get at the nest now; Mum was a spoil-sport. I gave her a hard, green stare and turned my attention back to the mice and moles that were back in force. Someone else could have the silly birds, for all I cared.

Grey cat Piglet and I hunted together for days among the fresh grass and flowers of the spring meadow next to our house. His bandage had long fallen off and his wound had healed. There were hundreds of butterflies and tiny lizards besides the usual rodents. Under the roots of a large tree we found a hole with young rabbits in it. I took one into the house for my family, but they put it straight back outside and locked me up for a whole day – well, no more presents for them!

Instead, another visitor began to turn up with annoying regularity as the weather improved: one of the neighbours had a goat. It was usually tethered to a tree by a long rope, but the spring weather seemed to have filled it with wanderlust and it regularly broke loose to come and visit us. The first time we saw the goat, it was following Robin up our driveway after school. I watched them from the safety of the deck. Robin didn't look too happy: he kept looking nervously over his shoulder and telling the goat to go home, but it wasn't listening. Fortunately, he knew better than to run, but I could tell he really wanted to.

Mum was taking the washing down when Robin and the goat rounded the corner of the house. Mum's hand froze in mid-air, clutching a peg. I didn't blame her. You don't get to meet a goat every day in your back garden. Robin, once he was within safe reach of Mum, ran and hid behind her, so she had to face the goat all on her own, armed with just the peg in one hand and a towel in the other. I was proud of her. She did really well at first, talking brightly to both the goat and Robin, but it wasn't long before the goat took a shine to the clean sheets on the line and started charging at them with its horns. Mum wasn't very happy about that and tried to push the goat off. That made it angry and it charged at Mum, head down and horns facing her. Robin, I'm sorry to say, abandoned her at that point and ran into the house. Mum, who clearly was in no mood to sacrifice her washing to the goat, threw the last of the sheets into the basket, picked it up and ran after Robin, using the basket as a shield against the goat, which was getting quite vicious by then. She just made it into the house and slammed the door shut as the goat's horns crashed into it.

I had wisely entered the house some time ago. Now the three of us stood by the closed door and listened to the goat bashing about outside. At one point it came around to the window, stood up on its hind legs and peered in at us. For an awful moment we thought it would break the glass, but then it trotted off and hung around the house until dark. When we turned on the lights, it came back and stared accusingly at us through the windows. Mum told us to turn all the lights off once more, so we sat in pitch darkness for a long time, whispering to each other and wondering where the goat was.

The banging of the kitchen door almost had us jump out of our skins. The goat had finally broken into our house! I was halfway out of my cat door to find myself a nice, safe tree when we heard Dad's voice from the kitchen, calling us. I had never been happier to hear his voice. We all ran to meet him. He laughed when he saw our stricken faces and asked what we were doing, sitting in a dark house. He had seen no sign of the goat.

16

WE HIDE EGGS, JOIN A HUNT AND HOST A GREAT PARTY

I woke up at dawn as Mum and Dad were rustling papers in the kitchen. When I got there, I found them packing coloured eggs and tiny chocolate rabbits into little paper bags. They looked smug and secretive and told me to be very quiet so the children wouldn't wake up. The three of us were going on a top-secret mission. Breakfast could wait.

Two minutes later, we slipped noiselessly out by the kitchen door. The birds were trilling their morning songs and the sky was pale blue as the sun rose behind the tall trees. It was going to be a perfect spring day. As the three of us tiptoed across the dewy lawn, I felt a sudden thrill of excitement in the air. Whatever we were up to was going to be fun!

We walked all around our garden, and wherever there was a good hiding place – under an overhanging bush or in the fork of a small tree, behind a fallen trunk or in the centre of a clump of yellow spring flowers – we placed some of the coloured eggs and chocolates. There were dozens of little nests everywhere by the time we had finished.

Back at the kitchen door, we turned around to see whether we could spot them. They were pretty well hidden, but if you looked carefully, you could just spy a speck of pink here and a splash of blue there. It was all very intriguing. I just hoped the real rabbits weren't going to find the chocolate ones and take them away to their burrows. Or, banish the thought, the goat didn't come back!

When the children woke up and came down for breakfast, they were pretty excited and kept looking out of the window, but Mum made them eat their cereal, followed by pieces of toast and hot chocolate. The meal seemed to go on forever.

We were saved by the sound of cars coming up the drive. Several families with young children spilled from them and rushed towards our house with waves and gleeful shouts. I sat on the deck to welcome them, but my dignified gesture went unnoticed in the noisy welcome. Soon everyone raced off down the garden together. The hunt was on; I followed on their heels.

For the next half hour, there were children everywhere, screaming and laughing, some spying hidden nests, some running right past them without seeing anything, some actually *treading* on eggs before noticing them. I don't think kittens could ever be *this* silly. Meanwhile, the parents got in everyone's way, clicking cameras and exclaiming in great surprise whenever a new nest was found. Mum and Dad seemed surprised, too. Unbelievably, they had already forgotten that it was us who put the nests there in the first place. I was clearly the only one in the garden who had any sense left.

It took them a long time to find all the eggs and chocolates, but once they were done, everyone sat down in a large circle to eat their treasures. That seemed a sensible enough thing to do; I quickly caught myself a small mouse and joined the circle. It was quite delicious, and everyone else enjoyed their snacks, too. Most of the children looked as though they could do with a bath when they had finished: they had brown faces and sticky hands. I made sure they didn't touch me. Since only the tail was left of my mouse, I wandered off to find my sunny spot on the deck, leaving the parents to clean up their offspring as best they could.

They stayed all day and ate lots of food. The adults had sparkly, bubbly water in tall glasses. The children played games, laughed, cried, sang, argued and generally made a lot of noise, so after a while I retreated to my mossy wood pile in a quieter corner of the garden to have a little snooze. Next thing I knew, the visitors' cars were filing past my hiding place, sticky hands waving from windows, goodbyes sounding across the garden as the sun threw long shadows on the lawn.

It was safe to emerge from my mossy wood pile. The garden looked a bit tired: here and there, squashed chocolate bunnies and the odd coloured egg lay scattered on the lawn, along with plastic cups and paper serviettes. Back in the house, Mum and Dad were resting on the sofa, looking exhausted, while the children were finishing up the last of their chocolates. I was finally able to have a peaceful meal, without having to worry about children tripping over me.

Later on, we tidied up the garden, the house and especially the kitchen. It had been a tiring day, but an exciting one, too. For a long time afterwards, I kept stumbling across forgotten nests of eggs and chocolates during my hunting expeditions. As the days grew warmer, the chocolate melted and oozed out of the shiny paper. The ants obviously liked chocolate; they feasted on it for weeks. It had been a successful party for everyone.

17

I AM HOME ALONE

A couple of days after the party, the travel bags made their appearance again. It was the first time after my traumatic experience in the cat prison some months ago. Naturally, I was aghast and ran straight under the double bed. They would not be able to prise me off the bedroom carpet; it was very thick and I had buried my claws deep in its pile. When they came to talk to me, I hissed at them and refused to listen. Soon five faces were lined up on one side of the bed, upside-down, smiling and cooing. I was not fooled. No matter what they promised me, I would stay put.

A visitor came in the afternoon, a young girl with long hair and a bright voice. I had never seen her before. Her face lined up next to the other five on the side of the bed. She talked to me for a long time, while I pretended to sleep. I stayed put right through dinnertime, even though my stomach was rumbling, and never moved even when Mum and Dad climbed into bed above me and everything went quiet. I slept fitfully, expecting the worst when dawn finally broke.

Again, faces appeared; I gave them a long, cold stare. Eventually they gave up. Bags were picked up, feet walked past the bed and out of the door, the front door slammed shut. They were gone. I was all alone in the house! They had gone and I could stay – and do what I wanted... Yes!

I shot out from under the bed and downstairs to the window overlooking the drive. They were just leaving. I gave them a little wave with my tail as the car disappeared in the trees. So that was that. I sat for a while, surveying the deserted garden, listening to the sounds of the empty house. Nothing but the ticking of the kitchen clock and the quiet hum of the fridge. Well, at least I was free, and I was home. I went to the kitchen, where I found a full bowl of food and one of milk; there was also a litter tray nearby, which seemed a little odd. But I was starving and set about eating first of all. I ate everything in one go, then started wondering where my next meal would be coming from. I hadn't thought about that while I was ravenous. Still, no use worrying about it now. I would go out and hunt. Catching my own food would be good. I would be totally independent of humans and look after myself like a wild cat in the bush. No problem – it would be fun! I ran downstairs to my cat door.

It was locked – in broad daylight! How could they leave me trapped inside the house, unable to hunt, unable to run or reach my favourite hiding places? Now I remembered the litter tray in the kitchen. I should have known! Well, we would see about that. I worked on the door for most of the day, using claws, teeth and everything I could think of. The plastic frame came off easily enough, but the glass panel was tightly fitted and stubbornly resisted me.

By the afternoon I was exhausted and had to take a rest on the sofa. This holiday was going to be no fun at all – only marginally better than the cat prison. I was bitterly disappointed in my family. They had gone off to have a lovely time, leaving me home alone without food, drink or access to mice. The unfairness of it all eventually sent me to sleep.

I woke up to the sound of the kitchen door opening. Judging by the position of the sun, which was just sliding down behind the trees, it was dinnertime. Were they back already? I ran upstairs to investigate. As I rounded the corner into the kitchen, there was the girl with the long hair and the bright voice. She called me by my name, then squatted down and waited for me to come over. At least she had manners. I walked across to her with my tail held high and allowed her to stroke me. It might pay to be friendly to her. She might know where my food was kept. Sure enough, after a while she went into the pantry and came back with my food, which she poured into the correct bowl. Then she added milk to my other bowl, just like Mum. It was a relief to find she was well-trained. When she had finished, she stepped back and invited me to eat. I was quite hungry and didn't need telling twice. While I ate, she sat down at the kitchen table and talked to me. Afterwards we had a little game in the living room. She was nice. I liked her voice and her shiny auburn hair that fell right down onto the soft, pink carpet when she lay down to play with me. She told me her name was Lily; it suited her. We lay together on the carpet for some time while she talked and I purred.

Unfortunately, Lily had to leave when it grew dark. I was sorry to see her go and tried to squeeze through the kitchen door after her, but she pushed me back gently and locked the door behind her. She told me she would come back the next day.

I slept in great comfort on Mum and Dad's bed. It was quite nice not to have them there, fidgeting and pushing me out of the way. I was able to stretch out as long as I liked. When I woke up, the house was still eerily quiet. I had my lonely breakfast, then waited for the girl with the long hair to come back as the kitchen clock still ticked the minutes away and the fridge continued to hum. She didn't come. It was pretty boring alone in the house. I decided to have another go at my door. Again I worked for a long time, squeezing my claws in behind the glass panel, pushing and pulling as hard as I could.

I was about to give up when grey cat Piglet appeared outside. What a stroke of luck! I explained the situation and he understood straight away. Now we worked together, he from the outside, I from the inside, four pairs of claws and a good many sharp teeth. In no time at all the glass panel was beginning to give and finally, with a satisfying 'plop', it fell on the mat outside. I dashed out of the hole and was free! Grey cat Piglet was very pleased to see me. I thanked him sincerely and we set off together for a great day's hunting.

We returned in the afternoon to see Lily with the long hair driving up to the house. Piglet said he had to go home, so I trotted up to the kitchen door on my own to welcome her. She stopped short when she saw me and seemed unsure what to do. She wasn't nearly as friendly as yesterday and did not bend down to stroke me. When she unlocked the door, I tried to walk in with her, but she shooed me away, slipped in quickly and shut the door. Strange creature! I wandered around the house to my cat door, jumped through and walked upstairs into the kitchen.

I might have been a totally different cat: as soon as she saw me in the kitchen, she was back to her usual bright, happy voice, said hello, stroked me, served dinner, played, trailed her hair on the carpet and seemed in every way back to normal. Humans! No use worrying about their behaviour too much. It could easily drive a cat crazy trying to work them out.

After Lily left, I went back outside for some night-time hunting, a rare treat, and then retreated to Mum and Dad's bed exhausted and ready for a long sleep. My dirty paws and the remnants of my last kill, a juicy bat, would have to wait until the morning. I was too tired to wash, and my meal would be alright on Dad's pillow.

There followed several more fantastic days of complete freedom and peace. Lily came in the late afternoons like clockwork, never recognized me outside the kitchen door where I waited for her, but was always full of affection when we met again inside the kitchen seconds after. She looked after me very well, even emptied my clean litter tray each day, and I became quite fond of her.

When my family came back, it was evening and Lily was with me. They looked pleased to see us getting along so well and had a long chat with Lily about me, my excellent appetite and all my talents. Then she told them about this other ginger cat who had apparently been prowling around outside every time she came to see me. Mum gave me a thoughtful glance, while Dad scratched the top of his head the way he does when he tries to solve a tricky problem. I blinked back at them in equal puzzlement. I had never seen another cat, except for Piglet and he wasn't ginger. How could I have missed an intruder on my patch? Lily said goodbye to us and seemed genuinely sad to leave me. I hoped she would come back again some time.

After we had waved her off, Mum and Dad took the bags upstairs while the children and I went to watch TV in the basement room, where it felt a little cool because my door had been open all those days. The children didn't mind, as their favourite show was just starting. Some loud exclamations from the bedroom above disturbed us at first, but we turned the TV up a notch or two and settled down. Not long after, Mum and Dad joined us. *They* noticed my open door straight away. Dad examined my work with expert appreciation, while Mum clapped her hands and screamed in delight at all the dead mice and moles I had lined up for her on the doormat. I purred at her and told her it was nothing. Then I helped Dad put the door back in its frame. I think he regretted locking it in the first place, because it was quite a fiddly job, especially without Piglet's assistance from outside. While we did that, Mum changed the sheets on the big bed and generally tidied up our bedroom. It was good to have them back, and best of all Mum said they weren't going to leave me alone again for a long, long time.

18

WE HAVE A SLEEPOVER AND I JOIN THE TEDDY BEARS' PICNIC

Caroline's best friend came over for a sleepover; they were both very excited. The three of us went up to Caroline's room to put up the spare bed. Then I sat on it and watched the girls give each other fancy hairstyles. They piled each other's hair up high in various ways to see how many pins and ties they could fit on their heads. The pins looked sharp and nasty, and I didn't like the look of the ties either. They had a tendency to shoot off from the girls' fingers like lethal projectiles, and I kept my distance until they had used them all up. Then they started painting each other's faces with little brushes and powder puffs. I checked all the different paints and powders with my paws and made pretty, multicoloured paw print patterns on Caroline's desk and on the carpet. Soon the room was full of pink and blue powder that made me sneeze. The girls looked a bit scary once they had applied lots of bright blue around their eyes, thick, black lines to their eyebrows and poisonous shades of red to their lips. When they approached me with a brush and one of the powder puffs, I retreated to the safety of the kitchen, where Mum was preparing dinner.

After dinner, we went back upstairs again to listen to music and to talk. I listened to the music while the girls talked. Emily and Robin weren't allowed in. When Mum came to say it was time to go to sleep, the talking changed to whispering, but it didn't stop. I nodded off at the foot of Caroline's bed to the sound of whispers and giggles.

I woke up in the middle of the night. The girls were just getting out of bed. I had a quick stretch before joining them. We crept silently past Mum and Dad's bedroom door, down the stairs and into the kitchen. The girls opened fridge and pantry and prepared a midnight feast on the kitchen table. The spread was magnificent: we had cheese, ham, crackers, biscuits and a whole giant bar of chocolate between us. The chocolate was delicious. I had never tasted any – Mum believes in healthy snacks for cats. Now I wished I'd eaten some of the chocolate eggs and bunnies at Easter.

When we had had enough, we went outside into the dark, silent garden. A full moon bathed lawn and trees in a silvery light. The bushes all around the lawn gave off a heady scent; their white blossoms looked like brilliant stars fallen from the sky. The air was warm and still. Somewhere in the forest an owl was hooting. The girls got bikes out of the garage and raced them up and down the driveway and round and round the house. Then they bounced on the trampoline. I expected Mum and Dad to appear on their balcony at any moment, but they never heard us, so I did a bit of hunting and caught another bat. There were hundreds of them flying around us. The big, yellow moon had set and dawn was just breaking when we finally crept back into the house and upstairs into our beds. This time the whispering and giggling stopped quite soon, and the three of us slept soundly.

The sun was high in the sky and the rest of the family looked as though they had been out and about for hours when we finally crawled downstairs. Mum was working in the vegetable garden, talking encouragingly to the lettuces, while Dad could be heard hammering in the garage. Emily and Robin were preparing a teddy bears' picnic. A blanket was already spread out in the shade of a small tree; tiny plastic cups and plates were arranged on it in a circle. About a dozen teddy bears had been jammed into a trailer that was being towed towards the picnic site by Robin in his little red jeep.

I went to join them just as the party arrived by the blanket. Emily and Robin sat the teddies down on the blanket, where they stared with glazed expressions at the plates and cups before them. I squeezed into a gap between them and received a plate as well.

Emily poured tea into the little cups and set a birthday cake down in the centre of the blanket. It had candles on it. Emily lit them with a match while Robin admonished the teddy bears, who kept tumbling over. We all sang 'Happy Birthday' to one of the teddies. He tried to look pleased but refused to blow out the candles afterwards, so Emily and Robin had to do it for him. Emily cut slices of cake for everyone and placed them on the plates. The feast could begin. Unfortunately, the teddies didn't seem to know how to eat and drink, so Emily, Robin and I helped them. The tea turned out to be water and tasted disgusting, but the cake was very nice. I had two pieces; Robin had at least five. He pretended to give them to one of the teddies, then popped them quickly into his own mouth while Emily wasn't looking.

When the cake was all gone, we played 'Pass the Parcel'. The teddy bears clearly didn't know how to play the game: they just kept rolling over whenever the parcel came their way. Emily and Robin had to help them constantly, which left me free to play with the little toys that came out of the parcels as they were opened – key rings, rubber balls and more pink hair ties. It really was a great party. As we rested on the blanket afterwards, I noticed that there was fruit in the tree above our heads – small green balls, some of them just turning a little red. Emily told me they were called plums, and that we would be able to eat them soon, once they were ripe. I thought I preferred birthday cake.

The party broke up soon afterwards: the teddies were jammed back into the trailer and Robin drove them up to the house, while Emily and I followed with the blanket and the picnic basket containing the tea set. It was a glorious early summer day – I fancied a little snooze on my mossy wood pile in the deep shade of the oak trees.

19

I FULFIL MY GREATEST AMBITION AND HAVE A FABULOUS FEAST

Summer arrived in full force. Some days were so hot and humid that hunting was out of the question after sunrise. All I could do was drag myself to a shady spot, stretch out on the cool earth and sleep all day. By late afternoon, there were often spectacular thunderstorms. I would run inside at the first distant rumble, then Mum, the children and I would watch from the safety of the sofa in the living room as the heavens cracked open outside. It was pretty scary: bright lightning flashed across the garden, thunder boomed above our heads and torrents of rain ran down the windows, completely blocking our view. Afterwards the garden smelt fresh and strong as each plant drank in the rain and breathed a sigh of relief after the heat. Mum opened the windows wide to let the cool air into the house. Back on the prowl outside, I had to zigzag across the driveway to avoid deep puddles, and the grass on the lawn was squishy under my paws. The trees had an annoying habit of dripping water on my head as I passed beneath them; in fact the whole forest was drip, drip, dripping all around me.

The mornings after a thunderstorm were always the best: the sky was bright blue and the air clean and fresh. One such morning I was sitting on the front veranda, surveying the garden below, when I spied a group of tree runners making their way across a big oak tree branch towards the little plum tree that had recently provided shade for our teddy bear's picnic. They took it in turns to jump from the oak tree branch on to the plum tree, pick a plum, jump back onto the oak tree and disappear up its trunk, cradling the stolen plum. One after the other they helped themselves to our fruit, more and more and more of them racing up and down the oak tree, greed written all over their cheeky faces. I was appalled – shameless burglary was taking place in front of my very eyes, in broad daylight. The plums were barely ripe! Worse still, I knew at that moment in my heart of hearts that plums were in fact my favourite food, much better even than cake or chocolate. I could almost smell the juicy fruit as it disappeared up the tree at an alarming rate. I could also smell the tree runners.

Fighting down the urge to run down to the tree and chase the thieves off, I swiftly plotted a battle plan instead. Had I not been waiting for such an opportunity for ages? Had I not realized long ago that greed was a tree runner's only weakness? My hour had surely come, but I had to be clever now. They were nimble, but I was smart. And so I lay low on the deck for some time without moving a whisker. The humans were out, there was nothing to disturb the tree runners in their thieving progress. I watched every move they made. As the little tree was gradually depleted of plums, it became harder for the tree runners to pick the remaining ones: only low-hanging fruit growing at the very end of the thin branches was left now, and the creatures' weight was bending the branches right down towards the ground. I had my eye on one particular plum, which grew right at the end of the lowest branch – the hardest one to get, surely. Soon it was indeed the only one left. I crawled down the steps of the deck in the shade of the hand rail. Inch by inch I crept up to the little tree, keeping my body close to the ground and using bushes and clumps of grass for cover. Not for one second did I take my eyes off the tree runners. I listened out for any sign of alarm amongst them, but they were too intent on their harvest to notice me. Besides, I am a masterful hunter. I was quite close now and settled down in the high grass, hind legs gathered under me, until the right moment came. I did not have to wait long. A tree runner had discovered my plum and was making its way towards it. The long, thin branch of the little tree began to bend down as the creature crept further and further out from the trunk. I could tell it was aware of the risk it was taking: the branch could well snap or bend all the way down to the ground, and it was a long way to the nearest big tree trunk. But it continued nevertheless, unable to resist that last plum.

It all happened in a flash: the branch dipped down low, the tree runner lost its balance and flipped over, holding on to the branch from below now, eyes on the plum, claw outstretched to pick it. Its back and tail were only inches from the grass. A quick wiggle of my bottom, and I pounced. In the split second as I flew through the air towards the creature, I saw its head turn and its eyes widen in surprise. Then my teeth closed around its neck and I heard the satisfying crunch of breaking bones. The creature was mine!

Holding the limp, warm body in my mouth, I marched to the very centre of the lawn, where I could be clearly observed by all its mates, laid the creature down on the grass in front of me and took a large bite out of its side. It was juicy and delicious; no plum could taste better. All around me, I heard tree runners screeching in alarm; no more giggling now – I had the last laugh. I licked the blood off my lips and continued my feast. From time to time I stopped to look around, but the screeches were fading as the scoundrels were scampering off to safety, letting the neighbourhood know that this garden was to be avoided in future. I was able to crunch away undisturbed.

I was halfway through my feast when Mum and the children returned from the shops. Mum came over to see what I was eating and was amazed when she realized I had caught a tree runner. She actually called it a squirrel when she told the children, who also came to admire me. It was all very satisfying, a real triumph. Looking back now I would say it was probably the highlight of my entire life.

By the time Dad came home, only the bushy grey tail was left of my tree runner squirrel. I thought he might like it as a decoration for his sun hat.

20

DAD AND I ARE IN CHARGE OF THE HOUSE FOR THE SUMMER AND DO A GREAT JOB

When the schools broke up for the summer, Mum took the children away on holiday. She left me and Dad in charge of the house. Dad had a long list of jobs to do while she was away. I was going to supervise everything and lend a paw if necessary.

He needed help before they had even left. As Mum gathed up their last few bits and pieces from around the house, Dad and the children took the suitcases out to the garage, loaded them into the car and got in. I waited outside for the spectacle of the big garage door opening. It was an automatic door and I loved watching it go up all by itself. This time, however, I had to wait: a lengthy argument was going on inside the car. Robin was asking lots of questions in a high-pitched voice and Dad was answering them in his low one, then the girls chimed in as well and everyone talked at once. Eventually, Dad must have had enough; he started the car. That meant the door would go up any second now – I craned my neck so as not to miss the moment. But the door stayed shut. Instead, the car came crashing through the closed garage door, sending splinters of wood in all directions. There was not much left of the door at all when the car came to a screeching halt on the driveway.

Dad got out to take a look just as Mum appeared at the kitchen door. She stood there silently with her mouth open. It had also gone very quiet inside the car. The garage door was in a bad way. Only one or two bits of wood were still attached to the frame, the rest were spread all over the driveway. The car had several dents at the back, where it had hit the door. Dad said a very short word, scratched the top of his head and looked upset. I walked up to him and leant against his leg to lend support. Mum joined us and patted him on the back. I could feel Dad's leg relaxing a bit. Mum bent down to say goodbye to me and told me to look after Dad. The children just waved quietly from the car. I watched them drive away with mixed feelings. I was looking forward to being in charge of the house with Dad, but the debris behind us didn't seem like a good start.

My misgivings were unnecessary: Dad and I had a great time together, even though it took us two whole weekends to repair the garage door. Reassembling all those pieces of wood in the correct way was a real challenge. Dad used lots of nails and several more very short words. After four days of solid work, the door still wobbled dangerously when it went up, so we added a few more thick pieces of wood for extra reinforcement. It didn't look quite as before, but at least we had a door again.

Once we had time to turn our attention to other things, we realized that most of the vegetables had ripened since Mum had left: the bean stalks were sprouting bright green fingers, the tomatoes were fat and red, and the rabbits had started eating the lettuces. There were dozens of ripe cucumbers as well. We picked an awful lot of vegetables. Dad froze the beans and ate cucumber and tomato salad every night. I tried some, but it was watery and slimy – definitely not something a cat would eat. Eventually he took some to work to give away. It seemed unfair that Mum should miss out on the harvest she had worked so hard for, and that Dad and I should end up with it all when we really weren't that keen on it.

At night, Dad and I slept together in the big bed – I had Mum's side. It was much more spacious than with the three of us, and we could snore as loudly as we liked without getting told off. On week days we had breakfast together, then Dad left for work and I spent the day guarding the house while snoozing in a shady spot until Dad's return. We ate our dinner in front of the TV, which we're never usually allowed to do. Our evenings were spent watering the remaining vegetables or sitting on the deck, reading the paper, appreciating each other's company. I sensed that killing the tree runner had been the beginning of my adult life. It had finally earned me respect in the garden. I had proven myself as a competent hunter and a guardian of our house. It felt good to be a grown-up.

21

I GET A NEW DINNER SERVICE AND ROBIN LEARNS TO READ

When Mum and the children finally returned from their long holiday, things became a lot livelier. Once their music practice started up again in the afternoons, I found myself thinking back nostalgically to the long, quiet summer weeks. I think Dad did as well. Another mellow autumn with vibrant colours and clear, blue skies replaced the summer heat, and the dark green foliage that had sheltered my favourite sleeping spots became lighter and sparser each day, until the cold winds finally blew it away altogether. I moved back into the basement room then, as I sleep better in the dark.

Winter came again and my family decided to go away for a long weekend of skiing. This, apparently, involved gliding along on snow with the help of two long, flat wooden boards, holding on to a couple of sticks. They showed me how to do it in the garden. It looked like hard work – at least the children made it seem that way; they were forever falling over or bumping into trees. Personally, I failed to see where the fun was in that. It was not an activity I envied them, and it got boring after a while.

I was more interested in finding out what would happen to me while they were gone. Would Lily come back to look after me? I reminded Mum of her promise that I could stay home whenever they went away, and she told me not to worry. I still did, though.

A couple of days before their departure, Mum returned from

72

the shops looking very pleased with herself. She placed a large box on the kitchen table and invited me to watch her unpack it. When we opened the flap, out came a set of two very fancy food bowls with elegant, blue lids. For me? Mum smiled and nodded, and explained to me that these bowls would allow me to feed myself while they were away, now that I was a grown-up cat.

I was intrigued to see how the new bowls worked. Might they perhaps enable me to help myself to extra food, now that I was a grown-up? Sadly, this turned out not to be the case. Still, they were pretty good: they knew when it was precisely five o'clock, my dinner time, at which point one of them clicked open to reveal my dinner of fish, kept fresh by the blue lid. The next day, the second bowl opened at the stroke of five. It was quite magical!

Of course, the downside of the new bowls was that you couldn't argue with them, or weave around them in a bid to get an early dinner, the way I do with Mum and Dad. No matter how much I shouted at them or tried to open the lids before five o'clock, they stayed firmly shut. They even tried to mock me by reflecting my own cross face back at me in their blue polish, so that eventually I took to turning my back on them until I heard the little click that announced dinner.

By the time my family came back from their skiing weekend, covered in bruises, the bowls and I had come to a mutually satisfactory arrangement: I left them alone and they refrained from showing me my cross face. It was a win: win situation. Everyone was pleased to see that I had been all right on my own. Why wouldn't I be? After all, Mum and Dad had even left my cat door open as a special gesture of trust, and I had done my best not to disappoint them: no fewer than three mice and one mole were neatly arranged on the mat for them.

From then on, my family often went away for long weekends and left me in charge of the house. I always enjoyed the peace and quiet after they left, but was equally glad to have them back after a few days.

It was during that same year that Robin had to learn to read, and Mum and Dad had to teach him. I could tell it was a tricky business to understand what all those little black marks on the page meant, so I didn't blame him for finding it hard, but I very much wished that Mum or Dad would continue reading to us in the evenings, as they had always done. Whenever Robin read, it took so long for one word to come out that I quite forgot what the story was about. It was no good going to Caroline or Emily's rooms for a bedtime story either: they had long ago learnt to read silently to themselves at night.

So Robin soldiered on throughout autumn, winter and into spring. He wasn't very happy when Mum or Dad made him read, and frankly I doubted whether he would ever learn how to do it. Then one evening, Mum relented and read to us to give Robin a break. She picked out a difficult book about a vet who could talk to animals. When she started reading, Robin and I were enthralled by the story about a man who apparently knew how to bark like a dog, meow like a cat and neigh like a horse. He could even talk to exotic animals like elephants and lions. I had often wished that my family, who are reasonably skilled now at understanding my simpler statements, could learn to speak my language, and here was a man who could! I wanted to hear more about him.

Unfortunately, Mum had an infuriating habit of stopping when she felt it was time for Robin to go to sleep. She would snap the book shut at the end of a chapter and declare that this was it for tonight. Robin and I were bitterly disappointed whenever she did that and always whined for more – usually to no avail. That particular night, she did it again, and Robin got very cross with her indeed, because the story was just building up to a particularly exciting part. When she would not give in, Robin grabbed the book from her hands and announced he would read it to me by himself. I admired him for his courage, but to be honest, I thought it was misplaced in this case, as he could surely never do it. So imagine my surprise – and Mum's – when he started reading, slowly at first, then more and more fluently, all the way to the end of the exciting bit. Then he fell back on his pillow, exhausted, and was asleep. Mum and I looked at each other in amazement. He had done it! He could read, and has done, ever since. The book about the man who could talk to animals is still my favourite, to this day, and Robin has read it to me many times over.

22

THE TIDES CHANGE AGAIN

Peace returned to our bedtimes, and to life in general, as the school year moved towards its end and the weather grew warmer. I felt very settled in our house and garden by now and thought we could be happy there forever and ever. I enjoyed my daily routine that changed with the seasons and therefore never got dull. We had all found friends and fun activities to do, and the things that had alarmed us at first − like the big yellow school bus and the disgusting tap water − had just become a part of life that we were able to accept. After all, nowhere is perfect, but our life very nearly was.

Sadly, nothing seems to last forever in my family. As spring turned into summer, I sensed the tides changing once more: there were the brochures again, the long discussions and finally the goodbye parties. Caroline and Emily were heartbroken at having to leave their friends behind, and Robin was upset about leaving his little red jeep. But for some reason, Mum and Dad had decided it was time to leave. Once again, all our belongings were taken apart and loaded into a giant container − it was twice as big as the one we had had when we came. I suppose we had all grown since then.

Mum told me it would soon be time to say goodbye to our house and garden, and that I would have to fly off on my own again, to be reunited with them in a while, back in Australia − back home! I was not looking forward to it. I had come to love our American house and the wild garden and forests around it. I loved the glowing insects of warm summer nights and the look of the forest on frosty mornings. I loved my hidey holes and my lookout point on the mossy wood pile. Even the tree runners seemed okay now that I knew I had to leave them. And what would grey cat Piglet do without me? It was not to be contemplated, and yet I knew I had no choice: my life was with my family, who needed me and relied on me for so many things. I had to go with them.

It was with a heavy heart indeed that I climbed into our car one morning to drive to the airport with Mum and Dad. I had said goodbye to all my favourite places in the garden and walked through the empty rooms in our house, remembering everything we had done in each of them and all the fun we had had. I had said goodbye to grey cat Piglet – who, disappointingly, seemed to be looking forward to moving back into our house with any new family that might come after us. And I had said goodbye to Caroline, Emily and Robin, who each hugged me in turn and told me to be brave.

I didn't feel brave at all, particularly when Mum and Dad delivered me to the check-in desk at the airport in my travel box, stroked me one last time, told me to be good, promised I would see them again very soon, and left me. I watched them walk away down a long corridor, getting smaller and smaller until they were just two little specks of colour, and I was so worried I would never, ever see them again. But that is another story.

PART 2

From Maryland to Melbourne

IN PRISON

I didn't have much time to miss Mum and Dad after they left me at the airport. As soon as they had turned the corner at the end of the corridor, a man came to take me away. We drove in a small vehicle along endless, bright corridors where bored people were wandering about aimlessly. From time to time, my travel container was deposited somewhere and I had to wait around before the next person came to move me on. I sincerely hoped they all knew where I was going.

Eventually I was taken to my plane to begin the first leg of my journey. It was the usual, joyless affair: I was squeezed in between boxes and blankets into a tiny space that felt quite airless until we took off, when some cooler air started circulating from somewhere – probably through a hole in the side of the plane. I was sure the contraption had seen better days. Everything rattled and shook; I felt quite sick. On landing, I had a short break in the airport building while several people studied my travel documents. I told each one of them that I was going to Australia, but nobody seemed to understand. They just smiled, nodded and wished me a safe journey. Was there any way of knowing where I would end up in all this confusion?

I was worried sick by the time I was lifted on to the next plane, but greatly relieved when I was welcomed by a friendly "G'day" from one of the crew. We were bound for Australia after all! I discovered further that I was going to travel in style: I was invited to sit in the crew's room, surrounded by their coats and luggage, and soon found myself the centre of polite attention. The captain came to welcome me on board and filled my water dish. Pretty air hostesses cooed over me whenever they had time and offered me tasty treats from the kitchen. It was all very pleasant. Even the noise and movement of the plane did not seem so bad when the service was so excellent. I dozed in between their visits and quite began to look forward to my return to Australia.

A long, long time later, we touched down in what turned out to be a cold, drizzly place – not the hot, sunny country I remembered. A man in a baseball cap and T-shirt of an unattractive reddish purple colour with bright writing on the front was already waiting for me in the airport building. I don't like reds of any hue – they clash terribly with my coat – so I stared at him sternly through the bars of my travel container and gave him the silent treatment. He seemed not to notice, called a cheerful welcome and loaded me into the back of his van, whistling all the time. Off we drove for quite a while. There were no windows in the van, so I had no idea where we were going or what the place even looked like. I hoped I was going straight home to my family; if not, then presumably they had booked me into a cat hotel again. I really wanted it to be my favourite one, where I used to stay years ago.

So imagine my disappointment when the van door opened to reveal a soulless, grey concrete block with bars at every window! Had the cheerful red man taken me to a prison? My dismay turned to alarm when he carried me into the building and down long, murky corridors lined with barred cells, where sad-looking cats were staring at us with vacant expressions. My journey ended in front of one of the cells. My guide joyfully announced that this was to be my new home now and opened the door for me.

Now, everyone knows that escape is most likely to succeed in transit. Once they slam the cell door in your face, all hope dies. So as soon as the man opened my travel container, I took off! Several days of being cooped up had made me a little stiff, but not too stiff to run like the wind back down the long corridor we had come in by. I had no idea where I would go once I got out of there, but I knew with certainty that I wasn't staying in this hell hole. Not after travelling in luxury in the crew's room; not after having lived in America; not after having had a loving family for so long. I did not belong here, and they'd better know it straight away.

The man threw his cap in the air in alarm and followed me at a gallop, yelling to his mates for help. Soon I had every red-clad person in the place running after me. The front door was locked when I reached it, so I turned right and tore off helter-skelter up and down corridors, past cells containing dumbfounded cats, around corners where people were lying in wait for me, leapt over them, scratched where I could, and actually really enjoyed a good run after my confinement. The cool air made me frisky, and although I could not discover a way out of the place, I was getting to know it pretty well after a while. Soon the other cats started yelling their encouragement, uniformed people were bumping into each other, food bins were falling over, spilling their contents – the chase was exhilarating!

After a while, the red brigade ran out of steam. They gathered in a corner, breathless and sweating, scratching their heads and fanning themselves with their caps. I was sorry they had given up so soon; I was just getting into my stride. But since the fun seemed to be over, I stopped as well and settled down by the food bins. The food that had spilled out on the floor smelled delicious. It reminded me of my bowl full of crunchy, tasty morsels back in our Perth kitchen – and suddenly I realized that I was, of course, back in the land of superior cat food! Much as I had loved being in America, the food there had never been to my taste. I inched forward carefully and tried a bit of the food: it was deeelicious! That's when I realized how hungry I was. Apart from the little titbits I had been offered on my flight, I had eaten nothing since leaving home two days earlier. Without further ado, I settled down to my unexpected treat on the prison's concrete floor and ate my fill. The food was fantastic. Surely, a place that served such food could not be all bad?

I gobbled up most of the food that had spilled from the bins. Then I found a bucket full of clean water and drank – again, deeelicious! Not the disgusting brown liquid tasting of iron that had been our lot for the past two years, but clean, fresh, wholesome water! I was almost reconciled with my surroundings by the time I had finished.

The red people, who had sat down on a long bench to recover their breath, were watching me from a distance in obvious bewilderment. No doubt they were impressed with my appetite. So was I, to be honest. I had never eaten quite this much before. When I was done, I decided to make amends for my earlier outburst and introduce myself properly to my captors. I strolled over to the bench and greeted them each in turn. They were delighted to meet me. Then I asked them to show me to my room, and they all led the way back down the corridors to its open door. I walked in and looked around. It was basic, to put it kindly – just a concrete floor, brick walls and a door at the far end which led out into my private yard, also concrete and completely enclosed by a sturdy wire fence. No climbing tree, no fish pond.

I came to the conclusion that I really had somehow, and for no reason I could think of, ended up in prison; a strange welcome to my home country. But on the upside, there were no dogs, and the room on closer inspection contained a very comfortable bed with a warm blanket. Considering also the prospect of more delicious meals and drink to come, I decided to resign myself to my surroundings for the time being. Surely my family would get me out of here once they heard where I had ended up. Mum would very probably shout at the red people when she came, just as she had shouted at staff in the horrible cat hotel in America. Meanwhile, I would make the most of my less than perfect situation by eating and drinking as much as I could.

My captors were plainly relieved by my change of heart and pleased to see I was no longer cross with them. I settled down on my new bed and slept away the remainder of my first day and all of my first night back in Australia.

2

I AM BADLY DISAPPOINTED

A great many days went by without any sign of my family. I had ample time to explore my new abode, but as it was small and unexciting, that was soon done, after which I began to get very bored. There was absolutely nothing to do! Inside my room, it was warm and cosy, but I could see nothing at all; it was only good for sleeping. Outside in my yard, it was cold and draughty, but I could at least see the other cats and have a chat with my immediate neighbours. They were pleasant enough, but just as bored as I was. Having travelled from various parts of the world, they were wondering what Australia was like. I was able to prepare them a little for their new lives by telling them about the crystal-clear pools they could expect in their gardens, the abundant wildlife, the endless sunshine and the excellent standard of holiday accommodation for cats. This information cheered them up, and together we looked forward to the day when our families would come to take us away from this dismal place.

The only highlight of our day came at dinner time, when the red brigade marched up with our bowls. The food was always excellent. My only complaint was the amount: there was never enough of it – never even half as much as I had eaten on my first day. At least there was always plenty of water, which tasted so nice I never even missed the milk I had become so used to.

For the remainder of the time, I day-dreamed about running through the field of long, green grass next to our house in

America, or along the shady forest paths, hunting moles and squirrels. Or of lying in the hot sun high up on the deck, watching my family at work and play down below. It all seemed so far away – so long ago! Oh, how I missed it all! Did they miss me, too, or had they forgotten about me? And if so, would I have to stay in this cell forever?

One night I dreamed I was being accused of having murdered a squirrel. A tall person in a red uniform was glaring at me sternly and telling me it was against the law in Australia to kill squirrels. He was holding up a plum and a squirrel tail as evidence of my guilt. All around the room, angry squirrels were nodding their heads when he accused me and demanded that I should spend the rest of my life in prison. I woke up in a cold sweat and decided I would give all squirrels a wide berth from now on. Then I remembered there weren't any in Australia and felt weak with relief!

The days dragged on and on. New cats arrived, jet-lagged and bewildered, and had to be settled down. Many complained loudly of their accommodation, but none of them, I am proud to say, came even close to my performance on the first day. One of my immediate neighbours was collected by her family. It was very moving so see them being reunited, and all of us left behind were doubly sad afterwards that we were still here. On that day, I crawled into my room and curled up tight on my bed, trying hard not to think.

Then one day as I was grooming myself in my yard, I heard familiar voices! They were coming from the direction of the front door, and they were drawing closer all the time. My heart started beating faster and faster, and I stretched my neck as long as it would stretch in order to see who was coming. But I knew, of course: it was my family, all five of them! They were being led by one of the red brigade, who let them into my yard by the gate in the wire fence. I could simply not decide whom to greet first, so I kept running from one to the other! For a long time, we just cuddled and stroked each other – I had dispensed with my rule number one (no cuddling!) the moment I saw them – then they sat down with me and we talked and talked. They had clearly missed me just as much as I had missed them. Their trip seemed to have taken a lot longer than mine – presumably they didn't get to sit in the crew's room on the plane – and they had only just arrived in Australia. That's why they hadn't come to get me earlier.

I could tell they disapproved of my prison, but Mum didn't shout at anyone. I encouraged her to make a fuss, but she didn't rise to the challenge. Well, I reckoned it didn't matter any longer, since we were going to leave anyway. I started to get ready. This didn't take long, as I had practically nothing to pack. It was while I was rushing about sorting things out that I became aware of a mood change in my family. There was no happy anticipation, as there should have been. Instead, I sensed sadness and regret, and they started stroking me in a good-bye kind of way. I was confused and looked from one to the other; they all shook their heads gloomily and Mum said something about rules and regulations that was way too complicated for me to take in. But the horrible truth began to dawn on me: I wasn't going home with them. Why, I could not imagine, since they clearly loved me still.

I was gutted. To have seen them and not be able to go with them was the cruellest thing I had ever, ever known. The children felt it, too. All three of them were crying when we said good-bye again, all too soon. They brought out some toys and several bags of treats so I would be less sad, and Emily gave me one of her sweaters to put on my bed, to remember her by. None of those things could comfort me; I didn't *mind* the treats, but what use were toys when I had nobody to play with? I was distraught when they left, and they knew it.

I slunk back into my room, wrapped myself in Emily's sweater and stayed in bed for several days. I did not want to see the other cats, who were calling for me outside. I did not even want my food when the man came at dinner-time. It stayed in the bowl until morning, by which time my tummy was rumbling so badly I simply had to eat it. But the hurt inside me did not go away, even after I had eaten.

Mum and the children came twice more to see me. Each time we sat and talked, they stroked me and left me more treats and more toys. Each time saying good-bye became a little harder. I think they knew that, which is why they didn't come very often.

By and by, I began to notice that some of the other cats' families also came to see them and then left again without taking them away. Many cats would cry for hours afterwards; it was heartbreaking to hear. Yet other cats were collected and left happily with their families. This gave us hope. Maybe one day our turn would come when we would leave our cells, never, ever to come back.

Well, you guessed it: my day came eventually! Mum and the children arrived, and I could tell immediately by their happy voices that I would be going home with them this time. I was right, as usual. We didn't sit down together for long. Mum packed up my toys and Emily's sweater, then she picked me up and I only just had time to call my good-byes to my neighbours before we walked out, past all the cells containing my fellow-sufferers, past the ever-cheerful red brigade who waved to us over their morning tea and biscuits, and out by the front door! I took a deep breath of fresh air – it wasn't actually very fresh, as I found myself practically in the middle of the city, but I just felt I should – then we climbed into our new car. It was a great big white car with chunky tires. We sat very high up, where we could look down on all the other cars, on the dogs and people, as Mum drove us right through the centre of the big city that was to be our new home. Caroline told me it was called Melbourne.

We arrived at our new house in time for lunch. Dad was there to greet us. The children couldn't wait to show me everything. It was a tiny house: just two bedrooms and bathrooms upstairs, one for Mum and Dad, the other one for all three children, and a large room downstairs with the kitchen in one corner and the laundry room, where my bowls and a litter tray had been prepared. I didn't like the look of the litter tray; I had hoped finally to be able to do my business outside again. But nothing could spoil my happiness for the time being: I was home!

3

LIFE IN A BOX

After a couple of days in the tiny new house, I was more than ready to return to the great outdoors. I had not hunted in weeks; I had had to use horrible litter trays instead of lovely, brown soil; I had had no exercise and was feeling sluggish and unfit. Mum was not keen to let me out: our house stood right by a road. That didn't scare me, though. I knew all about roads, since we had lived on a busy one when I was a kitten. Besides, there was a small fenced garden outside the living room for me to explore. We battled for several days: each time a member of my family left the house, I was right there, waiting to slip out between their legs; each time, they caught me. It was infuriating.

I tried to entertain myself with what little excitement was available, but the best I could get was a large, empty cardboard box that stood in the middle of the living room. Robin had rescued it from the recycling bin and was using it as a cubby house. There were pillows, books and a camping light in there. He also insisted on having all his meals in the box, so I joined him and we snacked on bits of cheese and an assortment of crackers, hidden away from the strange new world outside. I think Robin missed our nice, big house and garden in America just as much as I did. Above all, he missed his little red Jeep, which he had had to leave behind as he was getting too big for it. According to Mum, Robin was now almost eight years old – his birthday was coming up. According to Robin himself, he was only five if you didn't count the holidays.

Either way, the two of us sat in Robin's box, felt sorry for ourselves and waited for something interesting to happen.

It happened quite out of the blue, as these things often do, when Mum came back from the shops and proudly pulled what looked like a length of rope from her bag. She showed it to me and looked excited. How could you get excited over a bit of rope? On closer inspection, it turned out to be several bits of rope intricately knotted together. Still I couldn't imagine why she was showing them to me, but I feigned polite interest anyway, just to please her, by sniffing it appreciatively.

That was when Dad sneaked up on me from behind and picked me up. I was momentarily too surprised to struggle. At once, Mum pulled the string contraption over my head and around my front legs, effectively strapping me into it. Then she attached a lead to one of the strings, opened the glass doors to the garden and motioned me outside, a triumphant smile on her face. That's how, before I knew what was happening, I found myself being paraded around our front garden on a lead, for all the world to see, like a common dog!

I was stunned for a minute or two. Stunned, and totally humiliated. How dare she? The front garden had suddenly lost all its appeal. All I could think of was how to lose those strings. I threw myself on the grass and wriggled and wriggled until I sensed some freedom in one of my forelegs, then my neck, then the other foreleg – and I was free! Without missing a beat, I leapt over the small hedge separating our pocket-sized front garden from the next one and ran off. Mum was powerless to stop me, and she knew it. Her helpless yells were getting fainter as I cleared several more hedges and turned a corner, to find myself in a large car park. They would not find me there very easily: it was full of cars for me to hide under. I chose one that still felt a bit warm from having been recently driven and settled down underneath it.

It wasn't long before my entire family appeared in the car park and started looking for me on their hands and knees. Up and down the rows of cars they crawled, calling for me, waving treats and generally looking pretty conspicuous. Before long, they were joined in their search by other people, surprised to see two adults and three children crawling around a car park. It was an embarrassing spectacle, and I tried to look as though I didn't know them.

Of course they spotted me after a while. But really, all I had to do was move to another row and another car. It was too easy; we could go on doing this all day. Dinner time was still hours away. Until then, I would be quite happy in the car park.

My family must have reasoned along similar lines, because they gave up after a while and sat down on a low wall to discuss the situation. I could tell they were not happy. Mum was getting the blame for my escape, which wasn't entirely fair, because she had only been trying to help me, after all. I made a mental note to be cool towards the other four tonight, after I returned home. They sat there, arguing, for a long time, until Robin announced that he was hungry and wanted to go back in his box to have lunch. One by one, they reluctantly left the car park, until I was on my own with the cars and with the other shoppers, who soon lost interest in me, and I in them.

Finally, I was free to explore my surroundings. I did a quick circuit of the car park, walking on top of the low wall my family had sat on. There wasn't very much to see – just cars and a few small trees. I checked out the far side of the car park, where there were more little houses with tiny gardens, then I retraced my steps to our house via the neighbouring front gardens. They were all identical, small and very boring. Not even a bird's nest in any of them; not one mouse. Had I landed here a few years ago, I would have been desperate. Nowadays, I knew this could not possibly be our house for long: my armchair wasn't there, for one thing. So there was hope that we would move away before long, to a better house with a crystal-clear pool and a tin-roofed garden shed in a sheltered spot. For now, I had seen enough.

I leapt back into our front garden and strolled into the living room through the open glass door. My family were sitting around the dining table – all except Robin, who was in his box. I rubbed my side against Mum's leg in appreciation of her efforts, but ignored the others, before joining Robin for a bit of lunch.

4

WE HEAD FOR THE HILLS AND IT GETS EXCITING

Mum realized it was pointless trying to restrain me after my escape to the car park. She now left the glass doors to the garden open for me in the daytime and told me I was free to roam. Unfortunately, as I had discovered during my first walk, there was not very much out there to roam in; we were surrounded by houses and roads. Dogs walked past our front garden pretty much every day, and the cars on the road drove quite fast. I took to doing my business outside, which pleased Mum as she could dispense with the litter tray, and I snoozed on the paving stones when the sun was out. Once I visited the neighbours when their patio doors were open, only to find their house identical to ours and just as boring. I snoozed for a while on one of their beds, so as not to offend the lady who had shown me around, but really, there was nothing to be gained from our short acquaintance. I went back home and was almost as bored as before.

I started snacking to pass the time – something I had never done before – and craved more and more food. Mum tried to ration my dinner portions, but I complained so loudly that she usually gave in and added a bit more. Gradually, I noticed that jumping up on the beds required a little more effort than before, and once when Mum hadn't opened the glass door far enough, I almost got stuck. There was no denying it: I was putting on weight. But I told myself I would soon lose it again once we moved somewhere more interesting, and besides, I'd had a traumatic time in prison and deserved a little treat now and then.

Just as I had suspected, we didn't stay long in the tiny house. Within a few weeks, the bags were packed again and we were back on the road in our car. I sat with Caroline, Emily and Robin on the back seat; no more travel container for me! We were all very excited at the prospect of moving into a proper house with more rooms and a bigger garden. I was particularly looking forward to the crystal-clear pool and the hunting prospects.

We drove along endless roads lined by houses, houses and more houses. Melbourne certainly was a big place, but it looked pretty grey and uninspiring to me. I couldn't wait to see green fields and forests and was not disappointed, as we gradually left the greyness of the houses behind and headed towards colourful open country. I saw a park, a river and big trees, a small town that looked less forbidding than the city streets had done, and then our car climbed a steep hill and stopped right at the top. We all jumped out and looked around.

We were facing our new house. It looked inviting with its big windows and shiny front door; beyond it lay green, undulating hills. Dad unlocked the front door and we all filed in. There was a downstairs and an upstairs, with so many rooms that we lost each other frequently as we explored, but we kept meeting up at the crossroads, which was the kitchen. Though big, bright and glossily tiled, the kitchen lacked the vital bowls of food and water for me and was therefore disappointing. I also saw no sign of my armchair, normally positioned near a window for good light and views, or, come to think of it, any other useful items such as beds; just lots and lots of space everywhere. It was a bit eerie after the cramped house we had left behind.

The children didn't seem worried by the lack of furniture and happily took possession of their bedrooms. They were delighted to get one each, even if it only had a floor, walls, a window and a door. Meanwhile, Mum and Dad carried our things into the house. Even after everything was in, the house remained pretty much empty: all we had was a camping table and some hard chairs, some plates and, eventually, my bowls in the kitchen and a sleeping bag in each room, except in Mum and Dad's room, where there were two bags. It was almost as basic as my prison cell.

Fortunately, there was a basement room with a very high wooden corner table and some equally high stools. I didn't like them as they turned round and round when you sat on them, which made me dizzy, but they were useful for humans. There were lots of bottles on glass shelves behind the table, and a few glasses, making it look more lived-in than the rest of the house.

Once all our things had been brought in from the car, Dad announced that the sun had gone over the yard arm, and that we should have a drink in the basement room. I took a good look around the yard and found no sign of an arm, but we all congregated in the basement room anyway and Robin mixed us drinks: water for me, fruit juices for the children, and something from the bottles on the shelves for Mum and Dad. We talked about our new house and what we were going to do now we had arrived. It was all very exciting. There was a pretty picture of a golden crown surrounded by red roses on the wall above the table. Caroline told me the room was called the 'Rose & Crown'. I liked that name, and I liked the room, which became our family meeting place in the afternoons.

From the 'Rose & Crown', you could go straight out into the garden, which, being on a steep slope, consisted of several levels and was all fenced in as had been our garden in Perth. The views into the hills were lovely, but I could not find a pool anywhere. The children assured me we would build one soon. I could not imagine how we were going to dig such a big hole, particularly since we had none of Dad's tools, but decided not to worry about it until later. There were a couple of good climbing trees and, once I had scaled the garden fence, a welcome tin roof revealed itself on the other side that would do well for naps. I left the children to their games and tried my first snooze there, protected by the boughs of an old apple tree, with the smells of the outdoors all around me – at last.

That night, I discovered that sleeping bags on the floor are quite a lot of fun. Having everyone at ground level meant I could kiss the whole family goodnight, several times if I wanted to; I could walk over them easily and settle down in the warm folds of the bags of the quieter sleepers.

The children started school the very next day, leaving me with plenty of time to explore our garden and the neighbouring ones. Dad installed a new cat door for me in the patio door, so I was once again free to come and go as I pleased. Almost straight away, I encountered two scaly creatures on fat legs who lived in the shrubs under Emily's window. Their tails looked identical to their heads; only when they moved could you be sure which was which. They didn't seem too friendly; I pawed one of them, and it turned out that the head end was equipped with a good set of teeth. I saw no dogs and only one other cat, a long-haired female who assured me she didn't sleep on tin roofs, ever, preferring instead the softer surfaces in her house. She seemed to clean herself a lot and was not interested in hearing about my adventures overseas. In fact, she didn't seem to care whether there was a world beyond the houses and gardens of our neighbourhood. When it started drizzling a little, she looked alarmed and dashed off home. I thought of grey cat Piglet and the adventures we'd had together. Somehow, it seemed unlikely that this cat here could handle much excitement.

The other side of our garden bordered a public footpath, beyond which lay a field that looked as though it had hunting potential. Unfortunately, the footpath was quite busy: children used it on their way to and from school, and walkers passed quite regularly with their dogs. The field contained several big, long-legged animals with swishing tails; bad news indeed. I doubted whether the hunting opportunities outweighed the risks out there.

I confined myself to watching the goings-on from the safety of the fence, and to accompanying Mum on a couple of walks when the coast was clear. The path wound its way to the crest of the hill, from where we could see in all directions. We looked down on green, wooded hills. Houses and gardens nestled here and there amongst them. A long line of wires supported by big, grey towers led across the land from as far away as you could see, all the way up to our hill, back down again on the other side and off into the distance, where we could just make out the greyness of the city. The wires made a humming sound to accompany the twitter of birds perched on the tower just above us. Mum, being higher up, was able to see any danger approaching well before I could. Then she would tell me to run along, back to our fence and to the safety of our garden. When Mum was too busy to walk, I caught up on sleep and looked forward to mealtimes.

Before too long, a great big truck came puffing up our road and disgorged my armchair and all our other belongings. Now the house began to look and feel like our home at last.

5

I HELP TO BUILD A POOL

Even before our furniture had arrived, a succession of men had called at the house and walked around the top of the garden with Dad. They all pointed and talked a lot while Dad scratched his head, nodded and sometimes looked a little worried. I watched from the apple tree in some apprehension. Somehow I sensed that those visits would spell the end of my hard-won peace.

I was right: only a few days later, my morning nap was interrupted by the arrival of large, noisy machines, which moved to the top end of our garden and destroyed it completely, leaving a gaping hole where grass and roses had grown. The two scaly creatures I had met earlier on left their hidey holes in alarm and emigrated next door. So did most of the birds. When the machines had finished their work of destruction, they were replaced by men who lined the big hole with a crisscross pattern of iron rods, designed to trip me up every time I went in there to check on progress. Next, they produced a large hose that poured a sticky, grey substance into the hole. That evening, my paws sank right down into it; it took me hours to clean myself afterwards. The following day, however, it turned out it had all been worth it: my paw prints had dried solid and were displayed beautifully all over the hole, finally adding a bit of interest to the ugly site. The hole stayed like that for a long, long time. Lots of people were able to admire my paw prints, and the bottom of the hole gradually filled with rain and dirt.

The summer came and still our hole stood abandoned. Dad, who seemed frustrated by the silence in the garden, spent many hours digging up those parts of it that the machines had missed. He created deep trenches leading off from the house to the big hole. Soon our garden looked like a mole's playground. I fled to my tin roof, from where I could hear, but thankfully not see what was going on.

Eventually, the workmen returned to destroy my paw print artwork by covering it up with a fine paste of bluish colour. That night, I was prevented from making my usual inspection of the building site by Dad, who locked my cat door. I complained loudly, but he did not relent. By the time he let me out for my morning walk, the blue paste had set rock hard and no amount of walking over it left any impression whatsoever. Well, if he ended up with a soulless hole in the ground he had nobody to blame but himself! I left him to it and retreated to my tin roof yet again, the only place of sanity left for now. I was tired, having had little sleep in the night due to my efforts to get outside, and slept deeply.

I woke to the sound of splashing water as the sun was beginning its descent behind our hill. Intrigued, I jumped on to our fence to investigate – and looked down on an expanse of lovely, blue water. I was transfixed: in the time it had taken me to sleep off my early morning disappointment, the ugly hole in our garden had filled with water and transformed itself into the crystal-clear pool of my dreams! I jumped down and had my first, delicious drink from its side.

Over the coming weeks, paving stones were laid around our new pool, plants and boulders appeared in various places, and finally Mum carried out the deck chairs. Unfortunately, it was autumn by then and getting too chilly to swim. The children went in anyway, but I could tell they had trouble breathing in the cold water. From then on, the pool pretty much belonged to me, except for the times when Dad came to clean it or Mum tended the plants around it.

6

I AM PRESENTED WITH AN INTRUDER

Peace descended on the garden once again, and with it boredom of a kind I had never known before. I tried half-heartedly to hunt a little, but the tiny mice I managed to track down in corners of neighbouring gardens – our own garden having been pretty much depleted of all wildlife by the builders and their machines – were so pathetic I was almost reluctant to present them to my family. True, the ones in Perth had been no bigger, but I hadn't known anything else then. Now I knew the plump, shiny moles and the tasty squirrels that lived in the forests and fields of America. By comparison, everything we had here fell well short of the mark.

I realized with a shock that becoming a world traveller had spoilt my enjoyment of what might otherwise have passed as a perfectly good life. I now expected all the good things I had had in different places to be in the one place where I happened to be at the moment. And all the bad things I had experienced elsewhere no longer seemed to matter in hindsight: I no longer minded the disgusting American water; my flights seemed quite exciting on reflection; and I could not imagine why I didn't want to share my armchair with grey cat Piglet back then. It was all very confusing.

The children were back at school after the long holidays and Mum now had a job in the city, where she spent a lot of her time. This was new, and I didn't like it, because the house was very quiet without her. Fortunately, Dad was working from home now. He had a small office downstairs, next to the 'Rose & Crown', where

I sometimes kept him company, but it was soon covered in piles of paper, books, folders and bags, making it difficult to find even a small square of carpet to lie on. Plus, he kept blaming me whenever he lost something in the mess. So I spent nearly all my time on the tin roof or on my armchair and asked for more food whenever a member of my family showed themselves. Eventually, I had to face the upsetting truth: I had quite lost the spring in my step and had turned sad and glum.

Mum was worried about me. She bought me a little bottle of medicine and made me take a few drops of it every day. It tasted bitter and we had nasty fights over it that upset me and left Mum with scratches on her arms. After a while, we both agreed we would be happier without the medicine, and Mum stopped trying to cheer me up. I slipped back into my melancholy frame of mind, dozing for long periods and snacking in between.

I should have known Mum better; I should have guessed she wouldn't give up; perhaps I should even have pretended false cheer in order to fool her. But I didn't do any of those things, and so Mum took the children off on one of their shopping expeditions one day and they returned carrying a small box, which they set down on the carpet in front of me, smiling brightly. I was suspicious of course, but intrigued enough to drag myself off the armchair to see what they had bought. Clearly, whatever was in that box was meant as a surprise for me. I didn't hold out much hope, and I was right. Emily opened the box and lifted out – a tiny, white kitten! She put it down on the carpet in front of me; it crept closer and whispered a meow. I was struck dumb and immobile for a second or two, unable to believe what I was seeing. A kitten? Another cat? The ultimate insult! Competition for food, drink, attention – everything! My life was well and truly ruined now.

I did the only thing I could do, under the circumstances: I arched my back, demonstrated the full length of my claws to the creature and hissed at it. It retreated behind its box and the whole family tut-tutted at me. At me! How dare they? Wasn't this all their fault in the first place? I turned on my heel and marched off. They would not see me again until dinner time. I climbed to the top of next door's apple tree, where they would not think to look for me. Mum and Emily came out and called me, but I ignored them; let them stew. Perhaps they would see sense and remove the intruder before I returned.

Come dinner time, there was no sign of the kitten in the house and my dinner was ready. Relief washed over me: the creature had gone, thank goodness! All evening, my family made a fuss of me, and I reluctantly accepted their apology. That night, I slept at the foot of Mum and Dad's big bed, as usual, and thanked my lucky stars that I was still the only cat in the house.

The next day, however, started with a bitter disappointment: just as I was finishing my breakfast, Emily walked in, carrying the kitten! She put it down on the kitchen floor, and once again it scuttled over to me, wanting to make friends. I shrieked, jumped back and hissed. I would not share my kitchen with this – thing! I would not share my bowls, or, come to that, my Emily.

It seemed that Emily had other ideas. She crouched down between me and the creature and stroked us both with one hand each. I hid behind her and hissed at the kitten every time it tried to come near me. After a while, I jumped up on the kitchen worktop to get out of its reach and to have a better look at it.

It didn't seem very healthy: there was a large bare patch with a fresh wound on its side, and its eyes were sticky. It was also sneezing quite a lot. Perhaps it would die soon; but probably not before it had infected us all with some horrible disease. What were they thinking of?

Emily now produced a new set of bowls and placed them on the kitchen floor at some distance from mine, but not far enough, I reckoned. She filled one with food – my food! That was *my* food! – and the other with water; I didn't mind so much about the water. Then she set the kitten down in front of the bowls and watched it eat. It ate very slowly. I would easily be able to eat all my dinner and then the kitten's dinner as well, once we were left undisturbed. Perhaps the creature would have that one use, at least.

After breakfast, Emily took the kitten away again and peace returned to the kitchen, if not to my mind. I sat and pondered the situation. If the kitten was here to stay – if it didn't die of its disease, or get run over by a car, or eaten by a dog, all of which were well within the realm of the possible, I reassured myself – and if my family did not recognize the utter folly of their ways (which they rarely do), then what? My life would never be the same again, that much was clear. I would forever have the kitten following me, asking stupid questions, needing help, wanting to play when I wanted to sleep… It really did not bear thinking about.

I sulked all day on the apple tree, trying to think of a way to get rid of the kitten, but failed. At dinner time, Emily once again placed it near me in the kitchen and I had to watch it picking daintily at its dinner for ages, while I was still feeling hungry after gobbling mine up in a matter of seconds. I was hoping to be left alone with its bowl once it had lost interest, but Emily appeared from out of nowhere as soon as the kitten walked off and removed its half-full bowl.

Over the next few days I worked out where the kitten slept at night: in Emily's bed! It hid under her hair, in between her ear and her shoulder. There was no way I could get at it without waking her. I had no option but to retreat to Mum and Dad's bed. That, at least, was still mine and mine alone. I would have to get at the kitten during the day, but even then there never seemed to be a minute when Emily or another member of the family wasn't watching. What had happened to school? Or work? It was intolerable. I continued hissing at the kitten at every opportunity, while it continued trying to sidle up to me.

Over time I realised that the kitten was, in fact, a 'she'. They had called her Tammy, which starts with the same sound as my name, but in every other respect she was as different from me as she could be: brainless and over-eager to please, long-legged and scrawny. And she was bright white, for goodness' sake, apart from her head and ears, where she sported a silly little bonnet of grey hair, and her grey tail. She would stick out a mile in the russet forests of America! But, I had to remind myself, we were far from those forests, so it probably didn't matter what colour she was. In any case, it was clear she was a nuisance and always would be.

To make matters worse, it started raining not long after she arrived. No more escaping to the apple tree. I snuggled down on my armchair instead and tried to forget all about the kitten. It worked; I fell asleep and drifted into sweet oblivion…

I had a lovely dream. I dreamed of my brother lying close to me and licking my head in all those places I couldn't reach for myself. It was a delicious feeling – nobody had licked me like that in years, not since he died. I could feel the warmth of his body next to mine and felt him purr softy. He licked all around my ears and up my cheeks, in exactly the way I liked best, as only he could. I was in heaven and didn't want it to stop, ever! Moving my head a little so he could do my other side I half opened my eyes and almost fell off the chair. Strewth! It wasn't my brother at all who was snuggling against me and licking me; it was the kitten! I had a mind to jump up, clobber her over the ears and throw her off my armchair – only it felt too good to be close to her. I was confused.

I decided to gain time by pretending still to be asleep, and it worked for a while: she continued to weave her magic on my head, licking me slowly, rhythmically, until I was so full of happiness I felt I would burst. Just then, she held her own head out for me to lick… Now, that was going a bit far! And how did she know I was awake, anyway? Startled into activity, I had given her one lick before I knew what I was doing, then another, and it felt almost as good as before. Her tiny head lay against my shoulder and I could hardly believe how small her ears were. In fact, the whole kitten was so small I could almost lick her entire body in one go. There was something very vulnerable about her. I felt a little ashamed of having wanted to bash her. What glory could there be in beating up someone so small and helpless? So we continued licking each other for a while, before we both drifted off to sleep again.

She woke up first and embarked on a lengthy and vigorous cleaning session. The armchair shook with her efforts. I yawned and stretched before opening my eyes and watched her. All things considered, she wasn't actually as ugly as I had first thought. Her eyes, I noticed, were no longer sticky; they were dark and almond-shaped now, and she had the tiniest pink nose I'd ever seen. When she had finished her toilette, she skipped off on her long white legs, light as a feather, and seemed to have forgotten all about me already. There was no doubt in my mind that she would be trouble – and that she would need a lot of looking after if she was to survive the week! With a sigh, I heaved myself off the armchair and padded in the direction of the kitchen, where she was already helping herself to my water.

7

FRIENDS AFTER ALL

My suspicions turned out to be well-founded: Tammy did not have one grain of sense; she was completely green. The world for her was this happy place where no danger existed and everyone was kind and friendly. In short: she was an open invitation to predators and prone to all kinds of accidents. So who was expected to watch and teach her? Me. I was saddled with her before I even knew it.

Mum wanted Tammy to stay in the house until she was a little bigger, which suited me fine. I could at least get some me-time away from her outside. While I was out, I had to trust my family to keep her safe, and generally they did. Her tendency to creep into any box or shopping bag very nearly became her undoing a couple of times, but fortunately someone always discovered her before she was thrown out with the rubbish. She also had a habit of going to sleep on the backs of sofas and in other high places, and then falling off. Luckily, she was just about cat enough to land on her feet each time.

Eventually, Mum pronounced Tammy old enough to go outside under my supervision. She asked us not to go beyond the garden fence and warned me that Tammy needed looking after. As if I didn't know! Even so, she managed to fall into the pool and I had to pull her out. That was one of her nine lives gone. She didn't worry about it for long though, as she seemed to be incapable of remembering anything that had happened more than five minutes ago. Mum shot me a sharp look when I brought Tammy home looking bedraggled, dripping water all over the kitchen floor. What was I supposed to do? Keep her on a lead?

Even without a lead, Tammy followed me everywhere, like a shadow. At the same time, she was very easily distracted by, say, a passing butterfly or a crawling insect, and before I knew it, she had disappeared. Then I would get the blame if she was lost. She also had the tiniest little voice which nobody except me could hear. Generally, I would find her skipping about somewhere in a happy daze and take her home, but there was also that time when she climbed up into the chimney from the fireplace. I saw her tail disappear into the blackness and was appalled. How could I get her down from there? I realized I was no longer nimble enough to follow her up, and anyway, I shouldn't have to: I was a cat; cats didn't climb up chimneys. Not normal cats, anyway. When the children came home from school, they were greeted by an eerie wail that echoed around the fireplace. They froze in shock, so I ran to get Dad. He eventually located Tammy by shining a torch up the chimney, where she was perched half-way up on a narrow ledge. Dad and Tammy were both as black as chimney sweeps when they emerged.

To be fair, there were also good times. Tammy was agile and quick, which made her an excellent hunter. My own figure now being slightly on the heavy side, I was at a disadvantage in that respect, but she caught her prey every time. Once she even caught one of the fat, scaly creatures I had encountered early on, who had moved back into our garden after the pool had been finished. She carried it into the house through the cat flap, which was an amazing feat, considering how long the creature was. She had to ease it through sideways; it was expertly done. Unfortunately, Mum had no eye for Tammy's outstanding talent. She unceremoniously bundled the creature into a shoe box, where it thrashed about and hissed, and took it back out into the garden. Later that day, I watched it emigrate again with its friend, probably forever this time. It was a shame, because Tammy was only just getting into her stride.

Over time, Tammy and I developed a number of games that we played with each other. My favourite one was 'Chase and Tumble', where we chased each other around the house, and when I caught her we wrestled on the floor. The rules were simple: I won. The fact that I was much bigger and stronger than Tammy helped, and she was always a really good sport about it. Even when I bit her neck at the final climax of the game and dragged her across the floor she never complained. My family told me off though, when they saw me doing it, so we preferred to play in private. As time went by, Tammy got a lot better at defending herself and would often stand up to me quite bravely, landing a few punches of her own before I pounced on her for the final bite.

In the evenings, we shared the armchair and licked each other. That became my favourite time of the day. Mum lit some candles and sometimes the fire – she always checked carefully on Tammy's whereabouts before she did so – then we all had a cosy time together. Our family was very pleased with our new friendship and either all squeezed onto the sofa or sat on the floor to watch TV with us, rather than disturb us on the armchair.

I hated to admit it, but in spite of my earlier misgivings Tammy eventually brought fun and entertainment back into my life. I no longer sulked on the apple tree. I didn't have time even if I'd wanted to, as I was far too busy looking after her. Life was good once more.

8

CAROLINE TURNS 14 AND WE HAVE A PARTY

When we had left America, Caroline had been very cross with Mum and Dad because she didn't want to leave her friends. She had cried and cried and said she was sure she would never, ever make friends again, in Melbourne or anywhere else. I felt dreadfully sorry for her. Sure, I was sad to leave grey cat Piglet, but I didn't love him anywhere near as much as Caroline loved her friends. Her heart was breaking; there was no doubt about it.

I was therefore surprised to hear her ask Mum about having a party for her 14th birthday, not so long after we had moved. Who was going to come? All her friends were still in America. I was intrigued, particularly when Mum and Dad said yes and the 'Rose & Crown' was readied for the party. Judging by the preparations, we were expecting quite a few guests. The carpet was rolled up, Robin's train set was dismantled and packed away, and Dad removed all the bottles from the shelves. Caroline set up an elaborate arrangement of boxes connected by wires that played very loud music, while Mum prepared masses of food.

When the big night of the party arrived, I watched from upstairs through the banisters as Caroline's guests arrived. I didn't recognize any of them and they definitely didn't sound American, but they did produce a lot of noise. I went outside to watch them through the big windows at garden level. Tammy was too scared to come with me. It was just as well, because there were some wild games going on in the 'Rose & Crown', and the music was deafening. After a while, much to my alarm, a few of the guests discovered the door into the garden and decided to come outside, even though it was winter and quite cold. More and more of them followed. I hid under a bush.

At first, they just sat on a garden wall and talked. It was easier to talk outside, because the music was less loud, and they didn't seem to feel the chill. But the peace didn't last long. One of the boys discovered the small box that controlled a number of little black jets that squirted water on to the garden in summer. I knew those jets well and had learnt to listen out for the hissing sound which heralded their appearance above grass level just before they started squirting, early in the mornings. You didn't get much time to run once the hissing began, and some of them squirted quite viciously. There was one in the middle of the lawn that went round and round, pumping out water at a drenching rate. I'd had an encounter with it once and was not keen on a repeat. As the boy started fiddling with the little box, I jumped up on the garden fence to safety. Was I glad I did! There was the hissing sound – drowned out for the guests by the music and chatter – and then the black jet rose from its hiding place in the grass and began its mad dance. Round and round it went, shooting water in all directions, and particularly at the wall where Caroline's guests perched. There was a lot of screaming. One girl fell off the wall and landed in a shrub, legs in the air, a couple of boys leapt up and down on the wall as though that might stop the water coming; the rest ran back into the house. Soon Dad entered the scene with a spanner in his hand and received a good blast from the runaway jet before he managed to subdue it. It descended back into its hole with a disapproving splutter and the crisis was over.

The screaming in the party room subsided as the guests gradually dried off, but the thump, thump, thump of the music continued. I felt sorry for the neighbours and also for the rest of my family, who had to listen to the bedlam. The whole house was vibrating. Surely Tammy was a nervous wreck by now? I went in search of her and found her, as I had expected, in Emily's bedroom, where she was peacefully asleep on her bed in amongst the soft toys. If you didn't know, you would have taken her for a soft toy herself.

It was a relief to all of us when the guests' parents finally came to take them away. The 'Rose & Crown' looked as though a tornado had passed through it. There were gift wrappings, paper garlands, bits of food and drink everywhere. Those guests who had been outside when the watering started up had left muddy footprints all over the room and all down the corridor. Mum and Dad looked very tired. They said it was too late to start clearing up today, but that we would all be called upon to help in the morning.

I was the first one up as usual and went downstairs to make a start. There were some very tasty leftovers on the floor; I've never had a better breakfast. By the time Mum came downstairs with the broom and mop, I had already cleared away much of the food and decided to get out of her way, which is to be recommended whenever she wields those gadgets. On my way up I met Dad carrying the vacuum cleaner down – my enemy number one – so I was doubly glad I had put in an early shift. Anyway, I needed a drink after all that spicy food.

It didn't take Mum and Dad all that long to clean the 'Rose & Crown'. By the time the children got up, it was nearly all done. Caroline said it had been the best party ever. I was glad to see she had found herself some new friends after all, and that she had overcome her disappointment at having left America.

9

EMILY GETS A PONY AND TAMMY HAS A SCARY ENCOUNTER WITH A TRAIN

I returned from my early morning walk to find Emily in a state of wild excitement. She had already whirled Tammy around the room and made her dizzy; now she looked as though she might start on me. But I extracted myself from her grasp using my claws and called her to order.

She looked a bit sorry then and told me she'd just heard she was getting a pony. A what? Realizing I didn't know what she was talking about, she showed me a photo – it turned out to be one of the long-legged creatures that lived in the field next door. Whatever next? Were we to share the house with a hoof animal now? I wanted nothing to do with it. Emily assured me the pony would not live with us, but in the field next door, and that I didn't have to have anything to do with it if I didn't want to. I didn't; that much was clear to me from the start.

The pony arrived in the afternoon in a large box pulled by our car. Tammy and I watched from the relative safety of the garden wall as Emily guided the pony out of the box walking backwards and on to our driveway. Tammy's eyes grew rounder and rounder as the pony emerged; she was on the brink of panicking and running away. But curiosity got the better of her, and she stayed to watch.

The pony was brown and very chubby, with a large white patch on its face that covered one entire side of it. It didn't look as though it knew how much Emily had been looking forward to its arrival: it laid its ears back and aimed a couple of kicks in her direction. Fortunately, she was so in love with it already, she never even noticed, but walked instead to the front end that didn't kick and planted a big kiss on its nose. I could tell the pony was staggered by this welcome – I doubt it had ever been kissed before.

While it was still dazed by the experience, Emily led it off to the field next door, where it joined the bigger ponies who already lived there. Emily then unloaded a whole lot of equipment from the box and from the car. It seemed you needed a lot more things to keep a pony than you did for a cat. There were rugs and brushes, huge buckets, bulging bags of food, shiny leather straps and other strange implements I could not identify. She put everything into the wheelbarrow and wheeled it next door into a wooden shed. Then she set about brushing her pony until it got dark and she was no longer able to see what she was doing. Only then did she remember me and Tammy and came home, full of smiles but smelling oddly different – it was the smell of horse. We were to become very familiar with it over the coming years, as Emily's room would smell of it forever after.

Looking after the pony became Emily's main and favourite occupation. As soon as she came home from school, she put on her pony clothes – recognizable by their particularly strong smell and kept in a hairy pile in a corner of her bedroom – and ran next door. She brushed the pony first, then she put the leather straps on its head and a seat on its back, and finally she got on it and rode around and around the field for hours. There were a few painted logs in the field that she sometimes made the pony jump over. All in all, it didn't look very exciting to me. Emily, however, was thrilled to bits, so Tammy and I were happy for her as well. When she came back from riding, she changed her clothes and played with us before doing her homework. We were glad to see she hadn't forgotten us altogether.

Fortunately, there were others in the house to entertain us. Robin, for instance, had a new train set. He and Dad had built a wonderful landscape with tiny trees and houses, hills, roads and cars, and a train track that ran all around it and through two dark tunnels. There were several little trains that could run along those tracks all by themselves. I loved watching them from the sidelines and always made a point of joining Robin when he went downstairs to the 'Rose & Crown' to play trains.

While I was happy just to watch, Tammy wanted to explore the landscape on the set. She was small and nimble enough to pick her way through the little village without upsetting the houses, and she was careful to get out of the way of the trains, so Robin didn't mind her doing it.

One day I woke from my afternoon snooze to find that Tammy had disappeared yet again. I sighed and set about looking for her in all the usual places: Emily's bed, the chimney, Mum and Dad's wardrobe, the empty shopping bags by the front door – in vain. When the children came home from school, they joined my search, but we all drew blanks. There was nothing for it but to wait and see – and for me to listen out for the tiny voice from a totally unexpected place. Meanwhile, Robin and I went to play trains.

Robin got a couple of trains set up, then turned the knob on the controls and off they moved, in opposite directions. One of the engines – my personal favourite – had little puffs of smoke coming from its tiny chimney. I watched it closely as it puffed its way through the trees and into one of the dark tunnels. It gave a little whistle as it entered. Just then, a commotion began inside the tunnel and something white shot out the other end, followed closely by the little puffing train. Tammy! She had hidden in there and gone to sleep on the track. Now she looked scared and shook like a leaf. Robin thought it was hilarious. He laughed so much he rolled on the floor.

Tammy didn't like the train set any more after that, so Robin and I were left to play by ourselves – that's unless Dad joined us, of course.

10

A GLORIOUS SUMMER TURNS TO GLOOM

When summer came we were finally able to use the pool. The whole family moved to the terrace, where Mum had placed the garden furniture. The children splashed about in the water, Mum and Dad sat on the sun loungers reading the paper, Tammy and I lay in the shade, well out of the way of the splashing water, and watched. At the end of the day, Dad lit the barbecue and Mum brought out interesting food to grill. It was, as Mum said frequently, 'the life'.

Sometimes the children invited friends around for a swim after school. Nowhere near the pool was safe when the boys dive-bombed into the water, but the girls just swam, chatted and made a fuss of us, which was okay.

During the school holidays Mum and the children built a fish pond at the bottom of the garden. They dug a hole, filled it with water and added pretty stones and flowers all around it and some even in it. Then they released little red fish into the pond who darted about in amongst the plants and stones. They were fascinating creatures to watch. The pond became my second favourite place to be (the tin roof still retaining first position). I reckoned once the fish had settled in we could have fun together; a bit of fishing would be just the thing to bring colour into my life.

Spoil sport that she is, Mum told me I wasn't allowed to catch the fish. She made me look into her eyes and promise to leave them alone. I narrowed my eyes until they were mere slits and promised nothing. Tammy, on the other hand, wrapped her tail around Mum's neck, rubbed her cheek against hers and gave her one of her bright-eyed looks of sincere promise that never fail to charm humans. She didn't fool me though; she was just keeping away from the fishpond because she was scared of falling in.

No sooner was Mum out of the way than I went down to the pond for a spot of fishing. I knew, of course, to sit quietly for a while until the fish were used to me. I sat as still as a statue while the sun moved gradually past the tree shading the pond. Before long the fish had accepted me as part of the scenery and swam quite close. When the sun emerged from behind the tree and lit up the water, providing optimal conditions for fishing, I struck. My paw sliced into the water like a knife just by the biggest fish. According to my judgment, which is usually spot-on, I should have caught it easily, but no: my paw encountered no fish. For some reason, the fat fish of my choice had been swimming deeper down than it looked. Moreover, when I retracted my paw it was wet! Dripping wet! I shook it and shook it – scattering the fish in all directions below me – and licked it until it was quite dry again. I decided to try with my other paw, once the fish had calmed down, but – same result!

Fishing turned out to be much less fun and much harder work than I had anticipated. I could see the fish, I could smell the fish, I could even hear their little splashes when they came up to the surface – always in the middle of the pond now and well away from me – but I could not catch them. I had several more attempts from various positions around the pond with all four paws, in vain. When dinner time came, I returned to the house exhausted and disappointed, to make do with my usual bowl of boring, processed fish. I found it tasteless and uninspiring for the first time ever.

I was in a bad mood all evening and could not settle. In order to vent my frustration, I gave Tammy a good bashing, but Emily came in just as I was dragging her across the kitchen floor by the scruff of her neck. Emily told me off, scooped Tammy up and took her away to her room for a pamper session. Tammy-bashing was clearly no longer an option; it would have to be the armchair next. I sank my claws into its back, gave a good tug and was rewarded by the satisfying sound of tearing fabric. What I hadn't realized was that Dad was sitting in the armchair, reading the paper. He shot up, yelled at me and actually gave me a smack! I was speechless! Nobody had *ever* smacked me!

Really upset now, I marched down the corridor to Caroline's room. She would understand. I passed Emily's room on my way and heard her sing to 'darling Tammy'. It was a pretty stupid song. When I poked my head around Caroline's door, she was on the phone to one of her friends. I had been aware of phones for some time, of course – Mum and Dad used one frequently to speak to people who weren't there. I had never known a phone to be permanently attached to someone's ear, though, as had been happening to Caroline ever since her party. I hoped it wasn't anything to worry about. She was talking in a very loud voice, interspersed with high-pitched peals of laughter, and hardly looked at me as I entered. I settled down next to her on the bed, waiting to be noticed, and she stroked me absent-mindedly while bobbing up and down and talking non-stop into the phone. The person at the other end couldn't be saying very much – unless they were both talking at the same time, of course. It wasn't exactly what I had imagined in terms of sympathy for my situation. A particularly shrill exclamation followed by Caroline throwing herself down next to me catapulted me off the bed. This was intolerable! Did nobody care about me?

I walked back up the corridor – more cooing noises from Emily's room. How could Emily, my favourite human, take sides against me like that? Disheartened, I stopped outside Robin's door. It was ajar and it seemed Story Time was just beginning. Finally a stroke of luck! I joined Robin on his bed and we listened together as Mum read us the story of someone called Robin Hood, whose life, it seemed, was even more beset by trouble than my own. I decided to stay on and hear what happened to him and enjoyed it so much, I remained on Robin's bed for the night. He might not be the quietest of sleepers, but he was definitely the only family member worth spending time with tonight. It had been a gloomy end to my day – little did I know there was worse to come!

11

I MEET MY NEMESIS

I felt better the next morning. Sometime in the night, I had remembered my victory over the squirrel in America. This made me think that perhaps, sooner or later, I would work out an equally cunning plan to conquer fish. Once again, patience and the art of observation would be required, and I knew I had both.

Buoyed by such positive thinking, I made my peace with Tammy once she emerged from Emily's room. This was easy: she had already forgotten what had happened yesterday. We were soon settled in a patch of sunshine, licking each other, and the morning and early afternoon passed pleasantly enough.

After school, Mum, Dad, Caroline and Robin drove off somewhere while Emily went next door to ride her pony, so Tammy and I were in charge of the house. I patrolled the hallway and stairs while Tammy, never much of a guardian, slept on the armchair. It was to be our last few hours of peace for a long, long time.

I knew there was going to be trouble as soon as the car turned into the driveway. Peculiar noises were coming from it – howls, to be precise. But cars don't howl, do they? I stationed myself by the window on the landing and watched as Mum and the children got out. Then Mum went to open the boot. I froze to my spot when I saw what jumped out: a *dog*! And not just any dog, but the biggest version of its kind I had ever seen! It was huge, hairy and extremely lively. No sooner had Mum opened the front door than it came bustling in and was all over the house before anyone could stop it. It spied Tammy on the armchair and ran up to sniff her. Her face when she opened her eyes to a sharp set of teeth and a drooling jaw defied description – I thought she was going to have a heart attack there and then. But full points for speed to her: she was out of that chair and down the corridor in the direction of Emily's room faster than you could blink. The dog was dumbfounded; it looked around, wondering how she had vanished like that. Luckily, by then Caroline had caught up with it and prevented it from tracking Tammy.

My family had by now gathered around the dog and were encouraging me to meet it. Ha! As if! They made it sit down and held on to its collar, and for a moment it looked as though it might stay there for a while. I moved closer – but only to get within bolting distance of the corridor, from where I planned to join Tammy at the earliest opportunity. It presented itself without delay, as the dog wriggled from Mum's grasp and came bounding over to me. I was off! Where the corridor divided, I took a right turn towards Emily's room, dashed in and kicked the door shut behind me. Tammy was already on Emily's bed, pretending to be a soft toy. I joined her and we lay there together as our heartbeats gradually returned to normal.

Tammy had never seen a dog, so it was left to me to enlighten her on its kind and what its arrival meant for us. She was horrified and trembled all over. I licked her ears a bit and told her I would look after her. It was a lie, as I well knew: nothing would stop that dog from tearing her apart if it chose to, but it made her feel better. Before long, she dozed off next to me, leaving me to reflect on this new challenge in my life – the biggest yet, I reckoned.

I spent the next few days in a state of constant vigilance, expecting the dog to turn up at any time, anywhere. My fears were justified: the monster had the run of the garden and a sixth sense of knowing where I was hiding. It would come bumbling along out of nowhere, nostrils flaring, ears twitching, drawing ever closer. Ecstatic whenever it found me, it made little bunny hops and bowed down on its front paws in an invitation to play. No, thanks! I had no interest in the rough-and-tumble games it wanted to play; there was not the slimmest chance that I might win! Its paws were about the size of my head, and its wrestling style, which I had observed when it played with its favourite rope toy, was unsophisticated to put it mildly: brute force over skill. I really didn't fancy myself in the role of the rope toy.

It didn't understand subtle refusals either. When it dropped a slimy tennis ball in front of me – expecting me to throw it, no doubt – my well-practised look of daggers went completely unnoticed; it just howled encouragement at me. I had to leave it standing there and retreat to the safety of the house.

The dog slept in a large kennel just outside the back door, well away from the main expanse of the garden. Once it had been put to bed, it was possible to wander around the night-time garden relatively undisturbed – so long as I didn't make any noise whatsoever, because it had excellent hearing and came to investigate any shriek of a mouse or flutter of a bird.

Our one saving grace was that the dog was allowed into the house only under strict supervision. So while we stayed indoors, we were able to relax up to a point. The bedrooms were definitely out of bounds to it, which is why Tammy and I spent increasing amounts of time asleep on beds. As it was autumn, which meant long stretches of fine, mild and calm weather with the bluest skies imaginable, this was most annoying. It had always been my practice to sleep off my short morning walk in a sunny spot on the lawn at this time of year. That was now impossible. In fact, one day I even found a giant dog turd in the very spot I favoured. The dog had stolen every small pleasure I had ever had. No wonder I slowly but surely turned into an indoor cat and my waistline expanded further as autumn turned to winter.

Not surprisingly, Tammy kept forgetting about the dog. The very morning after its arrival she blithely wandered out into the garden without a care in the world. My warning call came too late; she was already half-way across the lawn when the dog appeared. Its ears shot forward in excitement as it spied her happily catching butterflies and sniffing at flowers, and it leapt over to her, delighted to have found such an easy victim. I could hardly bear to watch. When she finally noticed the dog, she panicked instantly and bolted, which as we all know is the one sure-fire way of getting a dog to chase you. It did. Once again, she owed it to her astonishing agility and acceleration – from zero to supersonic in about half a second, in any direction – that she escaped unharmed and came flying through the cat flap just before the dog crashed into the patio door behind her.

Tammy was quite beside herself. Her chest and flanks were heaving, her eyes bulging, her tail the size of Mum's feather duster. Once again, I had to explain to her about the dog and implore her to be more careful, knowing full well that my warnings fell onto deaf ears. Within minutes, she was contentedly crunching away at her breakfast, her near-death experience just a dim memory, to be erased completely by the time she reached Emily's bed for her mid-morning nap. Clearly, the task of mastering the dog would be mine, and mine alone.

12

THE OUTBACK BECKONS!

It was hard to believe indeed. At first I thought Emily had gone soft in the head when she told me, but soon the signs were all there: we were packing up and moving again! Why? As far as I could see, we had only just settled in this house, built a pool and a pond, acquired a kitten, a dog and a pony… What more could they possibly want?

In actual fact, it turned out to be the pony's fault. Emily was really getting into riding her pony and spent more and more time next door. She was also taking the pony away at weekends, returning dirty and sweaty at the end of the day, reeking of horse. It seemed our neighbourhood was cramping her style: she wanted more space to ride and a paddock of her own. For some reason, Mum and Dad also thought that would be a good idea. Nobody thought of asking my opinion. As usual, I had to either go with the flow or despair. My only hope was for a place with a very secure dog run, where the drooling monster would be kept locked up.

We had the packing down to a fine art by now. Mum had already given up her job in the city in readiness for the move. She gradually packed up the kitchen and the contents of all the cupboards. Soon the familiar sight of boxes became a feature of every room once more. Tammy and I played games of hide-and-seek in amongst them, which provided some welcome indoor distraction, and we perched on top of them whenever the drooling monster was allowed into the house.

It didn't look as though we were moving far this time, because Mum and Dad had decided we would do most of the moving ourselves. It turned out to be a lot of work. Mum and Dad made endless trips with the car and trailer stacked full of boxes while the children were at school, Tammy slept in the ever more sparsely furnished bedrooms and I patrolled the lines of boxes in the hallway. We were exhausted by the time the removal men came in their big truck to take the furniture away.

Mum put me and Tammy into my travel container, which was quite a squash. She also loaded the dog into the car boot and off we drove. I was cross not to be able to see much, due to being confined in the container, and complained loudly. I would have much preferred having the run of the car, as I usually do. But Mum explained we were going to a very big and wild property, which I should get to know little by little, so she preferred to have me contained when we arrived. Well, we would soon see about that. They could not possibly keep all the doors shut while moving furniture in, could they?

I was, once again, perfectly correct: the back door in the new house was a glass sliding door, which stayed open the whole time things were being carried in. I was out there within minutes of our arrival. The dog – praise to the new garden! – had been locked into just the kind of dog run I had visualized in my dreams, where it howled loudly and continuously. Tammy found a bag of some sort in Emily's new room, into which she crawled without delay in an effort to hide from the world, so I was free to explore the great outdoors all by myself – which is, believe me, the only way to do it.

And it was the great outdoors! I smelled it and felt it as soon as I set foot in it: we had moved to the outback! As it was a late afternoon in winter, night was already falling as I walked past dense shrubbery by the side of the house and across a sloping piece of lawn to the driveway which wrapped itself around our new house. Beyond the vegetation that lined the far side of the drive, I sensed more than I could see wide-open country falling away below: it was hilly country, and we seemed to be quite high up, near the top of a hill. The aroma of big gum trees lay fresh and spicy in the air. I took a deep breath and felt as though I had just come alive again after a very long time. It was a chilly evening, and still; no sound of traffic or humans, just a mournful whistle and rumble far away down the valley, far enough so as not to bother me. The birds were already winding up their evening song, but I could hear owls hooting in the distance, and from further up the driveway came the loud ribbeting of frogs! Remembering how much fun I had had with them in our Perth garden, I followed their calls and ended up at the top of a steeply sloping paddock by a large pond all covered in reeds.

There was a lot going on in and around the pond. Frogs were splashing in the shallow water, singing the familiar ribbeting song I remembered from my days as a kitten. There were other frogs, too, emitting hollow bong-bong calls that sounded like eerie drum beats in the night. All around the pond, ducks were sleeping with their beaks tucked under their wings. I sat down under a big old gum tree and soaked in the peaceful scene. I didn't feel like hunting; it was enough for now to watch, listen, and learn.

I could see there was much to learn in this place, which seemed even wilder and more remote than our home in America. I sensed forests here, too, and fields spreading out in all directions just beyond our garden fence. From behind me through a big hedge came the sound of swishing tails, the stomping of heavy feet and the rhythmic ripping of grass. Horses? No – the smell was different and unfamiliar.

The ground fell away sharply beyond the frog pond. It would be a steep climb back up; better to squeeze under the farm gate and continue my exploration of the level garden by the house. There were two huge cedar trees in the front garden, excellent for climbing. I scaled one of them easily – its branches were low down, quite unlike the trees in America, allowing me to leap up easily further and further until I was high above our new house. A few birds gave chirps of alarm as I passed their sleeping quarters, but they needn't have worried: I was too busy to pay them any attention. The two ancient trees reached right across the picket fence that bordered our property, across the wide grass verge in front of it, from where the delicate scent of early spring flowers drifted up to me, and over a dirt road that led up from the deep darkness of the valley, past our garden and on to the very top of the hill, where its final curve was bathed in moonlight. A huge full moon had just emerged above the crest of the hill. The animals in next door's paddock were sharply outlined against the grass by its silvery light. I took a good look at them from my new vantage point. They were about the same size as horses, but heavier-set with thick necks and short, sturdy legs. One of them in particular was huge and bulky, with an enormous head on its broad shoulders. It uttered a long, plaintive bellow that seemed to come from deep down in its throat and rose up into the still night, to be answered shortly afterwards by a similar call from across the valley.

Further down the paddock, the moonlight revealed a couple of ponds that looked deeper than our frog pond and were free from reeds. More animals were grazing down there – smaller, slender, with little heads and front legs, but large, powerful hind legs and tails. As I watched, one of them leapt off in big, graceful bounds and all the others followed. They bounced up the hill and fanned out into the trees, the sound of their feet landing on the turf providing a slow and steady accompaniment to the bong-bong frogs in the pond. The paddock went quiet, and I realized that apart from the larger animals there were hundreds and hundreds of rabbits about. I could not believe how many there were! The whole hillside seemed to be hopping with them. It was all very entertaining.

I thought the only place remaining to be explored on my descent from the tree was a big shed by the side of the house, but as I walked towards it, I saw another low building further down the hill, which seemed worth a visit. It looked quite derelict – always a promising prospect. All kinds of debris littered the rough dirt floors – rotting bits of wood, rolls of wire, a couple of filthy saucepans – and there were droppings everywhere. Some smelt of bird, but all the rest gave off the unmistakable aroma of rats – my speciality! I would tackle them in the morning. For now, I peed on some tufts of hay in one corner, to let them know I had arrived. It seemed fair to give them a warning.

After the rat house, my last stop was the big shed, which was already full of our things. It was also home to a colony of small birds who had built neat little nests in the rafters. There might be some potential here in spring, at nesting time. I reckoned I would have my work cut out in this new place of endless possibilities.

On emerging from the shed, I saw to my dismay that the dog had somehow managed to get out of its run. It was pawing at the back door and whining. The door was shut now, and the moving truck had gone. How had I missed that? I must have been so absorbed by all the sights and sounds of our new, fascinating home.

A car slowly rounded the corner of our driveway, and out popped a couple of friends carrying bowls of food. The back door opened and we all filed in, including the dog, whom nobody seemed to have noticed. There was much laughter and shouting. The visitors were shown around the house, stumbling over boxes, bumping into things, then Mum set the table in the family room – the only piece of furniture that was currently in its proper place, along with its chairs – and everyone sat down to eat, surrounded by boxes and an assortment of abandoned furniture. I discovered my food and water bowl in the pantry where shelves were already stacked with food. Tammy came to join me and we had our dinner to the sound of lively conversation from the kitchen.

That's how we arrived in our home in the bush, among the gum trees and – as I learnt later – the kangaroos.

13

ANOTHER NEW LIFE

Chaos reigned in the house for some time afterwards. It seemed that a move of a few miles was harder to accomplish than a move from another continent. Our new house was smaller than our old one – it was all on one level, no stairs, no 'Rose & Crown' – so it wasn't easy to fit everything in. Some pieces of furniture never made it in from the big shed and, frankly, I never missed them. I think humans own too many things.

The new house was actually very old. It creaked and the walls, which were various shades of muddy water, soared high up to ceilings shrouded in cobwebs. Could there be bats nesting in the gloom up there? Impossible to tell from where I stood, but an intriguing possibility nonetheless.

My family bravely set to with paint brushes, hammers and nails until the rooms emerged in lighter colours, revealing – alas – no wildlife. It would have been too much to ask. Tammy and I were constantly being moved from one napping place to the next. No sooner had we settled down on a pile of soft curtains or warm coats than someone came to take them away. It was very unsettling, and it took ages; much longer than on previous moves.

I have to hand it to them, though: when at long last they had finished tinkering with everything, the house was comfortable. It had a cosy sitting room at its centre, which warmed up nicely on cold winter nights when a black box similar to the one we had had in America crackled into action, and a bright and airy kitchen and family room, where big windows allowed lovely views in several directions. Sitting on the worktop while Mum cooked, I was able to look down through the crowns of big trees into the deep folds of the valley below, and across to the hills on the far side.

Caroline and Emily had been allowed to decorate their own rooms: Caroline's was sunshine yellow with pretty blue butterflies chasing each other up the walls, while Emily's was a soft, creamy shade that looked delicious, but sadly tasted quite disgusting. As an afterthought, she added a thin pea green border. It might have been wider had she not spilt most of the paint on the carpet. But she moved her bed to cover the stain, and no-one ever noticed it after that.

Robin's room was all panelled in timber and smelled of the forest. From its ceiling dangled an array of aeroplanes that circled overhead when the breeze moved them. His desk was bathed in sunshine in the afternoons, when we did his homework and occasionally nodded off together in the blissful warmth. It was a tiny room; he really struggled to fit in all his toys without the large expanse of the 'Rose & Crown' at his disposal. The train set had to stay in the big shed, where it was soon covered in dust, cobwebs and bird droppings.

If we lacked space in the house, we certainly had plenty of it outside. There appeared to be no end to the land we owned. On my first walkabout with Mum, I discovered another pond, a big old tree with a tire swing, a ring of pretty red toadstools and a huge rabbit burrow.

At the top of the hill stood a big old stable full of irresistible nooks and crannies. Straw covered the floor and bits of rotting wood and rusty iron lay scattered about in a mysterious muddle. My nose immediately picked out the scent of entire colonies of rodents who had lived here undisturbed for years; I would be more than busy! Huge cobwebs draped themselves across the rafters like dusty veils. Spiders the size of Mum's hand waited drowsily overhead in the cool breeze for their next snack. It was an enchanting place; I planned to return at night if I possibly could. As it turned out, the dog would actually do me a favour in that regard: due to its roaming habits, it was eventually put on a long lead by its kennel at night, which meant that Tammy and I were free to hunt after dark.

Dad installed a cat door which led out on to the wide veranda that wrapped itself around the house, so we would stay dry in all weathers when stepping outside. It was far from the dog's kennel; we had a clear getaway between dusk and dawn.

I know Mum would have preferred to keep us in at night so we wouldn't hunt for wildlife. But she realized the dog was a nuisance to us outside during the day, so she relented. We had the most wonderful times hunting rats, of which the rat house provided an unlimited supply, mice, bunnies, bats and even the odd sugar glider and bringing them inside for our family to find in the morning. They never failed to be impressed and became quite good at prising bats and sugar gliders off the curtains, to be released back outside for another time. Early in the morning of Mum's birthday, Tammy and I killed a bunny and arranged it on the kitchen floor for her to find first thing in the morning. Tammy even placed a lovely weed next to it as a finishing touch – she has quite a flair for that kind of thing. Mum was thrilled. It was her best present, actually; everything else she got looked pretty useless to me.

Tammy got lost in our new home just as she had done in our old one. On our very first night, she ran off and slept outside in the cold and damp. She looked and smelled filthy when Mum found her in the morning; white is a terrible colour to be. A short while later, she somehow managed to climb up to the roof of the house – nobody ever worked out how – and couldn't get back down, so she called for me through the skylight. I could see her little face peering down at us while the wind flattened her ears and rain dripped off her nose. Mum and the children were just getting ready for school, and in the chaos I had a job to make myself heard to alert them to the emergency. Dad had to get the ladder out and rescued Tammy in the pouring rain.

The dog loved our new home. The fences and gates were all old and mostly broken, so it was able to escape easily whenever it felt like roaming, which was often. I'm afraid the old dog run turned out to be quite useless at restraining it. It simply jumped the fence and was off. That was absolutely fine with me and Tammy. We hoped it would get lost and never return, but no: it would be out for hours and hours, then come bouncing back full of excitement, usually with blood and a few feathers hanging from its drooling mouth. When one of the neighbours mentioned that almost all of his chickens had been killed by something, Mum and Dad made valiant efforts to put a stop to the dog's expeditions. It was harder than they imagined; the dog was very inventive and kept finding new escape routes.

14

WE WITNESS A CRIME

Tammy and I were peacefully dozing in the armchair by the window in the family room; Dad was away somewhere with his suitcase; Mum had just started a new job and the children were at school. The dog was quietly howling in its kennel, where it belonged. Things were good; we were getting back to normal.

Through half-closed eyelids, I saw a strange car draw up outside our gate; a man got out and checked out our house. He walked up and down the fence for a bit, waving and calling. Fully awake by now, I waved back at him, but he didn't seem to see me. To my surprise, he then boldly opened the gate and drove his car down our drive. There was another man in the car as well. I went to the back door to see what they wanted.

The back door was locked, and the dog was sitting just outside. The men drew up and got out of the car. The dog, all teeth and noise with us, trotted over to greet them with a wagging tail as though they were old mates. The men had been apprehensive at first sight of the dog, but now they relaxed and patted it. One of them rummaged about in the car and produced a bone, which the dog received with delight and slunk off to gnaw, all thoughts of guarding our house forgotten.

The men lifted some heavy tools from their car and came up to the back door. First they tried to open it with a number of keys from a large bunch. When that didn't work, they smashed the glass with a hammer. Glass flew everywhere. A gloved hand pushed in through the jagged-edged hole and groped for the lock inside. I thought about scratching that hand – how dare these people damage our house! Then I thought better of it. It was the dog's job to protect us; why should I risk life and limb? My family might as well see what a hopeless guard dog it was. I turned and ran back to the family room, woke Tammy from a deep sleep and bustled her out of the cat door just as the men burst into the room in their heavy boots, shouting at each other in gruff voices. We fled across the lawn and raced up one of the cedar trees, from where we observed through the windows what the men were doing in the house.

It was very scary to watch. Tammy whimpered next to me, and my own heart was pounding in my chest. The men stomped all over the house, opening cupboards and drawers and throwing things out. Everything our family had only just put away was roughly pulled out and scattered all over the floor. We heard the sound of chairs and ornaments crashing to the floor, of doors banging and glass breaking. The men emerged from the front door, carrying armfuls of our belongings over to their car. We saw the TV and the computers disappear, Mum's jewellery box, Dad's leather jacket, Robin's precious hunting knife – just about everything they could carry was taken away. We were beside ourselves, yet completely powerless to stop them.

Meanwhile, on the far side of the house, the dog was happily gnawing at its bone, quite oblivious of the abomination to our property. I hoped the bone was poisoned. I had never seen a more pathetic guard dog.

When the men had taken everything they could, they drove off, leaving the gate wide open. The dog never gave them a second glance. Once it had finished its bone, it went to investigate the back door, where it cut itself on the broken glass. Blood dripping from its nose, it came to settle down at the foot of our tree to wait for Mum. It didn't look so happy now. I think it finally realized something very bad had happened. Still I detected no trace of guilt, just pain and worry about its nose. Tammy and I were so frightened by what we had seen, we stayed on our perch in the tree for the rest of the day. The light was already fading when our car drew up at the gate – at last we were safe!

Mum and the children had a terrible shock when they saw the broken back door. Robin started crying and Mum's face went white. They went through the house, looking at the devastation the men had left behind. Tammy and I crept down from the tree and ventured back inside. Mum was relieved to see we were all right. Then she set about bathing the dog's nose with camomile tea, while the girls tried to tidy up and Robin continued to cry. I didn't think she needed to rush to tend to the dog. After all, what had that dog done to help?

Mum made several phone calls. Soon a man came along to fix the back door, and the police called to look at the mess in the house. All evening Mum and the children tidied up and made lists of what the thieves had taken. I was relieved to find they had not stolen our bowls or any of our food. Nevertheless, we all spent a restless night thinking about the men rifling through our things.

The next day was Caroline's birthday, but it turned out the thieves had taken away all her presents. She was very brave, considering, and Mum promised to buy more presents as soon as possible. Still, it wasn't a happy birthday, and we all felt sad for her.

15

DOUBLE TROUBLE

Dad came back with his suitcase later in the day. Over dinner, we decided that something needed to happen to make our new property more secure. A sturdy new gate and a big padlock were first on the list. Then the children mentioned the dog and the sorry role it had played in the burglary, at which they were able to guess even though they had not been here to see it. I sat on the dining table, in the centre of the family counsel, in order to put my opinion across, which was to get rid of the dog in the face of so much uselessness.

I'm sorry to say my voice of reason was not heard. I expect I should have known my family better; they were infuriatingly stubborn. Having accepted the dog into our family, they were not going to send it away now, however badly it behaved. My objections fell on deaf ears, and the whole family closed ranks on me. Search me why. I was sorely disappointed and left them to it, in order to think things through in my armchair. If the dog was staying, I needed a battle plan.

Later on, when all was quiet, I went outside and sat down near the kennel to observe the enemy. If I was going to solve the challenge of the dog – and clearly, nobody else was going to – I had to get to know it better. I realized I probably should have done this before, but I had never been that interested in the dog, having naively assumed it wouldn't be around for long, given its bad habits.

In the course of the family council, I had learnt that the dog was a female, and that her name was Mishka. I had not even been interested in that much information before now. She was lying outside her kennel, attached to a lead, her twitching nose resting in the forked branch of a small shrub. She was surveying the night-time garden with a self-satisfied expression, her slanted eyes half-closed, probably plotting her next bad deed. She didn't look like a female to me: she was big, strong and very determined. Her thick, grey coat looked as though no claw of mine could ever penetrate it, and her mouth, when she opened it wide to yawn, was big enough to swallow Tammy whole. There was no doubt about it: she would be a tough nut to crack.

Just then, the breeze dislodged a large seed pod from a nearby tree, which landed on the dog's nose with a plop. It was a hard, knobbly pod and came down at some speed. With a yelp of pain, she jumped up and fled into her kennel, her tail between her legs. There she cowered, whining quietly to herself and peering fearfully at the black pod that lay innocently on the ground in front of her. She watched it for a long time, and when it did not move, she relaxed and settled down to sleep. But she did not come out of her kennel again until the next morning, when Dad let her off her lead. Even then, she kept Dad between herself and the seed pod and gave it a wide berth for the rest of the day, until Mum swept it away when she tidied up.

I returned to my armchair, much reassured by what I had witnessed. My nightly vigil had been well worth it. The dog had a weak spot, after all (how could I have overlooked the nose?), and she was a coward. Maybe there *was* hope for me.

Unfortunately, I had not reckoned with my family's next wild decision, which was, unbelievably, to get a second dog: one that was fierce enough to drive any thief away.

It won't surprise anyone to hear that they succeeded: soon we were joined by a streamlined, turbo-charged, razor-toothed killing machine by the name of Max. At the first sign of a visitor at the gate, Max was there and stood up on his hind legs, which made him easily the height of most humans. If anyone was foolish enough still to venture in through the gate, he took their hand in his mouth and marched them up the garden path to the front door, ready for inspection by Mum or Dad. By then, most visitors looked ashen-faced and pleaded with us to let them into the house quickly, while they still had both their hands.

The arrival of Max certainly solved one problem: we were as safe from intruders in our home as we would ever be while he was patrolling our fence line. The down-side for me and for Tammy was that this dog's brain was hard-wired to kill anything that moved, including us, and consequently we were no longer able to go outside unless he was firmly on his lead. While Mishka had been a bumbling nuisance, Max was a very real threat to our lives. Together, they were a pack of wolves, not to be trusted. After several scary experiences and a couple of near misses, even Tammy managed to remember that there were dogs outside, and a long period of self-denial began for us. We effectively became prisoners in our own home during the day and could do little except sleep and eat. The year basically shrank down to two seasons for us: sleep-by-the-fire season and sleep-on-the-veranda-right-by-the-cat-door season.

This seemed to suit Tammy fine. No amount of eating and sleeping made any difference to her long, skinny legs and lithe body. I, on the other hand, only had to look at a bowl of food to put on weight, and my regular nightly visits to the rat house required too little energy to make any difference: the rats were so plentiful, they practically ran into my mouth. And so I became even rounder than before. My family started calling me 'plumpkin' and other unkind names I won't even repeat here, when really my predicament was all their fault.

Luckily for us, the dogs were not allowed into the house. This definitely gave us an advantage on cold, wet days. Mishka didn't mind those: her coat was thick enough to withstand even the worst weather. But Max would have much preferred to be warm and dry. On bad weather days, he sat wet and bedraggled on the veranda and gazed longingly at us through the floor-to-ceiling window of the family room as we rested cosily in our armchair by the crackling black fire box. Often, Tammy and I played a chasing game around the room especially for his benefit. He became quite excited watching us.

Max was given his own kennel by the back door, next to Mishka's and, to start with, the two dogs seemed to get on wonderfully well. They played wild, snarling games on the grass while Tammy and I looked on aghast from the safety of a windowsill. They chased each other all over the place. They attacked a large and extremely venomous eastern brown snake and pulled it apart in front of our very eyes. This should have been the end of both of them, but somehow they got away without being bitten. They escaped together for entire days, leaving the whole family worried sick about what they might be up to out there. In short, they were a menace.

Our family had many discussions about the dogs, and I listened with interest to see just how far their good natures could be stretched. Quite far, it seemed. They started taking the dogs to training classes – to little effect, as far as I could see. Dad ran an electric wire along the top of our front fence to stop them from escaping, and it worked: once zapped by the electricity, they never jumped the fence again. Instead, they squeezed under it, wherever the smallest hole provided an opening. They were, apparently, unstoppable and untrainable.

In time, Mishka asserted herself over Max. I watched her attack him viciously over their dog treats and saw her try to steal his dinner from his bowl. She even pulled his bed out of his kennel and tore it to shreds in front him. He hardly defended himself. For all his fierce behaviour towards other animals or visitors, Max was gradually and visibly shrinking into subservience to Mishka. I observed it with interest and filed this fact away in my mind for future use.

16

THERE ARE MORE AND MORE OF US AND I MEET THE NATIVES

While all this was going on – and much of it without the knowledge of our family – Emily's pony arrived. Or rather, it wasn't the pony any longer. Somewhere along the line, probably while I was asleep somewhere, the fat brown pony must have been exchanged for a bigger one of speckled grey colour. It arrived at our gate in a big trailer and was soon installed in its paddock, from where it called unhappily for its friends across the valley.

Emily was in seventh heaven. At dawn each morning she went out into the stable to groom, feed and talk to her horse. Sometimes, when the dogs were busy having their breakfast, I went with her and sat on the fence to watch. After school, she rode out into the countryside for long hours and in all weathers, but still the horse remained lonely and unhappy. It was clear what had to happen: the horse needed a friend, and while we were expanding our menagerie on an almost daily basis, it really was no big deal for my family to get another horse.

Yet again, a trailer arrived at the gate to discharge a chestnut horse of similar size to the grey one. Whether the two of them got on or not is more than I can say. Confined as I was to the house most of the time, I had better things to do in my rare moments of freedom than to run all the way down to the horse paddock. But I did see the new horse leaving our property at a smart canter one day. I was just turning over in the armchair and there it was at the gate, presumably in pursuit of Emily and her horse, who were out on a trail ride. This was surely an indication that the two horses liked each other. The gate had been left open by mistake, so off he galloped up the road. Soon the whole family was out looking for him. They must have combed the length and breadth of the surrounding countryside because they looked weary when they returned hours later, leading the horse. After that, the gate stayed shut at all times, which was a good thing from any perspective.

In due course, we were joined by a flock of white sheep with black faces. I was well past caring by then. They moved into the paddock by the frog pond and turned out to be the least trouble of all the animals we had accumulated. Their peaceful grazing was pleasant to watch on dewy summer mornings, when mists lay in the folds of the valley and all was still and serene. That was before the dogs were let off their leads and charged up to the paddock fence, scattering the sheep in all directions, heedless of Mum's or Dad's yelled commands to leave them alone.

And so, almost before we knew it, we had acquired a small farm, and I was outnumbered about fifteen to one by creatures I never even knew existed. How did that make me feel? Take a guess! By now, had I been foolish enough to venture out during the day, I would have had to check first whether the dogs were on their leads, all gates shut, the horses and sheep safely in their paddocks... It simply wasn't worth the effort.

Our fish had moved with us from their pond at the bottom of the old garden to a new one right by the window of Dad's home office. Emily had spent hours catching them in a net – an ingenious idea that allowed her to trap them without getting her paws wet at all – plopping them into a bucket filled with water and, after transporting them to our new garden, introducing them to their new pond. This was very pretty indeed. A mass of tumbling blue flowers and spiky ferns surrounded this pond in no time, so it looked as though it had been there forever. The fish seemed very happy, and by and by a colony of tiny frogs came to join them. I sharpened my claws on Dad's carpet while watching them through the window. But of course, any real hunting efforts were frustrated by the dogs, whose kennels were nearby.

In any case, before long other visitors started dropping by, more dangerous even than the dogs, to foil my attempts: the first one appeared one sunny afternoon as I was snoozing on the deck, the dogs safely locked into the stable with Emily. A funny little rustling noise woke me up. It came from the ferns by the pond and didn't sound like any of the usual suspects: bird, rabbit or mouse. I crept closer to investigate. Something was moving in amongst the dark green foliage – something long and smooth. It was gliding down towards the pond from a point above the blue flowers, and suddenly the sun lit up a section of its golden-brown body as it coiled around the ferns: a snake! I knew to be careful of all snakes and even anything that looked like a snake, such as the garden hose. Back in America, I had shunned the black snakes who lived in the field next door, even though they were relatively harmless. But this snake, I sensed, was something else; one bite from it would kill.

I retreated soundlessly to the safety of the house and alerted Dad to the intruder. His eyes widened in alarm when he saw it. He reached for the phone to call the snake man, who arrived a while later and crawled about under our house, trying to find our snake and to take it away in a bag he had brought with him, but in vain; it had left as silently as it had come, without anyone noticing. So ended my first encounter, but it was by no means the last.

There were plenty more snakes in and around our property. They had been there long before us and were not going to go away just because we had moved in. A succession of them adopted our garden pond and the frog pond in the paddock as their drinking holes. You could never be sure whether they were about, as they moved perfectly silently. The eastern browns were careful of other species and slithered away as soon as they felt the vibrations of our footsteps, but the tiger snakes were bold and stood their ground. One of them, a regular visitor, lived in the paddock across the road. He was as big as the branches on our pear tree and very dark. His tiger stripes were barely visible, so I mistook him for a branch when I first met him on the driveway. With a sharp hiss he warned me to get out of his way and sent me scuttling up the garden wall. Then he slithered away under the fence without giving me a second glance, confident in the knowledge that everything around here belonged to him.

After that encounter, I decided to take a few extra precautions on my outings and avoided walking through high grass or dense shrubs. Even on the lawns, which were kept short or lost their grass altogether in the long, hot summers, it paid to rotate my ears and listen out for snakes. I met several more, but managed to save myself each time. So did all the other members of my family, including the dogs. This was a miracle, as Mishka liked to pin their tails down with her paw as they tried to slither off.

The amazingly colourful birds who lived on and around our property were noisy and greedy, but less dangerous as long as you stayed out of reach of their sharp beaks. At daybreak, flocks of brilliant white cockatoos with yellow crests and piercing, croaky voices swept across the valley like fluffy clouds and landed wherever food beckoned. They particularly liked the old pear tree outside Emily's bedroom window, which they stripped bare in a matter of hours. I watched from the safety of Emily's desk, powerless to stop them. Even when Mum and Dad covered the tree with a net the following year, the cockatoos still managed to get all the pears that grew on the outside of the tree.

Mum bought a big bird table and positioned it right outside the kitchen window so I could watch the birds as they ate the tasteless seeds and bits of fruit that were put out for them, poor things. A pair of king parrots regularly visited and had excellent appetites. When they had finished every last scrap, they whistled for Mum to put out more – what a cheek! I felt obliged to chase

143

them away a few times. Flocks of smaller lorikeets dressed in pretty rainbow colours took a shine to the stone bird bath in the middle of our front lawn. They sat all around its rim and took turns to splash in the water while the onlookers cheered. Strange creatures – fancy *volunteering* to have a bath! The bird bath was in full view of our armchair, but the presence of the dogs usually prevented us from getting anywhere near it. The dogs themselves were not particularly interested in the birds, which was surprising, since they hunted everything else that moved.

One night, pandemonium broke out at the back door by the dogs' kennels. The whole family was up in seconds and on the scene – of yet another crime, as you may have guessed. A prickly creature had chosen the spot just between the two kennels for its resting place. It was as round as the dogs' play ball and studded all over with long, sharp spikes. It seemed to have no legs, nose or eyes and must be fairly dim-witted to settle in between two large dogs, or else it was feeling suicidal that night. The dogs were attacking it even though they were doing considerable damage to their noses by biting into the spiky ball. Both had several spikes stuck in their noses by the time Mum and Dad pulled them off the intruder and locked them into the house for the remainder of the night.

The strange creature was still sitting in its spot between the dog kennels the following morning and seemed determined to stay there. It had uncurled a bit and now revealed a black, shiny nose and four legs. Interesting. During the brief family council that followed, I learnt that our prickly visitor was called echidna, and that he would have to be removed. Emily went to get thick leather gloves and tried to pick him up; he somehow managed to cling to the ground, using surprisingly strong claws. Dad tried to prise him off the ground using his pick-axe, but he resisted even that. While Dad was still scratching his head, the echidna, who had obviously had enough of us, started digging and slowly disappeared under our house. You had to admire his composure and his amazing claws. Mum's turn for action had arrived: she decided not to mess with the echidna, but instead picked up the phone and called someone who was knowledgeable about the species. The advice she received was to leave him alone until he decided to move by himself.

And so the back door stayed shut for several days; the dogs were grounded indoors. It was a brilliant time for me and Tammy, and I personally thanked the echidna for the service he was doing us. He was not a creature of many words. From the depths of his hole he gruffly informed me he would stay for just as long as it pleased *him*. I left him alone after that and went off to enjoy myself without the threat of dogs hanging over me. I visited the stable, the frog pond and the sheep paddock. The weather was beautiful: it was spring, balmy and breezy, the blossom was out everywhere and it felt like paradise.

Alas – just a short while later the echidna decided to move on. He emerged from his hole one night, gave a couple of sneezes and trundled off in the direction of the stable. I happened to be nearby, waiting for a mouse to emerge from its hiding place, and was very sorry to see him go. His departure spelt freedom for the dogs and the return to imprisonment for Tammy and me.

It turned out to be such a setback that the possibility of joining a nice, peaceful family of humans with a stable lifestyle and no other animals occurred to me for the first time ever. Life simply didn't seem worth living if all I could do was sleep and eat. What held me back was the startling realization that my family needed me more than ever now that they had become the hapless victims of not one, but two rude dogs, and that I actually loved them still, in spite of everything. Flight was definitely out of the question; I could not have looked myself in the mirror had I abandoned them to their fate – even though, it has to be said, they had nobody to blame for it but themselves.

So what was I to do?

17

I TAKE AN IMPORTANT STEP IN THE RIGHT DIRECTION

Quite unaware of my moral dilemma, my family carried on with their never-ending list of home improvements. When they weren't decorating rooms, they were digging up the dense shrubbery around the house, mending fences, removing rusty old gates or planting trees. They even built their own pool this time – a large oval structure that sat on a flat piece of grass by the big shed. It wasn't as nice as our old pool; I couldn't drink from it as its rim was high above the ground. But they had a lot of fun in there when it was finished, splashing and shouting, so I guess it may have been worth the trouble, provided you liked getting wet.

The dogs loved water and would really have liked to have a swim, too. They stood up at the pool's rim and looked longingly at the swimmers, but it was too high up for them to jump in, so they settled for barking a lot and chasing each other round and round the pool, getting terribly excited. Whenever anyone played with a ball in the pool, Max simply could not contain himself. He hopped around the pool on his hind legs like a kangaroo so as not to miss any of the action, and once he got so carried away he bit one of Robin's friends in the bottom and was banned from that part of the garden for the rest of the day. I was pleased to see this from my perch high up on the fence, well out of reach of the drooling squad.

After the pool, Dad built a timber deck next to the fish pond, the best place to sit on hot summer days: always shady, breezy, cool and elevated from the ground, which made it safe from snakes. A table and chairs soon appeared there for meals outside. Mum and Dad took to sitting there on summer evenings with drinks and nibbles, watching darkness fall over the valley, while Tammy and I watched them from the kitchen window, wishing we could be with them. Unfortunately, the dogs also loved the hour of the yard arm, mainly because of the nibbles that sometimes dropped from a careless hand to find their way into their greedy jowls. So we had no option but to stay inside and suffer in silence. Or so I thought…

While house and garden were taking shape, the dogs were bored and continued behaving badly. I could see that my family's feeble attempts at dog training had largely failed, while the dogs themselves went from strength to strength and did just as they pleased. This could not go on.

For my part, I had had enough of sitting in the house all day or fearing for my life every time I went outside. My reflection in the window told me I was getting ball-shaped; hunting was getting harder all the time. We had been living on our farm for longer than anywhere else I remembered – I could barely recollect life in America or even in our first house in Melbourne. It was an exciting place worthy of exploration, and we seemed to be set to stay. There was no way Tammy and I could remain prisoners here for the rest of our lives. It was time for me to take matters into my own paws.

From my observations I already knew that Mishka was the one who needed to be subdued. Once she obeyed me, Max would simply follow. I also knew her nose was her weak spot, and that in spite of her outward bravado she was a coward at heart. I therefore sharpened my claws and held back on the food for a little while, which I found difficult, but not impossible. When I felt ready, I walked up to Mishka as she was sitting in the sun and said hello. She jumped up immediately, ears forward, tongue lolling, a mischievous grin in her slanting eyes. I knew she was thinking we were going to have a great game involving snarling and violence, with me at the receiving end. She was wrong: I lifted my right front paw, shot out my claws and dealt a swift blow to her nose. She sat down heavily and blinked in surprise. I was pleased with the effect I had achieved and moved a little closer. She looked embarrassed now and shuffled backwards on her bottom. I lifted my left paw and hit her again. A little blood appeared on her nose and she slunk right up against the house wall. Whimpering softly, she lay down in front of me. I was satisfied with her progress and decided to call an end to her first lesson. Tail held high, I left her lying there and strolled off. I had earned myself a snack and a snooze.

The next time I walked up to Mishka, she looked uncomfortable, avoided looking into my eyes and moved a couple of steps back. Max was nearby and watched with interest. But he took his cue from Mishka, as I knew he would, and did not attack me. I still felt I should hit him for good measure and dealt him one of my right hooks; he just sat down and looked confused. I could not believe how well my two short training sessions had gone and how easy it had been!

From that day on, I was able to walk around our property undisturbed. I might have been invisible: the dogs pretended not to see me, even when I paraded right in front of them. I took to drinking water from their bowls, and they waited patiently until I had finished before taking their turns. Whenever they came too close for my liking, I gave them a taste of my paw and they shrank away. It was very satisfying.

My superior status now restored, I introduced Tammy to the dogs and made it clear she was under my protection. Max found it very hard to restrain himself and earned another slap from me for the greedy look he was giving her. He backed off immediately then. I encouraged Tammy to try her own paw at hitting the dogs, but she was too timid. I guessed she would find it easier once she grew a bit older.

Life became enjoyable again, and I realized I should have tamed the dogs a long time ago. My family watched the sudden change in the cat-dog hierarchy with amazement and a total lack of understanding. Humans are quite slow in these things. But they did realize that my new status as the dogs' guardian was freeing them up to do more work on the farm and lost no time in starting their final project: the renovation of the stable – the one project I personally felt was quite unnecessary, because there was nothing wrong with it at all.

A digging machine had already levelled a large piece of ground for Emily to ride on, but the stable itself had managed to retain its wonderfully tumble-down and messy look, no matter how much cleaning up she did. Apparently, this was not good enough. A flock of men in white suits came and stripped the whole building right down to its steel structure; it was awful to watch. Then Dad, assisted by the rest of the family, built new walls and windows and created a plain, level dirt floor robbed of its shady nooks, fascinating holes and mysterious piles of debris. It was a dusty job, and I was glad my supervising duties kept me up at the house, since the dogs were not allowed into the stable yard while the fences were down. But I went there every night to check on progress. It was sad to see the old place disappear, even though to begin with the hunting got better and better as the rats and bunnies had nowhere to hide from me once their nests had been destroyed.

The stable ended up very bright and orderly, with an area for the horses, one for storing hay, one for other feed and all the bits and pieces you apparently needed when you had horses, and a big room for Dad and his tools, where he was able to hammer and drill away. I liked the horses' area best, where sturdy timber stalls now enclosed each horse while they ate their dinner. Sitting in my elevated spot on a stall fence in the early evening, I was able to enjoy lovely views of the valley and the hills beyond while the horses quietly munched away below me. Sometimes I helped Emily prepare the horses' feed buckets, as did the dogs. Mishka in particular was keen to be involved and used the opportunity to steal food. She would creep out of the feed room with her cheeks bulging with horse feed and try to get away before Emily saw her. I always alerted her to what was going on, and Mishka was told off. That didn't seem to make any difference long-term, but at least it put a stop to her for the time being.

The stable renovation may have brought certain advantages to Emily: I could see that caring for the horses was easier for her with all the equipment at hand and the horses neatly separated at feed time. Nevertheless, I mourned the loss of the murky charm and heady scents which the old place had provided in abundance. The brightness that filtered through the clean skylights in the new roof had put an end to the mystery of dark corners and the prospect of delicious discoveries. Besides, the mice and rats had all but disappeared from the building once their ancient nests were gone. The spiders also missed their shroud of webs, but they stayed around and started weaving again almost as soon as the new roof was in place. Their webs never achieved quite the same luxurious weight and density as before, but they still made a reasonable living from them.

18

WE ENTERTAIN IN STYLE

With the hard work done and the dogs under my control, Mum said we could invite friends to share in our rural idyll. Tammy and I took action immediately and invited a fat rat from the rat house to visit. He was a bit reluctant to accept our invitation at first, but once we had coaxed him in through our cat door, he settled down well and lived happily behind the dishwasher, where it was warm with easy access to the kitchen bin under the sink and all its delights. Mum marvelled at how the chicken bones she threw away were suddenly picked so scrupulously clean whenever she came to empty the bin. Actually, I thought our friend was getting a little greedy; it never occurred to him to share those leftovers with me and Tammy, given that the bin was out of our reach. I thought he had perhaps outstayed his welcome and encouraged him to think about moving on, but he wasn't keen. It was winter and much cosier behind the dishwasher than out in the cold.

So the rat stayed, and by and by we quite forgot about him. There was plenty of other excitement going on: the children had also decided to invite their friends for a party. I remembered all the noise of Caroline's 14th birthday and was not immediately won over by the notion, but when they came up with the idea of a paddock bonfire, it turned out to be so much fun, even I had to admit there was more to parties than I had realized, and we ended up having one every winter.

Guests arrived from far and wide with sleeping bags and tents, which were put up under my supervision on Emily's riding arena, then Dad stacked up a big bonfire in one of the paddocks and Mum got the sausages out of the fridge. That was my cue to assist with the preliminary tasting, to ensure the sausages were good enough for our friends to eat. They usually were at that stage. Unfortunately, they tended to get spoilt later on, when the guests skewered them on to sticks and grilled them over the fire, where they either burnt them black or lost them altogether. What was left of them, they ate with bread, on which I'm not so keen, and tomato sauce, which I don't like at all. Fortunately, some leftovers could usually be found around the fire site in the days after the bonfire parties. The dogs were not allowed out into the paddocks on their own and Tammy was too scared to venture that far, so the tasty morsels were all mine.

After the bonfire, there was much singing, talking and laughing before everyone got cold and retreated to the warmth of the tents, where the laughing and talking continued long into the night. It was my job then to patrol the tent village to make sure all was well, and generally it was, although as the children and their guests grew older, they seemed to be more prone to sickness in the night, and one or two of them even had to be carried into their tents to sleep. In the morning, bedraggled figures with ghostly-white faces could be seen dragging themselves out of their tents and towards the house, where Mum prepared breakfast for everyone. Those were fun times.

In summer we had treasure hunts, when our property was swarming with youngsters looking for hidden clues and generally behaving oddly. One year, Caroline and I set up a treasure hunt with various challenges. The speed-eating of dry breakfast cereal turned out not to be my favourite thing, but the stringing up of doughnuts (much tastier than the cereal) on the washing line was fun. Once the guests had arrived and the hunt was on, however, the danger of being run over drove me indoors, where I watched the party unfold from Robin's desk. This provided an excellent view of the washing line, where the challenge involved eating the doughnuts dangling down without using hands. The guests were not very good at it – it had to be difficult when their faces were so flat. However, once the first team left the area, having hardly made a dent in any of the doughnuts, Max came along. He had no problem at all eating them without using his paws. In fact, he'd eaten all of them by the time the next team appeared. His jumps were really amazing.

Once or twice, guests brought their dogs along. Those were not good days for us cats. I don't think they were particularly good days for the visiting dogs either, as Mishka and Max shadowed them closely and jealously the whole time, allowing no slack for them to have a quiet sniff around. They always looked pretty harassed by the time they left, and none of them came back a second time.

Tammy was not at all into parties. As soon as the guests appeared, she vanished to her favourite hiding place among Emily's soft toys, or, if things got really perilous, into Mum and Dad's bed, where she crawled under the duvet and spent the day as a small bump in the centre. She did this even on very hot days, emerging almost roasted once all the guests had safely left.

The dogs, on the other hand, loved parties of all kinds and always participated in any way they could. They were generally banned from bonfires, as they could not be trusted with the sausages, and Max had to be restrained during races and ball games, where he got a bit carried away. But they were always around when food was served on the deck during summer parties. I think their job was to keep the ground scrupulously clean, which they did. Mishka in particular gobbled up anything that came her way, even if it wasn't strictly-speaking food: party hats, napkins, little charms and paper cups all made their way into her stomach, and she was never any the worse for it.

We also entertained a succession of grown-ups, but those were much quieter affairs where the real action was happening in the kitchen beforehand and later on by the barbecue when Dad put on his black apron and got out the big barbecue tongs, which he snapped together with little clicking sounds in time with the party music. Sometimes he tried to catch me by the tail with his tongs, but he was never quick enough for me and besides, I didn't have time for his little games; I was busy elsewhere. There was much to be had in the way of nibbles on the kitchen worktops once everyone had gone outside to eat. Although Mum has an annoying habit of tidying up before meals and covering up any plates of food, she sometimes forgets to pull the covers tight all around the plates, in which case it is just possible to get hold of a slice of ham or a piece of fish from the side and pull it out. This is particularly exciting as you never know how large a piece you're going to get. Some can be enormous – too big to eat in one sitting – , in which case it's best to push the leftovers off the worktop and on to the floor, where they may not be detected for a while in the general rush and confusion of a party.

One sunny afternoon in spring, Mum and Dad had friends over for tea. Mum had baked a lovely cake which was sitting on the kitchen worktop, hidden under one of those silly fly covers that so easily catch on your claws. The guests had arrived and were sitting outside on the deck, and Mum breezed in to get the coffee tray down from its spot on the freezer in the pantry. Now it just so happened that our long-term guest, the rat, had recently moved from behind the dishwasher into the pantry and was asleep on the tray. When Mum lifted it down and they were suddenly face-to-face across its rim, they were both equally startled. The rat panicked and catapulted himself off the tray while Mum jumped backwards and banged the pantry door shut, locking him in. I tried to tell her she wasn't being very nice to our guest, but she didn't listen. The party continued pleasantly enough and without any mention of the rat, but as soon as the guests had left, Mum assembled the family and asked everyone to help her catch him. It seemed like a churlish thing to do when Tammy and I had just been so

154

welcoming to their human visitors, though I agreed in principle that it was time for the rat to leave. So I remained neutral to begin with and left the humans to do what they felt they had to. The rat gave everyone a good run for their money, and it didn't look as though they would ever catch him. Eventually I had to step in. I told him the front door was wide open and suggested he might want to use it, which he did without delay. We never saw him again after that.

Mum had a quiet word with me and Tammy afterwards about not inviting strangers into the house without letting her know. Tammy listened with her trademark round-eyed expression of innocence, when it had actually been her idea to invite the rat in the first place! I complained loudly, but of course nobody listened.

I was completely innocent when it came to our next lodgers: the deck — or rather the fine beam structure inside its roof — had attracted a pair of furry, grey creatures with large, jet black eyes and long, ringed tails, who had built their nest in there. They sat on the beams in the evening and watched what went on below, ringed tails hanging down, and took a particular shine to one group of visitors who liked to make music and sing after dinner. The pair provided an appreciative audience, and our guests were enchanted by the friendly wildlife. Afterwards, the creatures were so roused by the performance that they played chasing games on the tin roof all night. It sounded as though we had a herd of elephants running overhead; quite scary.

19

WE HAVE AN EMBARRASSING ENCOUNTER WITH OLD MAN KANGAROO

Time passed, and once I had resumed my active life-style I soon lost my surplus weight and regained my athletic figure. The wildlife in the surrounding bush began to treat me with the respect I deserved – all except the snakes, who knew they had the upper hand on everyone and were smug about it – and my reputation was restored. Once again, I was able to observe a satisfying scuttle in the undergrowth whenever I emerged from my cat door. All was well.

I was strolling through the nature reserve at the bottom of our hill one late afternoon, minding my own business and keeping a look-out for interesting prey, when Mum and Max appeared at the end of an overgrown path, heading towards me. I faded quietly into the undergrowth. You can learn such a lot by watching.

Max was off the lead. I mentally tut-tutted Mum, as the rest of the family would if they knew. In spite of the fact that Max disappointed Mum's trust in him time and again, she never gave up trying to train him to be obedient. This time, she seemed to be succeeding: Max was trotting nicely next to her while she talked to him. They passed right by me. Max's nose twitched a couple of times and he turned his head my direction, but Mum called him to attention and he obeyed. They were almost at the end of the overgrown path where it joined the road leading up to our gate when disaster struck.

A small mob of kangaroos came bursting out of the bushes just in front of Mum and Max and bounced right across their path. Max froze only for a moment, tail up, ears forward, one paw raised and that mean killer look in his eyes, before he took off after the kangaroos. Mum's hand reached for his collar a split second too late and grabbed thin air. She stood, stunned, while the silence of the bush around us was shattered by the sound of cracking branches, the thumping of the bouncing kangaroos in flight and the sharp gasps of Max's breath in hot pursuit. Peering through the scrub, I saw the leader of the mob turn around and head Max off as his relatives fled on by themselves in the opposite direction. Max was confused at first; presumably he had hoped for a tasty young joey, easily caught, but then, never able to resist a good chase, he followed the leading male as he crashed through the undergrowth in big leaps. Up the hill they raced, then back downhill in a wide curve. Old Man Kangaroo was an excellent bouncer, and fast as Max was, he couldn't catch him.

Mum, meanwhile, had given up shouting Max's name and a few other names I won't repeat here and ran back along the overgrown path, across a rickety little bridge to a muddy forest pond. This brought her directly into the path of the chase as Old Man Kangaroo and Max came thundering down the hill. Old Man bounced right past Mum, heading straight for the pond and launched himself into its muddy waters, where he stood up in the very centre, submerged up to his chest. He was a big old kangaroo, easily as tall as Dad, with sharp claws on his muscular forelegs and an angry frown on his face. Everything about him told me he was not going to take prisoners. Mum made a fine but futile effort to throw herself on Max as he came flying by, but he deftly avoided her and jumped into the water after what he foolishly thought was his prey.

I scaled a tree for a better view of the pond; I hadn't seen this much excitement in years. Mum and I watched, one of us in horror and the other with growing interest, as Old Man and Max took turns to dunk their opponent under. At first it looked as though Max's teeth might gain him the upper hand as he clamped them around Old Man's throat and pulled him into the murky depths, but by and by it turned out that being able to stand up in the water gave Old Man an advantage over the furiously paddling Max, who, after spending a good minute or two pushed under water by an unforgiving claw, emerged coughing and spluttering, his fighting spirit temporarily diminished. Anyone could see he would lose this fight – well, anyone but him. As soon as he had his breath back, he wanted to go back for more.

Mum, however, saw her chance, and while Max was still recovering from his ordeal at some distance from Old Man, she started hurling anything she could find at Max's bobbing head: large and small branches, pine cones, prickly seed pods rained down on him and several actually hit him. I was impressed. Mum isn't generally known for her ball skills, but despair gave a mean edge to her throws, and eventually her efforts were rewarded: Max, who had judged himself free of Mum's restraining powers, suddenly realized she could get at him still, even in the middle of a forest pond. Or perhaps her blows finally cleared his head and he realized his game was up. He swam over to Mum and dragged himself through the mud to her feet. I expected her to welcome him with a lecture and a couple of good smacks, but she seemed to be too weary or too shocked for either. Instead, she wordlessly put him on his lead and marched him off down the path towards home, where she would definitely have to give him a bath: the stench of the muddy water still hung over the path for some time after they had left.

Old Man Kangaroo stayed in the water and gave a disdainful growl as he watched them go. I felt that at least *some*one in the family should demonstrate some manners, or else he might think we were all barbarians, like Max. So I slipped down the tree trunk, walked up to the edge of the pond, minding my paws where the mud began, and apologised sincerely for my family's behaviour – because, whether I liked it or not, I had to admit Max was a member of our family. Old Man stopped growling, but gave me a dark look of scorn that reflected the black depths of the pond and of the shadowy bush beyond and conveyed both the resigned wisdom of his years and a quiet contempt for lesser mortals. Then he jumped out of the water and returned at a leisurely bounce to where his family must be hiding somewhere up the hill.

As I strolled back home to check on the commotion that Mum's report of Max's disgraceful behaviour had undoubtedly created by now, I practised the look I'd seen in Old Man Kangaroo's face and stored it away for future use. It had been most impressive, and you never knew when it might come in useful.

20

MY FAMILY BEGINS TO SHRINK

We had lived on our property through many seasons, and it felt like home. The dogs had settled down so well under my care, they were even allowed into the house occasionally, where they were restricted to Dad's office, which had a tiled floor and a very old sofa that Max adopted for himself. It was my job to make sure the dogs did not step over the threshold into the carpeted lounge or, worse, into the corridor that led to the kitchen and our food bowls. Max never even tried, but Mishka trespassed whenever she could. Once she made it all the way to the kitchen and helped herself to a whole box of dog biscuits from the pantry shelf. While she was in there, she also gobbled up all the food in our bowls. I was thunderstruck when I discovered her and chased her back into Dad's office, where she settled down comfortably and licked her lips, well pleased with herself. Of course, Mum soon discovered the chewed-up box of dog biscuits and some tell-tale hairs on the kitchen floor. Everyone was cross with Mishka, but she was fast asleep after her big meal and didn't give two howls about being told off.

While we had all been busy settling down in our various ways, something odd had happened: the children had grown up. All of a sudden I realized that Robin no longer played with his Lego blocks and his toy cars, but instead spent hours on his computer; that Emily was in charge of big horses and wore reading glasses that made her look terribly clever; and that all Caroline's dolls and teddies had moved from her bed into cupboards some time ago, to be replaced by books, a telephone of her own and a range of sparkling party clothes, all of which she tried on every time she went out. There was no question about it: things had changed.

It all came to a head one late summer day, when Caroline and Mum pulled the big blue trunk out of its dusty corner in the shed, swept the cobwebs off it, gave it a good clean with soapy water and brought it inside. The big blue trunk belonged to Dad and was very old. It had moved with us wherever we went and normally contained the Christmas decorations, but now it was empty.

They carried it into Caroline's room, and over the next few days she gradually filled it with her belongings. This was an alarming development. I was well used to suitcases being packed from time to time: both Mum and Dad travelled regularly for work. They went off for a while, but always came back again, tired but happy to see us, the contents of their suitcases smelling of strange places. But the big trunk was something else altogether.

Tammy, who can never resist a good box or bag, let alone a big trunk, jumped at the chance of sitting in it whenever the lid was open. I, on the other hand, wondered exactly *why* the trunk was being filled. Call me suspicious, but I had been around packing crates and wrapping paper often enough to know what they generally led to. Would our happy lives be shattered yet again by the ogre of *change,* which seemed to follow me wherever I lived? Vigilance was called for.

To my relief, there were no signs anywhere else in the house that pointed to upheaval. All the packing was happening in Caroline's room only. So what was going on? Surely, she didn't want to leave us? This was her home; she belonged here, with us! True, I had noticed that her school uniform had been put away, to be replaced by new pairs of jeans, fancy tops and non-regulation shoes. She had also acquired new bedding, pots and pans. I had to face the fact that this could only mean one thing: Caroline was moving out. But if I felt gloomy about that, Caroline herself certainly did not. She was very excited and spent even more time than usual on the phone to her friends. Wherever she was going seemed to be a place of great wonder and thrill.

And so, one sunny morning in early autumn the big trunk was heaved into the car along with several other bags and, finally, Caroline herself. She seemed very pleased to be leaving home for her new life and gave Tammy and me a big kiss on the nose. She didn't kiss the dogs; she just patted them. I watched the car drive down the road, and then she was gone.

As I had suspected, the house became eerily quiet without Caroline. Sometimes you could forget we even had a telephone, it rang so rarely. Mum soon moved her computer into Caroline's empty room, and Tammy and I were able to sit on Caroline's bed and watch Mum work, just as we had watched Caroline. It still looked like Caroline's room, but without her in it, it felt different.

I was concerned that Emily would be next to leave. Tammy was quite beside herself when I mentioned it to her, as she could not imagine life without Emily. Fortunately, Emily decided to stay with us and with her horses. Her grey horse had been exchanged for a really big, brown mare, who was quite wild and not to be trusted. She trained her herself and seemed to know everything there was to know about horses and most other animals, so she was definitely in the right place with us. Therefore, even after she stopped wearing her school uniform, she and Robin continued to go on the train each morning and came back in the afternoons, as before, which was a relief. By and by, we all got used to life without Caroline, and of course she did come back to see us in the holidays, but it was never quite the same again as having her there with us all the time.

21

EMILY DEVELOPS UNHEALTHY INTERESTS AND LIFE BECOMES RISKY

Strange how life goes: one minute you're surrounded by innocent little children listening to good-night stories, and the next you are the victim of their attempts at growing up.

It dawned on me a while after Emily had finished school that whatever she was doing now between the time when she left on the train in the morning and when she came back in the evening might be bad news for me.

It began when she suddenly prised my mouth open one evening, as we were all happily watching TV, and announced that my teeth needed cleaning. Before I had even taken in what this might mean exactly, I was hauled off to the vet, who pricked my leg with a huge needle. I must have fainted with the shock of it, because next thing I knew, I woke up with a splitting headache and a mouth full of wounds. I couldn't eat a thing for days. My teeth did look much cleaner – Emily made me look at them in the mirror – but was it really worth the pain? Emily thought so. No sooner had my wounds healed than she tried to clean my teeth *again* with a little rubber brush. Well – let's just say we both soon realized there was no future in that. Instead, she produced a bag of new cat food that was supposed to keep my teeth clean. I was immediately suspicious: I don't like newfangled recipes and fancy ingredients. As far as I was concerned, the food I had eaten for years was fine. However, there was no arguing with Emily this time: my old food disappeared, and she made it quite clear that it would have to be the new food or nothing. What choice was that? I was finally persuaded to try a little of the new food, and then a little bit more. On my third try, I had to admit it was better than it looked; in fact, it wasn't bad as new foods went. I decided to choose my battles wisely and to accept the new food for the time being.

Next, Emily appeared with a strange contraption, one end of which she plugged into her ears while with the other she poked my tummy until she found what she said was my heartbeat. This took a long time, and at first she announced I didn't have a heart at all. The poking was very unpleasant. I tried to get away several times, but in vain. When she had finally satisfied herself that I did indeed have a heart and that it was beating, I was relieved, both to know I was fully intact and to be released from her vice-like grip. Emily then moved on to Tammy, who simply rolled over on her back and let Emily prod her tummy. She even pretended to be enjoying it. Emily made a huge fuss over how good Tammy was. She even gave her a treat while I was watching!

For a long time after that, every animal on our small farm had their heart rate and their teeth checked daily. We also had to submit to having our bodies prodded in search of organs, and our legs bent and stretched in all directions to make sure we had the right kinds of bones. I was fortunate to have the rat house, where I was able to hide well out of the way of Emily's instruments. I began to spend more and more time there. Others were not so lucky. The sheep were to be pitied more than anyone else: Emily invited her friends over to wrestle them on to their backs, where they were helplessly at the mercy of Emily's friends and their heartbeat instruments. I could tell the sheep were not at all happy about that: they began to run away and hide as soon as any cars appeared at our gate.

Every spring, Molly the ewe produced a tiny black lamb that

bounced about in the paddock, watched by its mother and all the other sheep. The lambs were no bigger than me when they were born and had funny little bleating voices. The spring when Emily first got her new toy, she tried to listen to the lamb's heartbeat almost as soon as it was born. She hadn't reckoned with Molly, though: she stamped her feet furiously and pushed Emily out of the way until she put the silly instrument away.

While Emily developed these unfortunate tendencies, Robin, not to be outdone, decided to learn how to shoot arrows. This was all Robin Hood's doing, of course – the man in the Story Book. He had been a really good shot, and Robin was inspired. Mum and Dad were somehow persuaded to buy him a long, slim bow and a set of lethal-looking arrows. He made himself a rainbow-coloured target from bits of wood, hauled it into a paddock and practised his shooting skills there every day after school. The whistle of the arrow as it flew through the air and the dull thud as it hit the target became familiar sounds to us. Every animal learnt to vanish when they heard it: the horses and sheep melted away down the hillside, the dogs disappeared deep into their kennels, and Tammy and I slipped through our cat door into the house.

Mum and Dad, meanwhile, were hardly ever home any more. Their suitcases were constantly being packed or unpacked as either one or the other took off for some far-away place. We were lucky if they overlapped at home for an hour or so. The household was in danger of falling apart. What choice did I have but to pick up the pieces? I sat with Robin every day while he did his homework; I reminded Emily when it was time to feed us; I kept a sharp eye on Mishka and rescued Tammy on more than one occasion; and I made a pact with Max to alert each other to the presence of intruders. My circumspection paid off: our existence, though precarious, was never seriously threatened, thanks to me.

22

WE'RE DOWN TO THREE, AND THE RAIN STOPS

I guess it was predictable that Emily should leave us sooner or later, and frankly, by the time her training had advanced to minor surgery I didn't object when she left. There are limits to my endurance.

Which is why, much as I still loved her and wished her well, I waved good-bye to her with a certain amount of relief when she drove down our road in her new car, towing the big horse box containing the mad mare she had never quite managed to tame, but from whom she could not bear to be parted. One last whinny of protest from the bowels of the box, and they were gone.

This left me with just three humans to look after, but with a whole lot of other animals, too, which was a concern, considering Mum and Dad's incessant travel. We could only hope there would always be *someone* left to provide the essentials needed for survival. Any luxuries we had been used to in times long gone, such as lazy afternoons spent by the pool or around the fire, bedtime stories and three-course meals with tasty leftovers, were things of the past. Now we had to get used to life in the fast lane.

Robin and Mum drove off in the car at the crack of dawn each morning – with Robin in the driver's seat! – and Mum didn't get back until it was dark again. In between, we were left at home with Dad, or else all on our own if he was away somewhere.

Tammy and the dogs took to sleeping all day, and I did what I could to keep things going.

Probably as a result of all the stress I was under, I developed a lump on my head that had to be removed, and Max got a lump inside his mouth. We both went to the vet on the same day to undergo the traumatic experience of what they called 'minor' surgery. It seemed pretty major to me: we each had to have several stitches. Our recovery was long and painful, but we became quite fond of each other as we shared the old sofa in Dad's office.

The final straw for me during that turbulent time was the removal of my armchair: Dad and Robin simply carried it outside and deposited it by the roadside one day. I just could not believe what I was seeing! My armchair had been my favourite sleeping place for as long as I could remember. It had moved with us from house to house, always a light at the end of the dark tunnels of the unknown. Tammy had come to love it as well. So what if I'd scratched it a bit on one side. Well…both sides. And that little bit on the top where the stuffing was hanging out – who cared? I loved that chair!

I ran outside and sat in my armchair by the side of the road, in silent protest. It was quite nice, actually, watching the world go by – except for the dust that blew into my face when cars went past. My armchair stayed out there for several days, and I spent every available minute in it, until a big truck came and took it away. It was a sad moment for me, and it took me years to get over it, in spite of Mum's assurances that they were going to buy me a lovely new chair very soon. In the event, no one thought to consult me on the purchase, and consequently they bought a useless piece of junk. It rocks when you jump on it; the material is so tough I can't even get my claws in; and it reclines with a noise like a machine gun. I refuse to sit on it.

The frantic pace of life continued, and now I didn't even have my armchair to recover in. One afternoon in spring, Robin fell off his bike and broke a bone that took a long time to heal. He was in a lot of pain and needed attention, so I moved into his room, where I slept on his pillow and made sure nobody touched him. Even when he was able to get up and resume his school work, I stayed on and provided moral support. Someone had to.

With Emily's mad mare gone, her lonely companion wasn't too pleased. He called and called for his friend until we were all upset. That was when Mum hit upon the idea of letting him into the garden. A persistent drought had just about killed everything there anyway, and the lawns were rock hard and brown, so she reckoned his hoofs would make no difference to them. I, on the other hand, knew they would make a big difference to *me*. Old Brandy had a mischievous streak and was known to charge at unsuspecting fellow animals when the fancy took him. I would have to be on my guard once again and wondered morosely how long it would take me to train a horse into submission; probably a very long time.

Brandy was of course delighted with his new status as a companion animal and spent his time happily sniffing and nibbling at shrubs and dead flowers as he circled the house. When someone called at the gate, he was there along with Max to greet the bewildered visitors. The bird bath became his favourite drinking spot, which he emptied in one easy slurp, much to the disappointment of the birds. When Mishka and Max played with their ball, he joined in with his tail held high, his head down and his ears back. Mishka was a little scared of him, I think, and gave up the ball much more readily when Brandy was involved. He also appeared by the deck whenever we had dinner outside, to check out the food and join in the conversation. He would have come into the house as well, but Mum's sympathy with his situation stopped at that.

Because of the drought, Mum and Dad decided to reduce our herd of sheep. Several of them went off on trailers to find new homes, and there were no more lambs. Our lush, green paddocks of earlier days had grown hard, brown and dusty, providing excellent camouflage for me whenever I went for a walk. Unfortunately, walking became very hard work in the heat at any time except at dawn. The remaining sheep knew that, too: they congregated in the shade of the big gum trees as soon as the sun was up and never moved all day. There was no point, actually: there was no more grass for them to eat. They had to be fed with feed from the stable every day, along with Brandy, so they just waited in the shade until dinner was served.

23

WE LIVE THROUGH SCARY TIMES

Summer seemed to go on for ever and ever that year; we all grew tired of the heat and the drought. Even the big water tanks were empty most of the time. Don't get me wrong: I do like heat. There is nothing nicer than to stretch out among the shrubs in the full sun, wriggle your back into the hot earth and feel its warmth seep into your body as you relax into a beautiful dream. But this was no ordinary heat. It was a searing kind of heat that sapped everyone's energy. Even the birds stopped singing by breakfast time and clung pathetically to the branches of the big cedar trees. The heat made the air above the paddocks shimmer like flames, and the fierce, hot wind burnt everything it touched. Whenever I poked my nose out through the cat flap, it felt as though I was walking straight into Mum's hair dryer (which I would never do, because I hate the thing). Mum tried to save her roses from certain death by collecting everyone's umbrellas and tying them to trees in an attempt to provide shelter from the wind and sun, but they rarely stayed put. We became quite used to the sight of umbrellas flying through the air, pursued by Mum and Dad.

Eventually, there came a horrible day when it was too hot even to go out before breakfast. Mum put Brandy into the stable and told him he had to stay there, where the shady breeze made it just bearable for him to stand quietly. The sheep looked after themselves in the shade of the trees. Against the protest of the entire family, Mum brought her worm farm into the house as she feared they would fry outside. So we all huddled in the house, windows and doors shut tight, while the air conditioning hummed and battled against the ever-rising temperature. It was an uncomfortable day; we all felt tense and irritable.

After lunch we saw black clouds billowing above the hills and Dad kept listening to the radio. Things were not good out there, that much was clear – but what could we do about it?

By mid-afternoon, the wind turned. The trees were whirling about wildly for a while, then the wind started blowing from the bottom of the valley, bringing cooler air our way. Mum and Dad opened all the windows and doors and a beautiful, refreshing breeze filled the house at last, pushing out the stale, hot air. There was a strong smell of bonfires outside, and much of the sky was black. Dirty yellow clouds hid the sun as it set, veiling the valley in a murky light. We were all exhausted and went to sleep early, windows and doors wide open to the cool breeze. Any burglars were welcome to help themselves to our belongings; we needed air.

The next morning, I woke to the sound of both radio and TV. This was unusual; something bad must have happened. I joined Mum and Dad on the sofa in front of the TV, which was showing tall flames and black smoke of the kind we had seen from our windows the day before. There were sirens and people running and sparks flying. I was glad we had stayed home and not become involved in whatever they were doing on TV. Mum and Dad looked very worried. They talked for a long time. Then they started moving around the house, gathering up a lot of things and putting them into the cars. Pictures disappeared from the walls, photos were packed into boxes, and I thought I caught a glimpse of my travel container being loaded up. I told myself not to panic, but remained on alert all day, watching out for hands trying to grab me, fearing the worst.

But the day passed and we were still in our house, doing all the usual things. The weather was cooler, almost pleasant. Brandy was allowed into the garden again, where he was up to his usual tricks. The sheep had moved from the shade of one clump of trees to another. The wind had died down almost completely, and the smell of smoke gradually disappeared.

The cars remained packed for a good while longer, though, preventing me from relaxing. I slept fitfully, usually hidden away in some dark corner where I hoped not to be discovered by searching fingers. The weather remained hot and dry, but never quite as hot as on that horrible day, and everything seemed to be on hold, waiting for a sound we had almost forgotten: rain.

When we finally heard the pitter-patter of rain drops on the roof one very early morning, it was like music to our ears. I ran into Mum and Dad's room, jumped on their bed with a loud meow and sensed their relief. We lay down together, listening to the rain until it sent us back to sleep. This time, it was a deep, sound sleep accompanied by the drumming of rain on the roof and water gushing into the flowerbeds from overflowing gutters.

By breakfast time, it was still pouring, but I ventured out anyway to have a look around. The hard, dry ground hadn't managed to soak up all the water coming down. There were little rivulets running through our garden, and the road past our gate was one big stream. I'm not usually a friend of water, as everyone knows, but after the long dry and fierce heat even I didn't mind getting a little wet. I walked down to the stable to check on Brandy, who was having a little trot around his paddock, shaking the water from his mane in a silvery spray. The sheep were on the move as well, for the first time in ages. The rain didn't seem to penetrate their thick coats at all. The birds were singing, and a group of them were splashing about in a puddle. Everyone was happy that the drought had broken.

When I got back to the house, I saw Mum and Dad remove the last of the boxes from the cars. We were back to normal.

24

THINGS COME TO AN END

I knew when Robin finished school, even though he didn't wear a uniform: he put all his school books in a big pile and kicked them out of his room. I understood how he felt. I was a little sick of those books myself, having spent hours lying on them as we prepared for his exams. I had almost forgotten the feel of the smooth timber surface of his desk under my paws. Mum and Dad seemed happy as well; they had a bubbly drink in tall, thin glasses on the deck that evening. When Tammy tasted it, as she likes to taste anything that comes in a glass, it made her sneeze.

It felt strange not to have schoolchildren in the family. For as long as I could remember, the pattern of school terms interspersed by holidays had marked our time together, along with the seasons. What would we do now?

Robin didn't seem too worried. He kept himself busy with all kinds of activities, none of which involved books and studying, and the summer passed pleasantly enough. My family went away on holiday together while we stayed home with Jamie, Emily's friend who came to our house a lot. She had trained him in everything he needed to know to look after us, so there was very little for me to do except watch TV and play computer games with him.

With the end of summer, however, I registered ominous behaviours: Dad started tidying up the big shed and Mum sorted out her wardrobe. Those were not chores they did very often, and it did not bode well that they should start now. Then people came to look at our house. Finally – and most alarmingly – Mum packed two large suitcases and left after long good-byes and making a big fuss of us. I told her not to worry; we were all quite used to her trips abroad and she would be back soon enough.

I was wrong: she didn't come back. She left us with just Dad, Robin and very occasional visits from Emily and Caroline. The house grew really quiet. I did what I could to support Dad, who had a lot on his hands and was quite irritable at times. I'd never seen him wield the mop and the duster so often, and so fiercely. Tammy spent nearly all her time hiding in Emily's room, and even the dogs behaved themselves.

Autumn came and went, and with the beginning of the colder weather, Robin packed *his* bags and left us as well! Would we be home alone soon, without any human company – an animal farm? For a while, Dad soldiered on by himself, but I could tell he wasn't enjoying being the only human. I watched TV with him every evening and slept on his bed, just like Mum, but he still felt lonely. Eventually, Emily took pity on us and came home. We were so glad to see her! Tammy didn't stop purring for days. Emily brought her horse home with her, which had to be a good sign. Brandy was beside himself with joy and happily turned his back on our garden, the ball games and the bird bath – much to the relief of dogs and birds.

Still, there was no doubt in my mind by now that big changes were afoot, and that we would soon be leaving. The dogs, Tammy and I had already made several visits to the vet, who had taken blood from our legs, a procedure I knew only too well, but which scared Tammy almost to the point of collapse. I would have my paws full looking after her when the journey began.

It came as a very pleasant surprise indeed when Robin and Mum returned in mid-winter. Dad had been tidying up and cleaning the house with a spring in his step, so we knew something was up. All of a sudden, there they were, and we had such a joyful reunion! They both smelt a bit strange, but they sounded the same as ever, and after a few days, once I had given their legs a good rub, all was back to normal. Not long after, Caroline came home as well. She brought a friend with her who was introduced to us as John and was very polite to Tammy and me.

Suddenly, we were a big family again – even bigger than before: in addition to Caroline, Emily and Robin we also had Jamie and John. The house became lively once more. There were long dinners with lots of talking, laughter and noisy board games, just like before. Mum lit candles and nobody minded if I tasted the food on the kitchen worktop – in fact, nobody even noticed. They were busy having fun, and we were spoilt for laps to sit on. During the day I helped Emily in the stable again and showed John around our property, but as the weather was cold and the days short, we snuggled down inside most of the time, basking in the heat of the fire and the warmth of our family around us. It was a happy time; as far as I was concerned it could have gone on for ever and ever.

Sadly, it didn't: all too soon Caroline and John left, and shortly afterwards so did Mum. Just before she left, we sat next to each other on the big bed, and she talked to me for a long time in a very serious tone. She showed me some pictures of a green place with flowers and big trees, which made her excited and happy. I purred to let her know I understood. Then she mentioned Tammy and the dogs. As I had suspected, she was asking me to look after them (as though I hadn't been doing that already, for years!) because they weren't as clever as I was – which I had worked out also. I realized all three would need my guidance on the long journey ahead, and I knew Mum needed me to be brave one more time, just *one more time* for the last move ever. Of that, she made me a big promise. Then she kissed the top of my head and left.

I stayed on the bed for a while longer to be able to watch Mum and Dad drive out of the gate and down the road. I had sensed Mum's sadness at leaving us and the home where we had been happy for so long, but also her eagerness to show me that green country that meant so much to her and Dad. I could not pretend to understand why they wanted to uproot us all again, but I did see that it was pointless to object, and I knew Mum was right in asking me to lead our little group on the journey. There was much I could teach them, and goodness knew they needed help! I resolved to be brave, just one more time. The green country looked okay in the pictures. With any luck, we would be able to settle down there and be content. I would do my best.

And so, while Dad, Robin and Emily started packing up the house in earnest, I went outside to say good-bye to the place I had called home. I walked up to the frog pond, but the frogs had long gone and all was silent there. Either the drought had got the better of them, or the tiger snake had eaten them all. I liked to think they had found themselves a deeper pond somewhere across the hills. I climbed the cedar tree, just as I had done on my first evening, and looked across the road at the neighbour's paddock, where the kangaroos were still grazing on what little grass they could find. The big animals that used to live there had gone for lack of grass, but down the hill I saw the tiger snake swimming smoothly across the pond, his long, sinuous body dividing the water into two sets of gentle ripples on either side. He could have his realm back now; not that he had ever relinquished it, of course.

The next morning Dad brought our travel containers into the house and Emily put us inside. Together they carried us into the car and off we drove, with the dogs panting in the back. From where I sat, I could just glimpse the silver tin roof of our house and the big cedar trees as we turned out of the gate. I said a last, silent good-bye to our home. My heart was heavy; heavier than it had ever been before. I had spent most of my life in this house and in this garden surrounded by hills and trees. From my very first walk on the first day I had loved this place with its wide views, heady scents and unlimited possibilities, and we had had so many adventures here. It was hard to leave, and I just hoped my family knew what they were doing.

We were taken to a cat and dog hotel where everyone seemed to know Emily. Even though I did not cherish the thought of being in an establishment with dogs, we were given preferential treatment throughout our stay, which made up for a lot of inconvenience. Emily came to see us regularly and reassured us that all would be well. I hoped she was right. Tammy had withdrawn into herself already and talked to nobody except me. I never saw the dogs, but reckoned they could look after themselves for now.

We stayed at that place for quite a long time. Tammy and I shared our accommodation, which was comfortable enough, but it was frustrating not to be able to go outside and hunt and play, and of course I missed my family. When a man finally came to take us away, I was almost relieved. On our way to the airport I had a serious talk with the dogs and told them what to expect; I had already tried to prime Tammy, to little avail. The dogs listened attentively, but I could tell they didn't really believe me when I told them we were going to fly to another country.

At the airport, there were the usual checks and paperwork, then the dogs were put into big wooden crates made especially for them, while Tammy and I went back into our separate travel containers. I was sorry not to be able to share a container with Tammy; she looked so small and scared all on her own. But I also knew we would be more comfortable on the long journey in a place of our own. So I just told her to be brave and that all would be well, and we set off on our next adventure – but that is another story.

PART 3

From Melbourne to England

WE FLY TO ENGLAND

Back home, Mum used to sing to us. She sang about our ears, the colour of our coats, the shape of our tails and about how clever and good we were. Our names came up a lot, and she stroked us while she sang. We always jostled to sit closest to her, so she could stroke us better, while Dad and the children rolled their eyes and winked at each other. Those were happy times. As we were waiting at the airport to board our plane to find our new home in the green country called England, I recalled Mum's songs and the touch of her hand on my body. I held that memory fast in my head throughout the whole journey, and it kept me going during what turned out to be the worst flight I had ever been on.

Although we had a room to ourselves on the plane – there being four of us – it was cramped and stuffy. Mishka howled for most of the first leg of the journey in an attempt to get released from her crate. I could tell we were fast losing the crew's goodwill because of the way she carried on. Eventually, the howls turned into short, high-pitched yaps that pierced through my memories of Mum's songs as we swayed towards our destination.

On previous flights, I had always been allowed to leave my travel container between the individual legs of my journey. It had been a welcome opportunity to stretch my legs and do my business in a litter tray provided for me. Not this time: we stayed on the same plane for the entire journey, and although it landed somewhere and all the human travellers got off, we were not allowed to leave.

There were cleaners moving about, wielding dusters and bin bags, and we were introduced to a new captain and crew. Everyone was very friendly, but I hardly listened, I was so desperate to get out, smell fresh air and go for a pee. As our plane lifted off again, I was able to hold on no longer and relieved myself in a corner of my travel container. It was lined with a fleecy material that had been nice and soft to lie on, but now the damp seeped through. It was disgusting. I sat up for a long time, trying to avoid getting wet and smelly, but eventually I grew so tired I sank down onto the soaking fleece. Looking across at Tammy, I saw that she, too, was lying in a wet patch. We exchanged sad looks while our journey continued.

A whiff of pooh was drifting across from the dogs' crates. Mishka had finally gone to sleep, snoring deeply, oblivious to the evil smells she had produced. The rest of us were just glad to have some peace and quiet.

When at long last the plane touched down and we were carried off into the fresh air, I knew I couldn't have survived in the cramped, fetid conditions for one minute longer. The sky was blue with little fluffy clouds; the air was mild, but fresh. The relief of feeling firm ground under our feet briefly revived us.

Once we arrived in the airport building, the dogs were allowed to leave their crates. They were given a wash before a man in a white coat checked them over and read the paperwork attached to their crates. Tammy and I waited and waited for someone to come and release us from our soaking containers, too, but nobody did. They checked our papers; that was all. The dogs looked much happier after their bath and smelt better, too. Or perhaps my own smell was by then so bad that all others faded by comparison.

After what seemed like forever, a stern-looking woman loaded us onto a trolley, while another one put the dogs on their leads and then, unprepared for their combined strength and bad manners, skidded along in their wake as they charged off and burst through a pair of swing doors to the outside world. We heard her yell as the doors banged shut behind them; then there was silence.

We were wheeled through more corridors on our trolley, and when we reached the exit, there – finally – were Mum and Dad. They were holding on to a dog each and looking embarrassed. There was no sign of the woman who had taken the dogs out; she must have escaped as soon as she could, to tend to her cuts and bruises. You really couldn't take those dogs anywhere. Tammy started meowing as soon as she saw Mum, telling her about the awful journey and how wet and dirty she felt; I just sat quietly, trying to be brave, as I had promised to be. Mum and Dad stroked us through the bars of our travel containers, but still they didn't let us out. I reckon they felt we were too wet and dirty to be let loose on the shiny new car that was waiting for us nearby.

All the way along the road to our new home, Tammy kept up her calls for help while I craned my neck to take a good look at this new country. I couldn't see much from where I sat, just big trees meeting overhead and small white clouds chasing each other across a blue sky.

Finally, finally the car stopped. Dad lifted our containers out and we saw our new house. It was tall and white, very different from our old one. He carried our containers inside and at long last opened their doors. We staggered out onto the cool stone floor of a spacious hallway. Dad showed us the kitchen, where bowls of food stood ready for us, but neither of us was in the mood for dinner. Mum took us upstairs into a bright, white bathroom and ran a warm bath with soapy bubbles in it. This would normally be my cue for vigorous resistance, but for once I actually welcomed being submerged. She soaped us down, rinsed us off, wrapped us in soft towels and rubbed us dry. The bad smell had not quite gone even then, but we felt so much better. Tammy crept into a little pink tent Mum had prepared for her in a quiet corner, curled up and went to sleep, but I couldn't rest yet. I stayed with Mum as she tidied up and followed her around our new house.

It was big and very empty: once again, we seemed to be starting a new life with the bare necessities. I remembered moving into other empty houses in other countries and felt the familiar excitement of new places and their intriguing prospects. What would we find here, and would I like it? There was an upstairs and a downstairs with lots of rooms. As we passed through the kitchen, I had a little snack and a long drink. The food and water were delicious. Refreshed, I was ready to explore the outside world and spied a cat flap in the back door. Mum made a feeble attempt to stop me, but I just weaved around her legs, jumped through the little door and – what bliss after my long days of imprisonment – found myself out in the open at last.

A quick tour of our new garden revealed a green and wild place with a range of opportunities. Big trees and bushes lined the edges of a wide lawn in an overgrown tumble of leaves and flowers, allowing intriguing glimpses into dark places underneath. The vegetation was so lush and bold! I marvelled at the softness of the grass under my paws, so different from the hard, prickly ground of our garden in Australia, and at the dense foliage of the shrubs and trees. Everywhere smelt green and fresh. My nose, confined for so long to the stale air of the plane, was assaulted by a bewildering array of scents from all directions. Only gradually did I manage to distinguish wave after wave of new and exciting aromas: the earthiness of a forest floor; the sweet smell of flowers by the fence; the fresh fragrance of tall conifers, a little reminiscent of the gum trees back home; occasional whiffs of rabbit, bonfire smoke and rotting leaves that reminded me of America. Tiny birds were giving their evening concert in timid little chirps and long, melodious solos; furry bumblebees were buzzing homeward; cars passed on a distant road. I rotated my ears in a happy daze, trying to take it all in.

The dappled light of the setting sun was weaving dancing patterns through trees in many shades of brown and green that grew beyond a tall hedge at the end of the garden. I scaled the top of a timber fence to take a look into the dark forest and to my delight spied a pile of mossy logs among the trees so similar to the one I had left behind in America all those years ago, I had to blink hard to make sure I wasn't dreaming. Where the forest ended, a field of long, wavy grass dotted with grazing rabbits stretched away into the distance. Not bad; not bad at all!

I was swaying dangerously on top of the fence; the long journey was catching up with me. Best return to the house and find a bed for the night that was rapidly falling. Mum and Dad were already in the bathroom, getting ready to go to bed. I was surprised to find they actually had one, complete with pillows and a soft duvet. It was easily big enough for the three of us, and I longed to be close to them after our long separation. As it turned out, so did Tammy. She emerged from her pink tent just as our little procession passed along the landing, and we all jumped into bed together. Tammy curled up on Mum's pillow, while I settled down in the soft folds of the duvet in the valley between Mum and Dad. Someone's hand stroked me gently as I drifted off into the first deep sleep for ages.

2

I GET BACK INTO MY STRIDE

Tammy and I slept so deeply, we didn't even notice Mum and Dad getting up in the morning. Not until the familiar smell of Dad's mid-morning coffee wafted upstairs did I feel Tammy stirring against me. Slowly we stretched, yawned and reminded ourselves where we were: tucked into Mum and Dad's bed in our new house, in the new country! The excitement of it all catapulted me from the bed. Tammy found it harder to embrace our situation. She peered carefully over the side of the bed and called for me to wait for her. Quick, then – there was no time to lose! A whole new world was waiting to be explored!

Nervously, Tammy followed me down the stairs, one step at a time. Stairs were a new concept for her, so I patiently waited on the half landing for her to catch up, and then again at the bottom. When she had finally made it all the way down with many stops, sniffs and starts, I led her into the kitchen. Our bowls were waiting for us on the counter top, well out of the way of the dogs, who were lying on the tiled floor, looking smug: they had never been allowed into the kitchen in our old house. Why had the rules changed? I would go and complain.

But there was no sign of anyone. Mum must already be at work. I couldn't find the children either and didn't remember having seeing them yesterday. Then again, yesterday was all a bit of a blur. I would look again later; breakfast first. My meal last night had been rushed, and Tammy hadn't had any food at all. We were starving. The kitchen was bright and cheerful in the morning sun. The coffee machine was spluttering happily and music drifted through the door from somewhere. We followed our meal with a thorough cleaning session, to rid ourselves of the remnants of the bad travel smells and Mum's bubble bath, after which I invited Tammy to accompany me outside. She was very reluctant. Just one look through the cat door and a sniff of the outside world were enough for her. Then she used the litter tray and ran back upstairs, presumably to find her pink tent and sleep some more.

I, on the other hand, was ready for a long walk. It was a glorious day, and I spent it almost entirely outdoors checking out every corner of our new garden, with only short breaks in the house for more food. I looked around for Dad and found him working at a make-shift desk. He was talking on the phone and didn't react when I told him that the dogs were in the house. The children were nowhere to be seen. That was disappointing, but I was too busy to mind much.

By the time the sun went down and Mum's car came up the driveway, I was happily installed on my new mossy wood pile in the forest next door, which being on a slope allowed excellent views of the field, the long driveway up from the road and our front garden. I ran over to greet her and told her all about my discoveries: the fascinating trail of strong scent that ran diagonally across our back garden, the endless forest beyond the hedge, my new mossy wood pile and – best of all – the presence of tree runners busily gathering nuts. I had already checked out where they lived and which paths they used for foraging. In my excitement, I completely forgot to complain about the dogs in the house.

Mum was very pleased to hear how well I was settling in and suggested we should go for a walk together in the forest while it was still light. We took Dad and the dogs and walked out through a convenient gate in the tall hedge at the back of our garden, straight into the forest. We climbed uphill for a little while before the ground levelled out and we entered a green wonderland of ferns and wildflowers, protected by big trees of many kinds. Some were excellent for climbing; all were great for sharpening my claws. We wandered around happily on soft forest paths covered in pine needles and leaves, taking in the unaccustomed scents with their underlying green softness in contrast to the pungent, prickly brown smells of the Australian woods we had left behind.

I had never been out for a walk with the dogs before. It was fun. They, too, liked to stop and sniff a lot, so our progress was slow, but we carefully took in every tree trunk, shrub and flower, and Mum and Dad didn't mind. When we turned back home, I led the way without hesitation.

As I drifted off to sleep that night, tucked in between Mum and Dad again, I began to feel that the terrible journey might have been worth it, and that we could be happy in this new world.

3

DAD IS GLAD HE HAS ME

If I had thought we were going to be left in peace now to settle into our new surroundings, I was mistaken. Dad had hardly put our travel containers away in the garage (never to be seen again, I hoped) when the first tradesmen arrived. They turned the house inside out, ripping up floors, hammering on the roof, measuring windows and wielding large paint brushes. It was way safer to stay outdoors between the hours of breakfast and dinner. The dogs thought so, too, and even Tammy was persuaded to join us occasionally, although she never ventured further than the edge of the wide stone terrace by the back door. The weather remained bright and sunny, which allowed us to rest on the warm stones while listening to the distant hammering, bumping and scraping in the house.

The tradesmen hadn't quite completed their jobs before our furniture arrived in two big trucks. Once again, box upon box was carried into the house and deposited somewhere, usually in the wrong place. In between the boxes, the men placed pieces of furniture in such a way that it was tricky even for me to get from one end of a room to the other; for humans, it was impossible. Mum had wisely packed her suitcase a couple of days earlier and flown off somewhere far away, Tammy was still catching up on her sleep, and the dogs were good only for getting in everyone's way. There was still no sign of the children, so I had no choice but to sit with Dad as he unpacked box after box and to marvel at all the things that emerged. We were pretty tired by the evening, as we sank into the sofa we had found behind a wall of boxes. I offered Dad my back to scratch, which never fails to relax us both, and we had a snooze before going to bed.

A friend came the next day to help us unwrap a staggering number of the kinds of things humans need to prepare their complicated meals. Were they really all ours? And did we need them? Personally, I reckoned a couple of bowls each would suffice, same as I have. But here they were, and soon the cupboards began to spill over. Dad said this kitchen was too small for us and our things would never fit, but I sensed he was just tired and fed-up with moving. You couldn't blame him. We had done this so often, and in the past there had always been Mum and the children to help. Now he just had me. That night, I put my paw on his leg as we sat side by side, watching TV across the sea of boxes and told him everything would be all right. He patted my head and thanked me for my moral support.

Over time, Dad gradually cut a narrow path through the boxes so he and the dogs could at least move around the house without having to climb over them. Tammy and I once again enjoyed jumping from one on to the next, and they provided a workout for Tammy, who was still sleeping way too much. The drifts of wrapping paper really woke her up: she dashed in and out of open boxes, hiding among the rustling, white sheets and startling Dad as he reached in to find things. She wasn't one bit interested in exploring the great outdoors I kept telling her about.

The number of boxes shrank only slowly, despite our combined efforts. No sooner had Dad cleared a small area than other boxes appeared from out of nowhere to claim the empty space. I could tell Dad was getting weary of it all; I'd never seen him scratch his head so often.

Fortunately, Mum returned home just as things were really getting on top of us. She emptied her suitcase and gave it to Dad to fill with his things, then he fled in a taxi and we were home alone with Mum for a change. The unwrapping continued day after day; I did not think we would ever get to the last box. But by the time Dad returned, things were beginning to look okay. Any unopened boxes left were scattered around the house rather than taking over each room. With Dad back in action, we made short work of the last few. The man with the paint brushes finished his job, collected up his dust sheets and drove off. Dad, Mum and I sat down on the sofa, looked around at our orderly house and took a deep breath. The move was over.

As if on cue, the weather broke. The mild, sunny days gave way to a period of cold and rain, during which I stayed indoors and explored the new and pleasant phenomenon of white panels along the walls of every room. They had a habit of warming up early each morning to a cheerful clicking sound, while a pipe by the back door puffed out white clouds of smoke. It was a grand spectacle deserving of close observation and also had the pleasant side-effect of warming up the house now that the sunny season was clearly over. The carpet right by the mysterious panels grew particularly warm, providing cosy patches for a snooze.

I was generally out on my first morning walk at dawn, long before the whole performance started and looked out for the tell-tale smoke signals from the vantage point of my mossy wood pile, sheltered from the rain and wind by big pine trees, while watching the village come to life and the first cars file down the road. Once the smoke appeared, it was time for me to run back home to alert Mum and Dad to the fact that the clicking panels were about to stir into action. I knew they wouldn't want to miss that. Dad woke up easily enough when I walked across his chest on my way to Mum's pillow. It took more effort to wake her: occasionally she was so reluctant to respond, I had to tug at her hair to make her get up. On those days I reflected wistfully that it really was about time the children arrived, to provide more entertainment in the mornings and a better chance to get my breakfast at the appointed time. But they remained elusive.

4

THE BATTLE OF THE STAIRS

Even without the children, though, our new house turned out to be almost perfect: wide window sills in the bedrooms upstairs provided excellent views of the garden and all the goings-on down there; the big kitchen had the added bonus of a floor-level fridge, handy for inspection whenever Mum or Dad opened it. But my favourite room of all was the cosy lounge with the black fire box, which I sensed we would need soon, in addition to the clicking panels. There was a real chill in the air already.

The presence of the dogs in the house remained the one disturbing feature of our new life. I raised this with Mum and Dad several times. They had been outdoor dogs in Australia. Their kennels on the veranda had been their beds at night and their resting places during the day. We cats ruled the house. Why had they suddenly attained the status of indoor dogs? Mum said the dogs were getting old, and Dad said it was too cold in England to leave them outside. They both promised that the dogs would not be allowed upstairs, to enable Tammy and me to put some distance between us and the dogs when we felt like it, but beyond that they would not budge. Objections were pointless, so the dogs made themselves at home in our new house.

They didn't even have kennels any longer. Instead, they were given nice, big beds in the hallway and the run of the downstairs rooms. Max was in heaven: he had never really liked being outdoors, especially in winter. Mum had had to make curtains for his kennel to keep the drafts out, and he'd always worn a coat at night during the winter months. Now he could be found stretched out on the soft carpet in patches of sunshine previously reserved for us cats, enjoying the luxury of a warm house. This wasn't a satisfactory arrangement at all where Tammy and I were concerned. Worse still was Mishka's drool all over the kitchen floor, where we had to pick our way carefully to avoid getting wet paws, and her habit of bulldozing everything in her path, including us.

The rule that said dogs were not allowed upstairs was quite a lot of fun to begin with. Tammy and I sat on the half landing to remind the dogs of our privileged status, while they looked up to us longingly. Even so, Max respected the new rule without question: wild horses wouldn't have dragged him upstairs once he had been told it was forbidden ground. Mishka was another matter. Forbidden ground was exactly what she was looking for. Doing things she wasn't allowed to provided a challenge for her and alleviated any boredom.

She first began to creep upstairs while Mum and Dad were out and had a good sniff around all the bedrooms. I told them as soon as they returned home, but they didn't believe me. Finally, one night she went upstairs while Mum and Dad were asleep and staked her claim to the new house by peeing on the carpet in one of the bedrooms. I'm glad to say the sheer size of the puddle immediately ruled out any suspicion that it could have been Tammy or I, and we all knew Max never went upstairs, so the culprit was soon identified and told off. Not that she cared.

But Mum and Dad became wary after that. They put various obstacles at the bottom of the stairs to keep Mishka out. Tammy and I had to weave our way through chairs and drying racks in order to get through. But not for long, because Mishka removed them almost immediately. This made a lot of noise, especially in the middle of the night when all was silent, and it woke Mum, who is a light sleeper. Mishka was sent back to her bed and Mum restored the barricade, eventually adding complex reinforcements such as elastic bands and bits of string. Now we had to jump over *them* as well as weave through the furniture. The reinforcements succeeded in making Mishka's job more challenging, but not impossible and definitely more exciting still. When Mum was away on one of her trips, Mishka managed to get through the barricade, creep upstairs and sleep next to Dad for one whole night. Tammy and I were appalled at her impertinence. It wasn't until the morning that her snoring eventually woke him. I've never seen him jump out of bed so fast.

When Mum heard what had happened, she bought a special gate that could be fastened to the bottom of the stairs. Tammy and I were still able to get through the bars, but for Mishka the sturdy gate spelled an end to her nightly entertainment. Hard though she tried to remove it, using teeth and claws, it was solidly fitted and never gave way.

This should have been the end of it really, and we fully expected to be able to settle down to undisturbed nights, but we hadn't reckoned with Mishka, who was frustrated, perhaps, but never beaten. After a couple of nights of brooding boredom, she chased Max from his bed and made him stand in the middle of the hallway. He did this patiently enough for a couple of nights, but eventually he grew so tired he had to call for help. I went downstairs and had stern words with Mishka – to little effect, I'm sorry to say. Grinning slyly at me through her slanted eyes, she continued growling at Max whenever he tried to return to his bed. I had no choice but to get Mum, who stormed downstairs, gave Mishka a good smack and settled both dogs back in their beds. It lasted for less time than it took me to go outside for a pee. On my return, both dogs were out of their beds again, and this time Mum *and* Dad were downstairs, looking tired and cross. We all agreed that Mishka was not an indoor dog and should sleep outside again. Mum bought a new kennel for her, the old one having been left behind in Australia, Mishka moved outside and Max gratefully crawled back into his bed. So did the rest of us.

5

WE HAVE THE KIND OF PARTY I DON'T LIKE

Mum and Dad decided to have a party to celebrate our arrival in the new house and the end of our big move. They began by moving all the furniture we had only just carefully placed, to make more space in the middle of the living room and in the kitchen. Apparently they expected lots of guests. Mum spent hours in the kitchen on the day, preparing little bites to eat. I tasted most of them: they were scrumptious. Dad went shopping and returned with bags full of clunking bottles. He neatly set out most of our glasses on trays in the kitchen. Then Mum gave the dogs a good brush, to make them look respectable. She said there was no need to do anything to me and Tammy, because we already looked great.

The guests arrived in dribs and drabs to begin with, and I welcomed them in the hall. Tammy took one look at the first arrivals and disappeared upstairs. I stood my ground for a while, but when more and more guests came in, and the ones I had welcomed earlier wouldn't move on from the hall, I began to feel uncomfortable. There were human legs everywhere, and the dogs were waving their tails in my face. The noise level rose and rose until my ears hurt. Eventually, I decided to leave them all to it and joined Tammy upstairs.

Even there, we did not remain completely undisturbed, as our guests wanted to see the house and were brought through by either Mum, Dad or the man who had wielded the paint brushes when we first moved in. Everyone ooohed and aaahed, but thankfully nobody thought of looking underneath the big bed, where we were hiding.

The laughter and yelling continued for ages, and by and by I needed to go for a pee. I crept downstairs to see whether people had perhaps settled down in the living room, leaving my path to the back door through the kitchen clear. The hall was empty enough, but once I entered the kitchen, I was faced with hundreds of legs and terrifying noise. There was food out on the table and all the guests were helping themselves. Mostly, they were moving in an orderly queue around the table, but there were those who went against the flow, and some were just standing around, chatting. My escape route was blocked in all directions.

I looked around for Mum or Dad, who might have carried me through the fray to the back door, but they were nowhere to be seen. I would have to make my own way through. At least nobody had seen me yet, so I had surprise on my side.

My best option was to run under the table, where there were no human legs, and then to plan my further escape from there. I dashed in between a few legs and made it to the safety of the space under the table. The buzz of human voices was now all around me. Plates were sliding across the table overhead and cutlery was clunking. A piece of ham plopped down right in front of me. What a bit of luck! Before the big, black shoe next to it had a chance to squash it, I dashed forward, retrieved it and settled down to my tasty snack. Under the table turned out to be a great spot. Shame I had to leave, but there really was no time to lose; I was getting quite desperate for a pee.

Peering out through the forest of legs and feet, some of them high-heeled and razor sharp, I could see that further progress would be tricky. I ventured out several times, only to be forced back by a maverick pair of feet crossing my path, missing my paws by a whisker. It was no good: I would have to proceed in stages. A lady was sitting down on one of the kitchen chairs nearby. Maybe

I could make a dash under her chair and on from there? It was worth a try. I ran over to her, dodging feet all the way and had almost reached her when she uncrossed her legs and planted them both squarely on the floor, blocking my access to the space under her chair. Too bad; there was no way I could stop. My momentum carried me right up her legs and on to the plate on her lap. I was in too much of a hurry to check what was on the plate. Besides, the lady let out an ear-piercing shriek and jumped up. Plate and cutlery crashed to the floor, while I catapulted myself off her lap in the direction of the back door. It may be that I sunk my claws into her legs for better grip, or else she was just a shrieking kind of person, but she really made a lot of noise as I tore through the air. Fortunately for me, the sound of breaking china had caused people to step aside, leaving the way clear for my escape.

I flew through the laundry room, where Mum was loading cakes on to plates lined up on the worktop. Her hand stopped in mid-air as she heard the noise from next door and watched me dive through the cat flap. The worried frown on her face was the last thing I saw before the cat door closed behind me with a reassuring click. The racket from inside subsided to a distant hum and gentle darkness enveloped me. I trotted over to my favourite bush, dug a hasty hole and abandoned myself to the sheer bliss of emptying my bladder. It had all been worth it for this!

Afterwards I stayed in the garden. It was a bit cold and damp, but definitely preferable to a return through all those legs. Plus there was no knowing what state the lady was in, and that again would determine the welcome I could expect from Mum and Dad. Mishka's new dog kennel stood abandoned while she was indoors, ingratiating herself to our guests. I went in there and discovered that its cushioned lining was actually quite comfortable, if you discounted the undeniable dog pong. I settled down and snoozed until I heard people drive off. The party must have ended; it was safe to go back inside.

Mum and Dad were washing the dishes while Mishka licked

the floor clean. I announced loudly that I was back and that I didn't like those kinds of parties. Dad just shook his head sadly – I suspected he hadn't enjoyed the party either – while Mum gave me one of her hard stares and some words of admonishment I didn't quite catch. I told them it was time to go to bed and retired upstairs to wait for them. It had been a nerve-racking evening and I was very tired.

6

THE SKY EXPLODES AND IT'S A SCARY NIGHT FOR MISHKA

Thank goodness I'm not given over to recklessness; I guess I owe that to my brother and his unfortunate accident. It would have been easy to become complacent once we had settled down to our new life: I had not enjoyed myself as much since we left America. There was so much freedom here and diversion from dawn to dusk. Nearly everything was perfect, from the abundant rodents around the house to the excitements of the forest nearby, and I was even able to enjoy it all without having to worry about the dogs, who were beginning to learn better manners from other dogs in the neighbourhood, snakes, of which there weren't any, or horses, whom we had left behind.

And yet I remained on my guard from long habit – and wisely so. Because once the warm, sunny weather had given way to frosty nights and shorter days, I became aware of strange goings-on in the neighbourhood. There was smoke in the air of an evening and the sound of many children laughing and shouting. It reminded me of our bonfire parties in Australia, and I was intrigued. Mishka was lying nearby, fast asleep in her favoured spot by the garden gate, oblivious of her surroundings. Why did that not surprise me? I would have to check things out by myself, as usual.

From the top of the garden fence I could make out a fire in the distance, sparks flying high up into the air. It was fun to watch from over here, but I didn't fancy being any closer. The flames were licking the air in long tongues of bright red and yellow; I could hear them crackling.

All of a sudden, I really missed our children. When would they finally come and join us, so we could have bonfires in our garden again, instead of me having to watch someone else's all by myself? We could cook sausages on sticks again, sing songs, get all sooty and smell of smoke for days after…

A loud bang scattered my melancholy reflections, followed by a bright fireball which zoomed through the sky to a high-pitched whistle before shattering noisily into a thousand multicoloured pieces that came tumbling down towards me. My legs were on their way to the back door before my brain had even had a chance to register what had happened. I crashed through the cat door and came to a halt in the dark kitchen, its walls lit up eerily by the multicoloured sparks still falling, falling outside. I looked for Mum or Dad, but the house was silent: they must have gone out. We were on our own with the nameless threat out there. I used all my will power to fight down a rising sense of panic and sat down under the kitchen table to think things through.

Mishka had also seen the lights now and began to howl to be let in. When nobody opened the door, she stuck her head through the cat door and howled into the house; it sounded scary. I told her I couldn't help her and suggested she should take shelter somewhere safe. A second, even louder bang must have convinced her of the wisdom of my advice. She retracted her head and ran off, howling and whining, in search of a hiding place. I myself retreated under Mum and Dad's big bed, where Tammy was already waiting for me. On my way upstairs, I caught a glimpse of Max, peacefully asleep in the sitting room and unaware of the emergency outside. He must be going deaf in his old age.

It was a long time before we heard Mum and Dad return. Carefully, we crept out from under the bed to meet them. All was quiet outside; the banging and bright lights had gone. Max went to the door to welcome Mum. I heard Dad call for Mishka in the garden, but there was no reply from her. It had started to rain. Damp, misty clouds hung low over the garden; a cold and miserable night to be outside. I felt a brief stab of sympathy for Mishka, but it was over by the time I had helped myself to a snack from my bowl. She would just have to look after herself.

Mum and Dad clearly didn't think so. They went out into the rain and mist to look for her and called for her many times. Only when they were thoroughly wet and cold did they give up. We all went to bed in a subdued mood, wondering what had happened to Mishka, and what our lives would be like without her. I reckoned Max's would be great.

It was not to be, though. When Mum gave Max his breakfast the next morning, we all heard a familiar howl. The sound of Max happily munching away by the back door had at last persuaded Mishka to give her hiding place away. The howl echoed wraithlike through the mist, impossible to locate even for me. Mum put on her wellies and took a large umbrella, then the two of us went outside on our quest to find Mishka. We stood in the wet grass and called her. When she replied, we tried to guess which direction the sound was coming from and followed her voice. It eventually led us behind the garden shed, where a jumble of undergrowth and rubbish discarded by previous inhabitants blocked our path and view. Mishka's howls seemed to be coming from right in there. Mum hitched up her dressing gown, abandoned the umbrella and climbed into the mess. I admired her for it, but decided someone had better stay with the umbrella. When she had almost disappeared in the jungley depths, I heard her call out in triumph: she had found Mishka. I heard her pull aside some bits of rotting wood and battle a bramble or two, then Mishka emerged from where she had been hiding, in between a rotten fence and the neighbour's garden shed. She was filthy and smelly, but otherwise fine and clearly looking forward to her breakfast. Mum and Dad set about the tricky business of cleaning her up with the help of the garden hose and several old towels, until she was fit to join us in the house. She was surprisingly keen to get inside. The garden seemed to have lost its shine for her, and she became an indoor dog again forthwith. Mum moved Max's bed into the library, where he was able to sleep in peace with the door firmly shut to keep Mishka out.

And the new kennel? You guessed it: it's mine and Tammy's now, for when we feel like spending time outdoors in bad weather.

7

I DEFEND MY TERRITORY

Due to all the excitement outdoors, it was a while before I had time to give our new garage my full attention. I had been looking forward to exploring it, remembering all the fun I had had in the big shed and in the stable in Australia. What was this new garage, which stood opposite our house across a wide courtyard, hiding behind its three big doors?

The doors opened automatically just like the ones in America. I secretly hoped for another time-consuming incident involving one of the cars and bits of wood flying in all directions. Dad and I had had such a great time putting that door together again. But for the time being, both Mum and Dad were careful to follow the correct procedure of opening the doors before reversing out.

My favoured scenario being unavailable, I had to content myself with looking around the garage when the door was left open one day. The space in there seemed disappointingly small to begin with: just enough for two cars and rows of shelves along the back wall, jammed full with all kinds of things that weren't needed in the house. Somewhere up high, I spied my travel container. It was unsettling to see they had kept it. Surely there was no need for that?

There was also an old wardrobe, its doors firmly shut, and a bookcase I recognized from Caroline's room. Instead of her neat rows of books and nick-knacks, its shelves now displayed rusty hinges, a cardboard box full of little bits of wood, an assortment of tools and plenty of dust. Cobwebs were appearing in its corners, a sign that spiders were universally busy creatures. I looked further up into the rafters and saw plenty there, too, although they could hardly compete with the Australian ones when it came to size and density. After all, the spiders themselves were tiny here and seemed quite harmless as well. I smelled no rats or mice, which was disappointing. However, since the outdoors provided them in such abundance, I decided not to upset myself unnecessarily at this shortcoming.

There was a smaller room separated from the garage by a sliding door that stood half open. It was pitch-dark in there; my eyes took a few seconds to switch to night vision. The room looked as though it might one day become Dad's wood workshop – his workbench and drills were all here – but for now it was a messy place where they had deposited everything they didn't know what to do with. I saw a number of unopened boxes as well as furniture still wrapped in brown paper and tape. I weaved in between them to get a sense of the size of the room. It would be all right for Dad once it was sorted out, though not a patch on his old room, which had easily been twice this size, with two windows. But it would be nicely out of the way for when he started making a lot of noise with his tools: watching Dad work anywhere except at his desk was generally a startling experience involving sudden bangs, ear-splitting screeches and deep roars that vibrated all through my body, therefore a room of any size well removed from the rest of the house was good news.

I emerged blinking from the little side room into the lesser gloom of the main garage and caught a small movement out of the corner of my eye at the top of the old wardrobe. It was just the hint of a movement, and it stopped as soon as I looked, but I knew it had been there. I went on strolling and sniffing around the garage for a while in order to lull whatever was hiding up there back into a sense of security before pretending to leave by the open garage door. Only I took a right turn instead and jumped up on to the roof of Dad's car, which stood in front of the wardrobe. My claws were well retracted – not just because Dad gets terribly upset when I scratch his car, but also to avoid noise. My scheme worked: there was no movement on top of the wardrobe to suggest I had been detected. But there was a black shape up there, and once I stood perfectly still I could also hear level breathing and at the same time caught the unmistakeable whiff of tomcat. Seriously bad news.

I had no way of knowing how big he was, since I could only glimpse the top of his back and a bit of one ear, but, my own size now being much trimmed down from my former, chubbier shape, I would have to be careful and rely on my agility and cunning rather than on brute force, just in case he turned out to be a heavy-weight. My big advantage was that he didn't know I was still here. But the fact that he had dozed off so soon after having seen me bothered me: it must mean that he was either quite old or a very seasoned fighter who did not fear competition.

All things considered, I simply didn't have enough information on my opponent to risk a frontal attack, particularly in the precarious and limited space on top of the wardrobe. There was nothing for it but to lie in wait for him somewhere on the garage floor. I found a hiding place behind an old roll of carpet and some buckets. A piece of the carpet was trailing on the floor, providing warmth and comfort. I reckoned I could be comfortable there for a while.

This turned out to be fortunate indeed, as my opponent was not in a hurry. I sat patiently on my piece of carpet while the weak winter sun crept slowly along behind the tall forest trees, now bare of leaves, before dipping listlessly down behind the hill, leaving our garden in gloom. It was very boring, but I was warm and the carpet was soft, and from time to time I dozed off a little – but never for long.

The tomcat didn't move until it was almost dark and my tummy was beginning to rumble. We probably had similar mealtimes and he wanted to be on his way home. He stretched, yawned and then climbed a little stiffly down from his perch. I was relieved to see he was no youngster; probably my age or older. I waited until he was down and on his way towards the open door before pouncing on him. I landed a swift right hook on his face before he even knew what was happening. He shook his head and rose up on his hind legs, as did I. I reckoned we were about the same height, although he was heavier and quite hairy in a messy kind of way. I dodged his paw when it came my way, caught him again on the nose and at the same time threw my weight at him and bit deep into his neck. He lost his balance and fell over, yowling loudly, and we rolled around the garage floor for a while. He bit and spat, trying to gain the upper paw, and gave as good as he got. At one point his claw caught my ear and I felt it tear, but was far too cross to feel any pain. Once we had ascertained that this was an even fight, we separated and circled, hissing abuse at each other. He told me he'd slept on this old wardrobe for as far back as he could remember. I told him it was now *my* wardrobe and *our* garage, so his presence was no longer wanted, and encouraged him to add that to the things he could remember. He grew furious at that and dealt me another blow, which I returned and saw to my satisfaction that I had drawn blood on his nose. A couple more punches and he was on his way. I chased him down the driveway and yelled after him never to come back.

When I was sure he had gone, I went home to see if dinner was ready. My timing was excellent: Dad was just serving it up. He noticed the blood on my ear and asked what had happened. I told him it was nothing; humans don't need to know about everything we do. He shrugged and went on to give the dogs their dinner, but when Mum came home he mentioned my ear to her. Of course she made a fuss, got out the camomile tea and the little cotton pads and grabbed me in a tight clinch. I held still for a little while and let her clean my wound, just to calm her down, before I wriggled out from under her restraining arm and ran back outside to check that my enemy was nowhere to be seen.

206

I needn't have worried: he never came back. A while later, Dad tidied up the garage, sorted out his wood workroom and got rid of the old wardrobe in the process. Now it really was our garage. As for me, I've carried the marks of my victory ever since, in the shape of a slit in my ear – a warning to any other potential intruders.

The story of my fight has become one of Tammy's favourites, which she asks me to tell her time and time again at night, before we go to sleep. She never tires of admiring my bravery and licks my ear while I relate how it received its slit.

8

WE EXPERIENCE WINTER AND A BIG SURPRISE

Winter arrived with a vengeance one night. Thick frost covered the lawn by morning, the leaves on bushes and trees sparkled silvery-white and it was so bitterly cold when I went outside that I feared my nose might freeze. A little later it started snowing, gently at first, then more and more. By lunchtime the snowflakes were as big as my paws and came down thick and fast. They covered the driveway in a thin, wet layer. Mum returned early from work. Dad lit a fire in the black box and we had a cosy evening together in the living room.

When I emerged from my door the next morning, the garden was covered by that same thick, white blanket of snow that I remembered so well from America. It was all just the same as before: the cold under my paws, the fresh scent and the stillness. Everywhere was white, even the air around me. It was still snowing. No cars passed on the road; the village was eerily quiet.

Our driveway was covered in snow so deep I could hardly keep my head above it as I ploughed across. I had to abandon my usual walk at the fence, where a snow drift nearly swallowed me up and looked instead for a sheltered spot where I might do my morning pee. There weren't many bare patches left anywhere in the garden. I ended up right under a bush, while the heavy snow load on the branches above me threatened to come down on my head. I was glad to get back into the warm, dry house.

Mum couldn't go to work, because her car was snowed in. She and Dad worked together on their computers in the library. We all moved in there for warmth and company as more and more snow piled up outside. The flowerbed outside the window wore a white cap so high we could barely see the driveway over it. The entire garden gradually disappeared before our eyes in deep, deep snow – far deeper than I had ever seen in America. It was beautiful, but icy cold. Nobody came to visit; not even the postman in his little red van.

We didn't really mind. After lunch Mum and Dad took the dogs out for a long walk through the deep snow. I opted to stay home and watch from the comfort of the living room as they trudged through the back garden to the forest gate, wrapped up in hats, scarves and thick gloves. The black box was on and Tammy roasted happily beside it in her little bed. We had a peaceful snooze while the red flames licked the window of the black box. When Mum and Dad returned, they brought with them the fresh scent of the frozen forest. Mishka loved the snow so much, she didn't want to come in and spent the afternoon lying in the garden, snapping at snowflakes and occasionally having a joyful roll. Her fur is much, much thicker than mine and keeps her warm even in very cold weather. Max was less sure about the snow and was glad to warm his paws by the fire.

It went on snowing for a very long time. Tammy was miserable; she had decided it was just not possible to go to the toilet in the snow. Mum tried to teach her to dig a little hole under a bush, like I do, but it was no use. After a couple of failed attempts, Tammy was given a litter tray and was much relieved.

The snow had stopped falling when we got up the next morning, so Mum and Dad set about clearing the driveway. I followed them outside to supervise. Dad sawed an old door in half, and they used a half each to shovel up the fluffy, white snow and tip it over the fence into the paddock next door. It didn't seem to be too hard a job, but it is a long driveway and they only managed to do half of it before they came back in, red-cheeked and steaming hot, to where I was already waiting for them in the kitchen. It was time for lunch. They continued again afterwards, but I was too tired by then to join them and had a well-earned snooze by the fire instead. By the time darkness fell half-way through the afternoon, they had cleared the whole driveway and even scattered some sand over it. Then they ventured out in the car and returned with shopping bags full of food and drink, enough to keep us fed forever. Now it could go on snowing for as long as it liked.

And it did: the following morning, the driveway was once again covered with a good layer of fresh snow, with more coming down all the time. The tire tracks of the day before were soon swallowed up again.

Now that we had all this winter wonderland right outside our windows, Mum began to decorate the house with fir tree branches collected in the forest and brought the Christmas decorations in from the garage. During a brief break in the weather, they brought home a tree and put it up in the living room. It smelled wonderfully like the one we'd had in America and looked magnificent once it was covered in baubles and lights. There was an air of happy anticipation in the house, of what I wasn't quite sure, but I looked forward to it anyway.

I guessed we were having house guests, because of the way Mum had been cleaning and making up beds in between rushing off to work whenever the roads were clear. I wondered who might be coming to stay with us. One very early morning, Mum and Dad left in pitch darkness, taking both cars. They were out a long time, well past our usual breakfast time, and the dogs were getting very fidgety when finally we heard the cars purr up the driveway. I ran outside just in time to see all our children spill from the cars, along with Jamie and John. Now I understood the reason for all that snow: it was to set the scene for a magical white Christmas for the whole family!

Dad unlocked the front door and the dogs nearly knocked him over in their eagerness to say hello. They jumped about, wagging their tails, upsetting suitcases and tripping people over while Tammy and I rubbed against everyone's legs and purred. It was the best Christmas present anyone could have given us.

The celebrations began. We had so much fun together, just like in the old days: the kitchen was always full of delicious food and tantalising smells, the living room a scene of laughter and games, there were sing-songs around the piano in the library, and even the dining room, otherwise rarely used, became the setting of long meals with candles, pretty glasses and that one alarming and quite unnecessary accompaniment to Christmas meals: the cracker. We were joined by lots of other people as well; the house was full to bursting. When everyone sat down to dinner, the big dining room table was crowded. Tammy and I sat underneath, admiring all the pairs of legs around us. There wasn't enough space left for the dogs to squeeze into the room, but they lay in the hall, close to the open door, and watched with dreamy expressions as meal after meal unfolded. Occasionally, they tried to trip Mum as she carried large plates of food across from the kitchen, but most of the time they were well behaved. It was Christmas, after all.

The wintry weather continued all through Christmas, and everyone thought it was wonderful. The garden saw many snowball fights. The dogs chased each other around bushes and through snow drifts, knocking people over and barking a lot. They rolled in the snow until their coats were covered in icy fluff and snapped at the snowflakes falling from a leaden sky. Even Max seemed to be happy out in the cold. The children built a strange snow creature and put a hat on it. I had about as much fun out there as you can have when you're almost buried in snow, as I was. Mostly, I watched from the sidelines or from a window. But when everyone had come inside and it was safe and quiet in the garden once more, I strolled around the snowy tunnels created by the others and marvelled at the bluish whiteness all around me.

211

Sadly, as I've discovered in my long life, nothing lasts forever, not even the good times. One day, the snow began to melt and soon afterwards everyone packed up and drifted away. I was sad to say goodbye to them all. Again and again, I watched the car go down the drive, taking some of my children away. Only Robin seemed set to stay with us; he sorted out his room and made himself at home. We were relieved to be able to keep him at least, and I happily resumed my responsibility of looking after him. I made sure he got up in the mornings, supervised his breakfast, showed him secret places in our garden and in the forest and advised him on the maintenance of his mountain bike, which had once again taken up residence in the garage. Tammy and I adopted his new bed as our favourite place, night and day. I don't think Mum and Dad minded. They were busy back at work.

9

A TRAIL ACROSS THE GRASS

It was a fine, cold day in late winter. Even though the snow had all gone, there was a touch of frost on the grass where I walked: it crunched very slightly when I put my weight on it. The smell was all of damp moss, leaf mould and something I couldn't quite identify: a strong scent of wild creature. As I was doing my business under the shelter of an overhanging bush, I saw it: a dog, crossing our back lawn. I was alarmed to begin with, but soon puzzlement took over. Dogs didn't smell like that – not that harsh and musty. I remembered smelling this before. It was the strong scent I had tracked in our garden on my first day. So who was this intruder? He was about my colour and had a pointy nose, and when he turned I saw a very bushy tail. I had a feeling I had seen similar dogs in Australia, though only ever from afar. Emily had watched the lambs carefully when they were about, because apparently those dogs liked lamb for dinner.

He stopped, sniffed and continued on his way diagonally across our back lawn. He must have come in from the forest. I decided to stay quietly under my bush and watch as he slipped in between the high conifers that marked the eastern boundary of our garden and scrambled up on to the fence. Dogs didn't jump that high, surely? I heard a slight bump as he landed softly on the pine needles on the other side, then silence.

I waited for a while under cover, hoping for further developments and was rewarded: before long, the forest dog's pointy nose parted the conifer branches once more. After a moment's hesitation, he emerged fully and retraced his path across our garden in the direction of the open forest. He perched for a minute on the fence, took a good look around our neighbours' gardens as well as ours, then disappeared into the gloom. I breathed out: for a second there, I had feared discovery. His sharp, cold eyes seemed to miss nothing, and I sensed that a confrontation with him was best avoided.

I stayed motionless, camouflaged by the winter foliage, in case he came back again. He did, several times: each time he followed the same path from the forest fence to the conifer hedge and back. He didn't seem to be carrying anything, but he was definitely on a mission of some kind. Finally, he disappeared in the forest for the last time. His departure left me worried. What had the strange dog been doing? The spot where he had jumped over the fence was very near my mossy wood pile. I would need to check him out. But it could wait until later, once his strong scent had faded and his presence no longer loomed over the garden.

I went inside and joined Dad in the library. He asked me whether I'd seen the fox, and what I thought of him. A fox? So that's what it was? And what *did* I think of him? I settled down on the sofa to ponder the question. I knew precious little about foxes beyond what I had just seen, but it was enough to make me uncomfortable. As for my mossy wood pile: I had no idea whether the fox and I might find a way of sharing that part of the forest, or what I would do about it if we couldn't.

I was extra careful the next time I went outside and stayed close to the cat door until I was absolutely certain that there was no scent of fox in our back garden and no paw prints on the frozen lawn. Only then did I venture further out, all the way up to the fence, and jumped lightly to the top. Still no sign or scent of the fox. I jumped down, gingerly crept over to my mossy wood pile and scanned the surrounding forest. The frost sparkling on the bracken covering the forest floor was undisturbed. A couple of squirrels were chasing one another up a pine tree, the rabbits were all out on the field for their morning graze: all signs of normality and the absence of danger.

I inspected the undergrowth around me in more detail, keeping to the cover of the bracken with my belly to the ground. It didn't take me long to pick up the fox's trail. It led to the far side of the slope, where the ground was bumpier and scattered with broken branches and rotting leaves. I hadn't been this way before because of the difficult terrain, and my progress was slow. I didn't fancy this part of the forest; too wild and messy. The fox was welcome to it. His scent ended at the base of a large pine tree and there, well disguised by undergrowth and fallen branches, was an excavation that opened into the side of the hill among the tree roots: the fox's home? It had to be, judging by the strong scent all around it. I took a careful look inside the deep hole: nothing but blackness and the powerful smell of long-standing occupation, but no sign of recent activity. Was Mr Fox in there? I would have to be on my guard from now on, but at least I had the advantage of knowing where his den was.

Slowly and carefully, I retraced my steps, hung around for a bit on my mossy wood pile until I saw the unmistakeable smoke signals rise from our back door, then went home for my dinner. As I chewed my fish meal, I wondered idly what Mr Fox liked to eat. I was to find out soon enough.

10

ROBIN LEAVES, SPRING ARRIVES AND I'M VERY BUSY

What is it with this family? Nobody ever seems to stay in one place for any length of time. It's very unsettling. We hadn't enjoyed Robin's room for long before he started packing up clothes and a whole lot of other things like kitchen tools, lamps and books. They were all piled into the car until it was full to the roof. It took me back to the time when Caroline left us to go to university, and he was almost as excited. There were pictures of aeroplanes all over his desk, and when he wasn't packing, he was flying planes on his computer. The thought occurred to me briefly that he might be going off to learn how to fly real planes. But no – surely not! How could anyone want to do that for a living? Wild horses wouldn't drag *me* onto another plane. I decided it simply couldn't be and put the niggling worry out of my mind.

Even so, when Robin said good-bye to us and drove off in the car with Mum, I was distraught. How would he cope out there, all on his own, without me to see to his safety and productivity each day? How could Mum and Dad let him go? Didn't they realize he was way too young and had had self-harming tendencies all his life? I was disappointed by their irresponsible attitude. Once the car had disappeared down the drive, I went upstairs to Robin's room to inhale his familiar scent, which lingered strongly everywhere. At least he had left us his comfortable room and bed.

He had also left many of his things behind, a sign that he would come back to us one day. The prospect was comforting. I turned my attention to his bed with all its comfy pillows, well positioned to catch the sun streaming in through the window, and set about keeping it warm for his return.

I didn't have to wait so very long: as it turned out, he's been coming back quite regularly for a few days at a time. Nowadays, instead of his old jeans he wears a smart black uniform with golden stripes on the sleeves, which he whips off and puts away as soon as he arrives, even before Tammy gets a chance to lie on it. And yes, there is an unmistakeable smell of aeroplane about him, so I guess my hunch was correct and he's flying planes after all. Well – what am I to do about it? Maybe humans enjoy flying. They are quite strange in so many ways; why not in this? I just hope someone looks after him out there. Meanwhile, we give him a really good time whenever he comes home to us by hardly leaving his side, to make sure he feels welcome and appreciated.

But I'm getting ahead of myself. Not long after Robin left in the car with Mum, I noticed a change in the weather and in the season. The air became warmer, the days longer, the snow finally melted, the sun managed to crest the trees at the top of the hill for a little longer each day and began to heat up the stones on our terrace. Small, green shoots appeared on the trees; big, golden flowers opened up all over our lawn, proclaiming spring. It was fun being outside again.

I resumed my walks in the forest with Mum or Dad and the dogs. Each time we discovered something new and interesting. One day we came upon a small girl sitting high up in a tree. She was holding a little black dog in her lap and called down to ask whether I was a cat. What did she think I was? Mum introduced me to her to clarify the situation. Even then, she seemed very surprised to see me out walking. Well, to be honest, we were surprised to see her sitting in a tree, so there.

Another time we discovered a wooden bear leaning against a

tree. He looked a little worse for wear; one of his forelegs was missing and his face was lined with deep grooves. I think he was quite old; I wondered where he came from and what he was doing there. Maybe he was the guardian of this forest? He never moved, mind you, just stood in the same spot always, so he wasn't exactly patrolling the place. I'm sorry to say Max peed on his leg.

Unfortunately, we also met other dogs. The first time it happened, I was taken by surprise, having assumed that the forest belonged to us, just as the paddocks in Australia had been ours. But Mum explained that this forest was open to everyone, and that we would just have to be careful and on the lookout for other walkers. Fortunately, with the start of spring the undergrowth in the forest began to burst forth. Before long, I was able to disappear under a dense canopy of bracken fronds whenever a strange dog came our way. The others would then hang around the spot where I was hiding until the danger was past and we were able to resume our walk in peace.

Tammy greatly admired my courage to walk out into the wild forest with the dogs. She listened wide-eyed to my adventures, but there was no way she would be persuaded to join us. Our garden was large and quite exciting enough for her to explore. She loved playing hide-and-seek behind flowers and shrubs, darting about like a white flash until I felt dizzy watching her, racing up trees with great energy and determination, only to look vaguely puzzled when she got to the top, as though she couldn't remember why she had climbed up there in the first place, and how she did it. She also took a shine to Mishka's kennel for her afternoon naps. Its interior was sheltered from the wind and a luxurious sun trap.

So I went off on my own to find tasty rabbits, juicy mice or the odd bird to take home as gifts. Even though the forest was teeming with squirrels, I had made a conscious decision not to hunt them any more. Killing the one in America had been fun, but once was enough. Ever since my nightmare in prison, squirrels hadn't seemed worth the effort any longer. Anyway: who needed squirrels when there was so much else to hunt? I enjoyed myself tremendously as it was and felt brimful of energy. Sunbathing just wasn't my thing.

All the exercise was giving me an excellent appetite, yet I felt my body grow leaner all the time. I was practically flying over our fence, my muscles were so lithe and there was so little weight on me. When Mum picked me up, she remarked that I was as light as a feather. She seemed worried about that. How typical! For years, while I was housebound and getting badly out of shape due to their dogs, the whole family had made fun of my chubbiness. Now I was fit and lean, for some reason that was no good either. There's no pleasing humans. I for one was perfectly happy with my new shape.

11

I AM TRICKED

It's a sad truth that a cat cannot allow himself a minute of distraction, even in his own home. Mum caught me in one of my rare off-guard moments, as I was snoozing in the morning sunshine. I was immediately suspicious when she picked me up and briskly carried me into the kitchen, humming one of her little soothing tunes for added subterfuge, feigning cheerfulness. I was not fooled for a second; my claws were out and ready for battle.

Even so, it came as a shock to see my travel container standing open on the kitchen table. I had firmly believed we had a deal that I should never see its interior again. I struggled heroically, but she had already slipped me inside and banged the door in my face before I could get my claws in position. Then she carried me outside to her car. I was seething with anger at her trickery. She had put some little treats into the container to mollify me. I threw them out one by one as she got into the car next to me, and I hissed and yowled all the way down our driveway, along the open road and into the unknown, reminding her of her promise that there would be no more trips. No more! She made happy noises and continued to drive. I began to suspect she had gone insane.

At least our journey didn't last long. We turned into a car park, Mum stopped the car, lifted me out and carried me into a house. As soon as we entered, I knew what this was, because there's only one place that has that heady mix of disinfectant, fear and pee: we were at the vets. Actually, I've never minded the vet. Once they open the travel container door, there is much to occupy an inquiring mind. A wealth of intriguing equipment is just waiting to be explored: cupboards filled with little bottles and boxes, bowls containing dog treats or soft cotton wool pads, interesting posters on the walls illustrating my insides, and of course the scent of hundreds and hundreds of other animals that have passed through the consulting room before. Should I ever run out of things to investigate, which happens rarely, then there's always a comfortable white plastic platform to one side where I can curl up and doze while Mum and the vet talk about me.

Of course, before the interesting part begins there is usually a wait in an open area where other patients – including dogs – hang about and often misbehave. There was one this time, desperately scared and unashamed to show his fear to all the world. He had already peed on the floor, and when that had been cleaned up, he proceeded to howl and beg for mercy. His owner was almost in tears by the time the vet opened the door and asked them to come in. Dogs are so pathetic.

When it was my turn, I strolled from my container to commence my usual round of exploration, occasionally interrupted by the vet, a nice young lady, who insisted on prodding my insides and listening to my heart with one of those earphone things Emily used to annoy me with. It was only mildly uncomfortable and didn't interfere much with my main agenda. Plus, the vet admired me, stroked my head, back and tail, checked my teeth (cleaned only just the other year, so no need to look again!) and talked at length to Mum. Then she encouraged me to step on to the plastic platform on the side. I wasn't really ready to settle down there – I hadn't had time yet to look at the area over by the sink – but humoured them by sitting down on it for a minute. The vet fiddled with the buttons on it and then spoke to Mum, who looked worried. But Mum is easily worried, so I didn't pay much attention to the long conversation that followed, and during which I continued my investigations of the room. I discovered a

221

fascinating model of a cat just made of bones, no flesh or coat; it looked weird and smelled of nothing but dust.

Before I had time to check it out properly, the vet picked me up and carried me into another room to meet the nurse. Between them, they produced one of those long, sharp needles and took some blood from my leg. I knew the drill and held still; it's easier that way. When we got back to Mum, I was ready to return to my travel container. I had had fun, but it was time to go before they thought of anything else. How well my instincts always serve me: just before I slipped into my box, the vet opened my mouth and pushed a large white tablet down my throat. I was so stunned, I swallowed it before I realized what it was: a worming tablet! I hate those things and never take them if I can help it. Disappointed by the vet's deceitful behaviour, I withdrew behind the bars of my travel box and turned my back on her.

Mum received a mysterious plastic bag, then we were out of there. Back in the car, Mum opened my container and gave me the run of the car while we drove home. It was so much better. I actually enjoyed the trip, checking the car over and looking out of the window as we sped along, just like I used to do years ago. We saw a row of shops, people and dogs out walking, a train passing over a bridge – all very entertaining. I settled down on the soft platform in between the two front seats, just by Mum's shoulder, and helped her find our way back home.

Tammy was waiting for me in front of the house. She looked so relieved when I jumped from the car. As usual, her imagination had got the better of her, and she had feared the worst for me: another move. I told her all about my visit to the vet and she was totally impressed by my adventure.

That night, Mum bustled about secretively before bedtime, then carried me out into the lobby – a small room by the front door – and locked me in there. I was confused. Why would she do such a thing? We'd had our adventure for the day, surely, and it was time to go upstairs to bed. How could I sleep in the lobby with its cold stone floor? True, she had prepared a blanket for me in one corner and a litter tray, but why? I wasn't aware of having done anything bad. I had even taken a worming tablet at the vets, for crying out loud! I walked back to the door and called and called for Mum. It didn't take long before she came back, looking guilty, as well she should. She opened the door a crack and slipped into the room next to me. I started making my case and asked her what she meant by her behaviour. Put on the spot, she explained she needed me to do a wee in the litter tray, for the vet. That was all? Just a simple pee? Why didn't she say so straight away? Humans are so *complicated*. I walked over to the tray, stepped inside, squatted down and did a big wee. There; done. Now was she happy?

She was! She absolutely beamed at me and called me her clever cat. So were we going upstairs to bed now? We were, thank goodness. I watched Mum pour my wee into a small plastic tube and close it with a stopper, and then finally we climbed the stairs together.

Whatever message my pee had given the vet resulted in a bottle of tiny pills. Mum put one in my dinner and told me to make sure I ate it. It was quite tasteless and small enough not to bother me. I've taken one each day since then, and while it hasn't helped me put on any weight, it seems to make Mum and Dad happy, so I guess it's worth it.

12

WE GET A HOUSE SITTER

Early summer is an amazing time of year here. It makes you forget that you've just spent an eternity curled up by the heater, gazing out on to bare branches of uniform brown and a tired, waterlogged lawn. Once the sun warms the soil, a veritable explosion of greenery transforms the world outside, turning stark branches into waving green clouds. The borders fill with all kinds of colourful shrubbery, and when Mum's flowers open up you know that the good times really have begun: sleep-on-the-terrace time is on!

That's in between the hunting, of course: the abundance of greenery is matched by the proliferation of rabbits and mice in the field next door. Alas, new humans have moved in across the field, much livelier than the ones who lived there before, and they have a dog, so my forays over the fence have had to be restricted to very early mornings, but no matter: entire families of small bunnies come over to us through a hole in the fence. All I have to do is sit there and pick them off one by one as they emerge. It's almost too easy. I take them to my secret hiding place behind the house, where I can munch them undisturbed, substituting my poor diet of dry food and a bit of fish in an effort to put some meat on my ribs, while keeping our garden rodent-free.

At the start of our first summer in the new house, Mum decided to stop working so she could spend more time with us. She also wanted to plant more flowers and make various other changes to the garden. This suited us fine: we enjoy watching her work. Tammy likes to stretch out on her back near Mum, wriggle into the smooth soil and soak up the sunshine. She was delighted with the new rhythm of Mum's life. Mum's friends were, too. We had a constant stream of visitors, and as a special surprise Caroline came back for a little while. We were all keen to spend time with her. Mishka, over-eager to get more attention than the rest of us, hyperventilated and ended up getting a bloated stomach, so she had to go to the vet and missed out on a whole night of Caroline's visit. It served her right.

A little later Robin returned with all his things and moved back into his room for a while. We enjoyed long, lazy lunches on the terrace under a big umbrella. Cocktail hour was resumed when Dad found another yard arm somewhere behind the shed, and sometimes the hammock was put up on the lawn – always a magnet for Tammy, who loves to snooze on people's stomachs as they rock from side to side. It was a long, warm summer, and we all made the most of it.

Once the shadows began to lengthen again, Mum and Dad announced they were going on holiday. Needless to say, this filled me with misgivings, given our track record of poor cat hotels in countries other than Australia. I quizzed Mum thoroughly to ensure she had thought this through, and by the time they packed their bags, it seemed she had. We were to stay home with a house sitter.

While this was unquestionably the lesser evil, several concerns remained: would this house sitter know where our food was kept and when to feed us (I am quite particular when it comes to food times)? Would this human be able to handle the dogs, or would I yet again have to do everything myself? For a while, I fretted, imagining all kinds of disastrous scenarios. Then I remembered Lily and relaxed a little. If luck would have it, we might just end up with someone really nice like Lily with the long hair back in America. Now *she* had been a lot of fun. Best to approach Mum and Dad's departure with an open mind.

The house sitter Mum had chosen for us this time turned out to be a kind, conscientious lady called Betty, who stuck meticulously to my schedule and never once forgot our dinner time. Full points to her for that alone. She didn't have long, brown hair, but I reckon you can't have everything.

Betty groomed the dogs with great abandon. They loved their regular beauty treatments so much that Tammy and I longed to have a turn ourselves. Next time the brushes came out, we lined up behind the dogs and were duly slotted into the grooming programme. The feel of the tough dog brush bristles on our skin was surprisingly pleasant. We asked her to do it every day from then on, and sometimes twice.

I made Betty feel welcome from the start by bringing her little gifts and leaving them outside her bedroom door. Had she left her door open like everyone in our family always does, I would have taken my mice and bunnies right up to her bed. As things stood, my gifts risked getting stepped on and squashed by an unobservant foot – and did, twice, to begin with. After that, she was more careful when she opened her door first thing in the morning, and my gifts remained intact.

Tammy took a long time to get used to the presence of a stranger in the house. She ventured out from under Mum and Dad's big bed only when Betty wasn't around and refused her fish at dinnertime. I didn't really mind that, because it meant two dinners for me, but Betty was worried. She sat down at a safe distance from Tammy and spoke to her quietly for ages, until Tammy's eyes returned to their normal size and she agreed to try a little dinner. Regrettably, it didn't agree with her: she vomited everything up again in the night, in front of Betty's bedroom door. It ended up being quite a mess when she stepped in it in the morning, having looked out only for my gift, not Tammy's, but we kept her company while she cleaned the carpet.

Sadly but not surprisingly, the dogs tried to play tricks on Betty. They pretended that Mum and Dad always fed them treats from the table and that Mishka slept upstairs at night, but I explained that they were lying. As an extra precaution, I saw to it that no food was ever left out on the kitchen worktops, particularly in the middle of cooking if Betty ever had to leave the kitchen. She was amazed when she returned from a phone call and found everything cleared up, spick and span. Encouraged by my example, Betty became almost as good as Mum at putting food away immediately or covering it up.

Our days without Mum and Dad passed very pleasantly. Betty was nearly always home with us, cleaning, grooming, wandering around the garden accompanied by us or cooking interesting meals as I watched. In the mornings, she took the dogs for a walk one at a time – wisely, she didn't trust them when they were together. Even on his own, Max proved quite a handful for her: he took her for a really long walk one day, so long we didn't think they were ever coming back. Betty looked hot and a little scruffy when they returned and went straight upstairs to have a bath and a lie-down. Another time, Max attacked another dog and we had its owner banging on our garden gate, promising revenge. I felt a lot of tension in Betty's legs that night as I sat on her lap when we watched TV.

By the time Mum and Dad came back, looking tanned and relaxed, Betty seemed ready to get back to her own home. I reckon she was looking forward to having a rest. We all lined up by the front door to say good-bye and to thank her for all she had done for us. Sadly, we didn't see her again for a very long time.

When eventually she did agree to look after us again, I sensed the kind of wariness in her dealings with our dogs that most humans tend to develop around them. She no longer took any chances at all with them on walks and watched them like a hawk even at home. I helped her by alerting her to any irregular behaviour during those brief moments when she nodded off on the sofa or was otherwise distracted, so while she may not have had a relaxing time with us, things worked out fine.

Until, that is, Mishka decided she wanted Max's dinner as well as her own and attacked him viciously one night as he was happily crunching on his dog food. The attack came quite suddenly, the only warning a snarl and a hoarse bark, before she was all over him. Once recovered from the first shock, Max defended himself bravely, and within seconds my favourite time of day had disintegrated into a noisy bedlam, the two dogs hell-bent on killing each other by tooth and by claw, while Betty wrung her hands and Tammy hid behind the kitchen bin. I reckoned my bowl was out of harm's way up on the worktop, so I continued eating while keeping one eye on the battle, which raged for some time. It was impossible to say who was winning until Max aimed a decisive bite at Mishka's cheek. Suddenly there was blood everywhere and Mishka ran off, howling, on a tour of the house.

Betty remained admirably calm: she went to find Mishka, washed her wound with camomile tea the way Mum does, and cleaned all the blood off the tiles and off the living room carpet. Then she phoned a number of people to get advice on what to do with Mishka, who seemed to be at death's door. I told her not to worry too much: Mishka is pretty tough. But that didn't stop her playing the dying swan for several days, while her wound healed. I could tell by then that Betty was fed up with our dogs.

The next time Mum and Dad went on holiday, we got a different house sitter, Danielle, who was strict and somehow managed to keep one step ahead of the dogs, like I do. They behaved like lambs for her when she took them out for walks, always together and sometimes even with other dogs! I fully expected more bloodshed and possibly a death or two, but they always returned looking docile, their long tongues lolling happily. She clearly had the magic touch. Minor incidents in the house – such as Mishka gobbling up her food too fast and then bringing it up almost immediately on the living room carpet – marred Danielle's time with us a bit, and on one or two occasions she just wasn't fast enough when I announced an urgent call of nature in the night, which began to be a bit of a nuisance for me around that time, but otherwise she did well.

All in all, both our house sitters looked after us well whenever Mum and Dad decided they needed a break, and being able to stay at home made up for minor inconveniences, so we hardly missed them at all.

13

MORE VISITORS

Autumn brought more and unexpected visitors to our garden. A large, colourful bird flew in one morning, uttering a warbling screech of alarm as he crash-landed on our lawn. He wasn't a very graceful flyer. His size may well have been a hindrance to his flying skills: he was bigger than next door's chickens. When he had regained his composure, he strutted about and painstakingly inspected Mum's flowers one by one, shooting his beak forward at each careful step to peer at a bloom in great surprise, only to retract it disapprovingly before moving on.

I waited, well camouflaged by the autumn foliage, to find out what the bird's final verdict on Mum's efforts would be, and used the opportunity to observe him from a safe distance. I had little experience with large birds beyond the cockatoos of Australia, whose beaks were so sharp I was never tempted to take one on. This one had a much smaller beak, though it looked sharp enough, and fairly big claws. But the really startling thing about him was his truly magnificent plumage: the feathers on his body gleamed in many shades of gold and ended in a long, slim tail which he carried at an arrogant angle. His neck shimmered in dark blues and greens, quite at odds with the general colour scheme, while his face was a splash of bright red. I'd never seen any creature quite so strange, yet so beautiful. I sat and admired him as he continued his assessment of our garden.

Up and down he pranced, peering closely at the pink flowers, taking stern objection to the purple ones and preening his shiny feathers a little in between. On second thoughts, he seemed a bit vain and indecisive. Mum's flowers are pretty as far as I'm concerned, and she's certainly worked hard to make them grow. I thought they deserved at least *some* praise.

I was getting a little hungry in my hiding place. It was time to go in for dinner, but the bird was taking his sweet time, very much in my path. I waited until his back was turned before I emerged from under my bush and crept slowly across the lawn, taking care to avoid any noise or sudden movement, my ears rotating towards the bird for surveillance. A sudden screech made me jump. Looking back, I saw the bird running after me, his slim neck and red-faced head now elongated menacingly in my direction. I broke into a trot, but the bird's long legs worked like pistons to catch up with me. In the end I had to take great leaps in order to stay out of range of his beak and made the cat door with no time to spare. As I dived through, my ears rang with the hysterical warbling of the bird as he charged past. Stunning though he looked with his gleaming feathers and elegant tail, the bird would have to go on my list of undesirable visitors, along with the fox and the fluffy black cat.

I barely had time to get over my encounter with the bird before a small dog invaded our garden and peed on every tree. I saw it from upstairs, where I'd been snoozing on Robin's window sill. Where were our dogs when you needed them? I went to get Mum and Dad. While the dogs snored peacefully in the living room, Dad went outside to meet the vagrant, who was absolutely delighted to see him, jumped high, yapped and panted. It took Dad ages to get a grip of its collar to see its tag and who it belonged to. When Mum opened the door, the dog cheerfully transferred its attention to her, jumped up to give her a big kiss on the lips and a black mark on her white shirt, then ran into the house to greet *me*.

Now, being chased by a bird in the garden is one thing; having

231

my home invaded by a wayfaring scruff is quite another. While I may be half the weight I was back then, my claws are as sharp as ever and I can still fluff myself up to a good size. A couple of yowls and a few right hooks later, the dog was happy to go back outside. Dad used one of our dogs' leads to take it away; Mum washed her face and shirt; I felt ravenous after the adrenaline rush of my defence of our realm and tucked into my food with gusto; the dogs continued to snore.

14

I FIND THE BED OF MY DREAMS AND DECIDE TO MAKE MORE USE OF IT

Mum has always been resourceful when it comes to providing me and Tammy with comfortable sleeping places. In every house I've lived in – and there have been many – she's created cosy corners and interesting viewing platforms for us. From the little fleecy bed placed next to the big black box that is Tammy's all-time favourite on cold winter nights to the folded baby quilt on the window sill with views of the garden, she has excelled herself many times.

Sadly, there have been failures, too. She tends to get carried away by glossy leaflets from pet shops showing cat models enjoying all kinds of useless beds. I don't think she realizes those cats are getting *paid* to look pleased, when in fact they loathe, like I do, beds with raised sides that allow no views of the surrounding area, even if – or maybe precisely because – they have pictures of me printed all over them. Or the raised platform bed precariously suspended from the radiator by two thin brackets. How do I know it's safe? It doesn't look it. I might be warm up there, but I might equally well drop like a stone in mid-snooze. No way am I going on there. Tammy has tried it a couple of times – she doesn't think ahead the way I do – but even she couldn't take to it long-term.

The truth is: custom-made beds are bad news. They cramp my style; they *will* me to get into them, and I feel trapped straight away. It's as though they were made expressly to lure unsuspecting felines into fake consumer cosiness. I won't have it. Why spend money when it's far easier and vastly more comfortable to improvise with what is readily available naturally: a pile of clothes, casually thrown on a bed; an open newspaper on the breakfast table; Dad, asleep on the sofa. All perfect – and free! In Australia, I used to find the washing basket really comfortable, particularly when it was filled with clean, dry clothes either waiting to be ironed or already folded into neat, sweet-scented piles. Then Dad remodelled the laundry room and the basket disappeared, though to his credit he replaced it with a draught proof corner under a cupboard that was almost as good.

Pillows make excellent resting places. Mum's, preferably, but just about anyone's will do if she's not available. Ever since we moved here, Mum and Dad's bedroom door has remained open. In other houses it used to be shut, but there we had other bedrooms and other members of the family to sleep with. Now we just have Mum and Dad, so they had no choice but to let us in; I made sure of that. One large pee on the carpet in front of their room, and the message seeped through – literally. So now I can sleep on Mum's pillow whenever I want to and purr into her hair, which smells reassuringly of all kinds of things I like.

Absolute sleeping perfection, however, was not achieved until Mum went on a shopping spree and returned with a purchase which fulfilled all the criteria for a perfect bed: it wasn't a bed; it was flat, allowing 360 views, while also being luxuriously soft and warm; it went on the floor in Mum and Dad's bedroom; and nobody expected us to sleep on it. We've both been sleeping on it ever since. It's white and fluffy like a big, silky-smooth, furry friend, and we love it. It's absolute indulgence. Full points to Mum for this one; she can take all those other cat beds away.

Our new sleeping quarters didn't come a minute too soon. As it turned out, I was in need of a good rest almost as soon as our new furry friend made its entrance into the bedroom.

One memorable day in late summer we were taking our usual

stroll around the forest when a man and his dog stopped to have a chat. I faded into the bracken as usual, but the dog picked up my scent. I knew straight away that my cover was blown and took off in the direction of our garden with the dog in hot pursuit. He was fast, for a dog. I weaved in and out of trees, dived under bushes and flew over fallen tree trunks, the dog's rasping breath never far behind. I knew I couldn't afford any wrong turns or hesitations – fortunately, I knew the forest well by then. But I realized I wouldn't have time to stop, take measure and jump up onto our fence with the creature so close behind, so I chose instead to use a convenient rabbit hole under next door's wire fence for my return to safety. From there, it was an easy few strides to the top of our wooden fence and down in between the conifers to the wide expanse of our lawn, while the dog sniffed up and down the path, whimpering and wondering how I had managed to vanish like that. It felt good to have outwitted him, but it had been a close shave; I was desperately out of breath and my heart took a long time to stop thumping in my chest. Should age be catching up with me a little? Surely not. It was simply a matter of not venturing out quite so far in future.

Yet I had to admit to myself that I hadn't been able to run as fast as I used to. Sure, I'd outrun my pursuer – he was just a dog, after all – but I wasn't at all sure I could do it again if the need arose. So it was with a heavy heart that I decided not to walk in the forest again. Instead, I took to staying behind when Mum, Dad and the dogs went out and called after them to remind them not to stray too far; they are so careless when left to themselves. I was always relieved when they came back unharmed and I was able to greet them at the gate.

Over time, even my forays next door to my mossy wood pile became fewer and fewer as I chose safety over adventure – a totally new concept for me, but one I felt I was ready to embrace now that the furry rug in the bedroom beckoned so enticingly on sunny and rainy days alike.

15

JUSTICE PREVAILS

Isn't it wonderful how some problems just resolve themselves? As autumn closed in and the shooting started up again in the forests around our village, my enemy the bird spent more and more time in our garden. No doubt he felt safer with us than out there in the path of the guns. However, given our last encounter, I was uncomfortable with his warbling, sharp-beaked company and really wished he would go away, so I could at least have my garden back now that I had given up on my forest walks. Little did I know that the solution to my problem was only just around the corner.

The fox and I had developed almost cordial relations over time: we knew of each other's existence, but kept to our own patch and each minded our own business. I was relieved to find he wasn't the slightest bit interested in my mossy wood pile. He did like rabbits, but there were plenty around for both of us and besides, I prefer the small springtime bunnies to the larger rabbits he took. I was still wary of him, his feral scent and sharp, white teeth, but he never paid me much attention, so we got along just fine on those occasions – less and less frequent – when I ventured over the fence into next door's pine tree grove.

The neighbours at the bottom of our garden have chickens, and I regularly observed Mr Fox staring at them longingly in the early mornings. He tried various ways to get at them, but failed every time: their coop is sturdily built and they are protected by a dog who sounds the alarm whenever there's danger. I could tell he was really annoyed by the presence of the fat hens just inches from his nose, and frustrated that he couldn't kill them.

It was on one of those mornings, as the fox had been circling the chicken coop in vain since dawn that the big bird flew in again. I had just settled down on Robin's window sill after my early morning walk and first breakfast, and found myself in the best possible position to witness his arrival. As usual, he wasted no time on diffidence, broadcasting his arrival with a flutter of wings and an indignant warble. I thought he was making a mistake; the fox was very close. Sure enough, he rounded the corner of our house in a heartbeat, crouching down and gliding forward stealthily, soundlessly, an admirable hunter, just like me in the old days. The bird had embarked on round one of today's flower inspection – so silly, as there were hardly any left at this time of year – and noticed nothing untoward. The fox crept nearer.

I could easily have warned the bird with a tap of my claw on the window, but frankly: why would I? The foolish, indecisive creature who had unfairly criticized Mum's flowers and tried to jab me with his beak in my own garden deserved to be taken down a notch.

The fox seemed to share my view. He had crept as close as he could and now stood frozen in picture perfect stalking pose, one paw lifted slightly, his long, pointy nose almost to the ground, a model of poise and focus, the only movement the morning dew trembling on his whiskers in anticipation of his tasty breakfast. His ears were tilted forward at the perfect angle; his cold eyes never left his prey even for a second. It was a textbook performance.

I knew of course that we had reached a crucial moment: if the bird saw him now, he might still get away. He had wings, after all, and even though he was a pathetic flyer under normal circumstances, with a fox in pursuit he might yet develop unimagined skills. I did a quick ear scan of the house: nothing. Mum and Dad were still asleep; good. Their interference at this important point would have been embarrassing. Goodness knew they'd done it to me often enough. No need to humiliate the fox as well.

The bird had completed his inspection of the shrubs in Mum's new border, her particular pride and joy but not, it seemed, up to the bird's exacting standards. He turned haughtily away, dismissing a late flowering bush with a flick of his arrogant head, and made to strut off.

The fox's timing was faultless – I expected nothing less of him by now. Like a flaming arrow he shot across the lawn and connected with the unlucky bird. His jaws closed on the gleaming neck before the bird even knew he was there. The beginnings of a warble of alarm died in his throat. I could almost hear the crack as his neck broke, almost feel the warmth of its feathers and blood in my own mouth. What a superb kill! Mr Fox was a true expert at his game. I felt privileged to have witnessed such a masterful performance, if only from the window sill.

The fox did not hang around. With the bird's long neck hanging limply from his mouth, he trotted off, jumped the fence in the direction of his den and was gone. I was so thrilled by what I had seen and felt so energized at the thought that the annoying bird was forever gone, I couldn't go to sleep for ages and just sat on the window sill, reliving the excitement while staring at the empty garden, where a solitary tail feather was all that was left of the snooty bird.

16

BACK TO THE PRESENT

So here we are, and my tale is coming to an end. Several seasons have passed since we arrived in England. The new house has become our home, where we belong. I know every little nook and cranny in it, and every inch of our garden at all times of the year.

Tammy and I like the summer best; I reckon Australia is still in our blood after all. When the grass is lush and green, when all the flowers open, dispensing their sweet scents, and when the bees lull us to sleep with their hum as we lie on the sunny stone terrace, soaking up the warmth, I sometimes dream of our home back on the hill among the gum trees and kangaroos, of the spicy aromas of the bush, the prickly, parched paddocks and burning sun. I wonder whether another cat lives there now and explores our stable, the rat house and the frog pond? It seems like part of another life, such a long time ago.

Personally, I've always had a weakness for the autumns on this side of the world – I so approve of the colour scheme. Looking out from Mum and Dad's bedroom window at the riot of warm colours in the forest beyond our hedge, I am transported back in my mind to the forests of America – the bright shades of red, yellow and brown that provided such perfect cover for me on my hunting expeditions. Our forest here is very similar: even the musty autumn scent is the same, and just smelling it makes me feel young and vigorous again. I also think of my friend over there, grey cat Piglet, and hope he's had a happy life, just like I have.

I feel the cold these days; winters are difficult. I spend my days curled up next to the heater in Dad's library and avoid doing my business outside. There have been more and more 'accidents' in the house, and Mum finally relented to the point of providing a litter tray for my use upstairs, so I can at least stay in all night (I have to go a bit more often nowadays). And – strange thing – the world seems to have grown quiet around me: I really have to strain my ears so as not to miss the sound of our bowls being filled at dinner time. Fortunately my sense of time has not been affected, so I still know with precision when they are due to be filled and line up the others, who are often fast asleep and unaware of the pending excitement of food.

I don't stray from our garden any more. The fences are high and there are too many surprises out there. I reckon I've seen it all anyway, so why expose myself to danger at my age? Mind you, I'm still agile and could probably give Mr Fox a run for his money – if I wanted to, that is, which I don't. He's welcome to my mossy wood pile now.

Mishka is getting old: she can hardly get back on her feet after lying down for a while, and sometimes she limps badly. She has also gone completely deaf, poor thing. I have to shout in her ear to attract her attention. On the upside, I hardly ever have to hit her any more, because she's fast asleep most of the time, so no more bad deeds. I marvel now that Tammy and I were ever scared of her.

Even Max has gone very quiet and spends a lot of time curled around Dad's legs as he works at his desk. All three of them rely on me more and more to tell the time and generally to keep them in order. Goodness only knows what they would do without me.

Christmas is coming. I can tell from the smells that drift in from the kitchen, where Mum is once again baking little sweet things. A tree was put up recently, along with all the other decorations that always turn our house into a magical place for a while during this time of the year. Tammy and Mum wrapped presents the other day, and the following morning the children started arriving: first Caroline and John, then Robin and finally Emily and Jamie, who came with so much luggage it makes me think they may have come to stay. Did I mention that Emily is now a vet? That means we will have our very own live-in vet and no more scary trips down the road in the travel box. Fantastic.

Now we will have party food, songs, games and laughter again, and a house full of all my favourite people. I think I can even put up with the crackers this year, for their sakes – and besides, they may have become a lot quieter, along with everything else.

I will sit on the sofa, surrounded by my children, as they drink the hot wine that smells of Christmas, while the fire crackles in the big black box, and thank my lucky stars that have brought them back home to us. I've missed them so much.

EPILOGUE

Tigger left us on a breezy day in mid-March 2014, barely three months after his story ends, and only a day after he and I had put the final touches to his last chapter. He now rests in our garden in one of his favourite sunny spots.

As he predicted, his tightly ruled household is now a shambles: 5 o'clock comes and goes, and without his noisy reminders none of the other animals wake up in time for their dinner. The rabbits have taken to visiting our garden and are nibbling at the flowers. Tammy is lost without his regular admonishments. What was he thinking of, leaving us like that?

Thankfully, he left this book as his legacy to us, his restless, roaming human family. Of the many gifts he gave us during our eighteen eventful years together, it is the most precious.

We will miss him always. He was a very special cat.

Mum

ACKNOWLEDGMENTS

My thanks are due to my fellow writers, both in the Writers' Cooperative at the Eltham Living and Learning Centre in Melbourne, Australia and at West Dean College in West Sussex, England, for their great enthusiasm for Tigger's adventures and their many helpful suggestions for improvements; to my family for their creative input and constant encouragement; to Cathy and Keith for so expertly reviewing and proofreading my manuscript; and of course to Connie, who persuaded me to complete Tigger's story and to make this publication a reality.